FIREBIRD

FIREBIRD

THE STORY OF ROMAN

A MEMOIR BY SERGEY FETISOV

Charleston, SC
www.PalmettoPublishing.com

Firebird: The Story of Roman
Copyright © 2022 by Firebird Production, Ltd.

Hardcover: 979-8-8229-0319-7
Paperback: 979-8-8229-0320-3
eBook: 979-8-8229-0369-2

Dedicated to

all persons who have suffered persecution
because of whom they love

Contents

Introduction

S ix years ago, we met Sergey Fetisov and made a promise to him that we would do everything in our power to share his memoir, *The Story of Roman*, with the world. Inspired by Sergey's words, we created *Firebird*, the breakout independent film that captures the true-life romance between Sergey and Roman. Set on an Air Force Base in Soviet occupied Estonia, they risk everything to be together at the height of the 1970's Communist rule. *Firebird* went on to global success, and we have had the opportunity to share Sergey's life story with millions of people. Now, we are fulfilling the second half of our promise by publishing Sergey's memoir.

The Story of Roman has so many incredible moments which we were unable to squeeze into the film. We had to carefully choose which pieces of his life to include and which to omit. Even if you have seen *Firebird*, this book offers many new moments from Sergey's life. We also added the social and political context of the time into the film, as Sergey wrote his book in the early 1990s, for Russian audiences who were more than familiar with the realities of Soviet life – fear, repression and persecution of minorities.

It is our wish to uplift LGBTQIA+ voices and stories to ensure they are heard around the world. Sharing first-hand memoirs like Sergey's is one of the most powerful ways to support our community and to incite positive change. In a world that is currently pushing back against the LGBTQIA+ community with new anti-queer policies, telling these true stories has become more vital than ever. We have seen the change *Firebird* has created around the world, and are sure that publicising this book will support the message: "love is love."

We trust you will be as moved by Sergey's life story as we were. If you have not yet had the opportunity to see our film, please visit **firebirdmovie.com**

Much love,

Peeter Rebane
Tom Prior
Filmmakers of *Firebird*

SERGEY FETISOV
THE STORY OF ROMAN

PART I

I

Black thorns and roses, smiles and tears,
They're sown together and grow so near.
Apollon Maykov

As the evening falls, the soul is relentlessly tormented by memories. They slowly, almost unwillingly, creep into the room with the first breath of twilight. They hide in quiet nooks and corners waiting until darkness settles, and then, just as you lay your head on the pillow wishing for comforting sleep, they viciously attack to reward themselves for their long patience and restraint. And no matter how hard you try to convince yourself that it's time to sleep, that it's all in the past and long forgotten, a long procession of faces, characters, destinies, and situations are hurriedly moving in front of your eyes, nervously bumping into one another. And then, all of a sudden, the barrage of images stills. Your memory latches onto the face that is the true object of your longing, the one that caused this chain of recollections. I once read that human memory should never be perceived as an old lady who greedily fills her basket with whatever she happens to come across. It is in its selectiveness rather like an old wise man who carefully examines every single morsel of experience, weighs it in his palms, and then decides what to take with him. At this point I still don't know what I will take with me and what I will leave behind as I embark on this long and painful road of memories about a man who entered my life unexpectedly and will remain a part of me forever. And I am not sure what form this story will take. Will it consist of diary entries? Will it be a collection of separate fragments? Maybe brief flashes of emotions? I cannot tell how it will turn out in the end. If I forcefully try to keep my story within a framework of a certain genre, I will destroy everything that my memories have brought to life.

He arrived at the army base with a group of young lieutenants who not that long ago were still trainees. His looks immediately drew everyone's attention to him: he was a blue-eyed giant, almost two metres tall, with dark and wavy hair, cheeks that would easily blush bright scarlet, childlike dimples, and a cleft chin that, instead of spoiling his looks, added to his features a more masculine touch. The few ladies of the garrison openly admired him and didn't even try to hide their longing, impassioned looks. This unwanted attention made his blush even brighter. An embarrassed smile would appear on his lips, enchanting those who were watching him, and he would hurriedly leave—a feat that his athletic build made easy to accomplish. The ladies started calling him the Prude and always sought an opportunity to check whether they were, in fact, right. However, they never managed to achieve what they wanted. Once the test flights started (oh!), it quickly became clear that he was on the way to becoming a leader, and it indeed happened soon enough.

But why do I…I guess I'm afraid…it's always easier to remember the unimportant details, but it's scary to dive headfirst into the water. On the other hand, a pleasant feeling of warmth is spreading throughout my body, and it keeps the memories burning. My heart is beating faster and faster still. There is no point in checking the pulse; the heartbeats may soften or resonate with an all-encompassing echo, but they could never catch up with what we were feeling. Not that long ago we were strangers, and then we found each other. Roman! Do you remember all this? If you do, let this story become our confession for those who are yet to experience love. And if, after reading this, they won't curse us but will choose to embark on their own treacherous path of getting to know one other, then we have not lived in vain, Roma. Then we have not loved in vain. Thank God, we never had to prove anything to anyone. We just believed that Mother Nature was not mistaken in giving us this love. Roma, give me your hand! Let's go! Help me remember and once again relive everything that we experienced. Help me tell this story to commemorate the past, to commemorate you, my only true love. You were never afraid of anything. You told me that there can be two lives, but you can't die twice. Probably those who are now as young as we once were and believe in the call of money rather than the sound of two hearts beating as one will laugh at me. But I am not afraid, and I don't blame them. They are the children of their time. Let time be our judge.

II

Waiting for joy is joy in itself.
Lessing

I would prefer not to look at the past chronologically, but it is impossible not to remember the first time he appeared at the doorstep of the flight house. I was surprised and delighted to find the confirmation of an idea I once heard—that the presence of an unadulterated and powerful male beauty can create the feeling of never-ending vastness. That is what I felt when he first came into the room where I was fulfilling my duties and evaluating the flights. When I heard the knock on the door, I yelled, "Enter!" I replied to the greeting without seeing who was talking to me (I was allowed to carry on working irrespective of who came into the room). Then I understood that it was not just a curious pilot and definitely not a technician who wanted to give me the latest report. It was the person who...

Invisible beams coming from the depth of his beautiful eyes shone through me like x-rays and made me raise my head. Once our eyes met, I saw his soft and kind smile. It was not a fawning smile like the ones I often saw. It seemed to absorb and evaluate the person it was addressed to. I had heard about him but only then saw him for the first time, and I looked at him with open curiosity. I remember comparing him to a ray of the sun—a rare visitor in late autumn—who had also sneaked into the flight house. The ray settled on his face and froze. Roman slightly narrowed his eyes, took off his helmet and hat, and looked at me, his smile unaltered. In that one moment, I forgot about my work, the flights, the maps, and the evaluations. It was not without a reason. His dark hair and clear-blue eyes—images of lakes reflecting the sunlight—pulled me in stronger than a magnet. My inner voice persistently kept telling me to stop staring at him but couldn't convince me to lower my eyes. Apparently, Roman was used to similar reactions. His cheeks burned scarlet like the setting sun. Suddenly, he frowned. I tried to move my eyes away from his face and realised that my hand was no longer holding the pen. I mumbled an apology and bent down to look for it but almost immediately hit my forehead against Roman's; he had bent down at the same time and already found my pen. We were sitting halfway under my desk, and our eyes met again. His eyes, reflecting the bright flickers of the sunlight, were smiling, and his hand reached toward my forehead to softly rub the place he had hit. Oh!

Love, you ruler of the hearts! What are you doing to us? I immediately wanted to get up, but his eyes kept me glued to the place and even made me lean against the foot of the table.

"Don't hurry; let's talk," said his eyes, carefully studying my face.

"Someone can enter," my eyes unwillingly told him, turning toward the open door and then back to his face.

"That's all right. We are just looking for a pen, right?" his eyes tried to reassure me.

"Yes," I replied with only my breath. My eyes were slowly melting in the golden light of love created by the two hearts that had found each other, and they were looking for confirmation that I was not mistaken. We were so close that I started breathing in time with him. There was a secret path that was about to unfold between us and show us that we had, indeed, been looking for each other for the longest time. His gentle smile made my head spin from the powerful emotions. His clear-blue eyes, the colour of the sky, softly invited me into this newly discovered and wonderful world. In my confusion I had forgotten to be careful. I decided to quickly stand up. His palm swiftly covered the back of my head and softened the blow, which once again made me sink down. He let out a good-natured laugh, offered me his hand for support, stood up, and finally introduced himself—Roman. It was enough to break the spell, so I introduced myself and once again felt free. We used this moment of clarity to start talking about everything we could think of.

It was dinnertime, but we forgot about it. When it was time to part, we realised that we hadn't told each other the most important thing: we were no longer alone in this life. The ugly and scary world of the army no longer frightened us because…There were a lot of things we didn't tell each other that time. We felt there was a vast ocean of days in front of us that we would cross together. However, the late autumn, the November that had brought spring into our lives, decided to test us through separation. Soon after our first meeting, Roman's company was temporarily relocated, and for the whole month, our only communication was through letters and phone calls. Who knows how everything would have turned out if…I still don't understand how the commander of the regiment (the Old Man) guessed, but when he asked me directly if I wanted to see Roman, I answered "Yes" without the slightest hesitation. The Old Man broke into a sly grin, playfully pinched my nose, and…a day later the door of the flight house burst open with such force that, had there been time to think about it, I would have concluded that a violent storm was raging outside. However, before even a single thought had entered my head, two strong hands touched my shoulders and then my chest, and a warm unshaven cheek gently pressed against mine. Burning lips whispered something into my ear in husky tones—words of endearment or greeting. Before Roman possessed my lips, I threw my head back and noticed that the door was slowly closing, and behind it I glimpsed the satisfied smile of the Old Man. Romka also noticed him, but he almost never let those around him influence his behaviour. Now he was my Romka, my Roman. It was the end of December 1971.

III

Thus, suddenly two hearts have met.
Both in love and looking for answers...

N. Apuhtin

There was a ball! On December 21 at nine o'clock in the evening, the officers' club started filling up with people. They came with families, they came alone, they came in couples. It seemed the ancient building understood that a celebration of this magnitude takes place only once a year. It was scrubbed clean and decorated, and while the old floorboards creaked, the building rejoiced in the commotion and sang, twirled, and danced together with the people, forgetting its age and uncomfortable state. We also easily forgot about it. Being so far from the rest of the world, that night everyone wanted to be invited to the ancient manor—the officers' club. As a rule, we had to find our own entertainment. This event was no exception. Within three days I managed to find the musicians, the singers, the dancers, and the poetry readers and organize such a performance that even those who were demobilized later recalled in their rare letters the exuberating celebration that took place on the eve of 1972. But that happened later. Meanwhile more people kept arriving. Our kindhearted Old Man, having just received a commendation for the consistent safety of the flights, brought to the ball everyone who was not on duty. The main hall was buzzing like a beehive. The happiness radiated also backstage, but we couldn't contain our nervousness. Despite the unforgiving cold of the winter evening, we were unbearably hot in our freshly ironed uniforms. The programme of the evening that I managed to put together in just a few days had been checked and confirmed a thousand times, but of course, there were last-minute changes. Dripping with sweat, I was running between the hall and the stage looking for new talent. And then the concert started. For the first twenty minutes, the audience was getting used to the environment, looking around and trying to recognize their neighbours, but once they settled down, everyone excitedly waited for every new performance and shouted "Encore!" whenever they particularly liked something. I had the nagging feeling that soon enough they would grow tired and stop paying attention. When my prediction came true, I went all in and invited on the stage the person everyone really wanted to see. Out came Roman in an impeccably ironed uniform and a guitar in his hand, looking like a Greek god. Before going onto the stage, he came up to me and, using the cover of semidarkness (as always, the mess hall manager was showing his magic tricks, just this time on the stage), firmly kissed my lips for courage. He then announced that he was ready to perform. After brief applause dedicated to the illusionist and my announcement that it was time for the surprise I had promised earlier, Romka casually strolled onto the stage. His name was not mentioned in the hurriedly printed programmes of the evening. The Old Man and I had both tried to persuade him to participate, but we received no definite answer until the morning of the performance. And now…the hall immediately fell silent. The ladies who were sitting farther in the back leaned forward, almost crushing into those who were sitting in front of them; however, no one seemed to notice. The wives of the higher-ranking officers filling the first couple of rows finally sat up straight in their chairs. I could see from the backstage area that Romka's cheeks were burning bright red, but he managed to calm his nerves. With the first chord played on his guitar and the sound of his velvety baritone, Romka managed to melt the hearts of those who were initially not particularly keen on hearing him (I mean the husbands) and to fully enchant those who had been longing to hear his voice. He was playing a sentimental melody. He sat half-turned on the chair that I had brought in for him. While his body belonged to the audience, his eyes were only mine. He openly sang to me, to us, about us. He never changed the lyrics of the song but expressed his thoughts and feelings through the beautiful poetry. "I was waiting for you…" Into this one performance, he managed to pour all his half-Cossack passion and his gentle Russian soul. His voice was breaking and pausing, as if he was testing his feelings, but then it rose again and filled the hall with declarations of love that were spilling out of his heart and soul. In his strong arms, the guitar resembled a child's toy, and it wept and laughed together with him. Those who were in the hall dared not move or breathe. They listened to his secret confession and felt his suffering:

> Please, understand that in this life of sorrow
> Each moment I will try to spend with you.
> I love you! Love you to the brink of madness
> And all my happiness is bound to you.

The last chord slowly dissolved in the air. Romka got up, took a bow, and quickly left the stage. Had I not caught his arm, his emotions would have driven him to leave the building. For a couple of seconds, complete silence fell upon the hall. When Roman turned around and I finally saw his face, I was stupefied. His always-smiling and clear eyes were filled with tears. They continued to sing about love, about the fact that there were just the two of us in this world, in this cursed army, and that he didn't give a damn about anything or anyone as long as I was near him and loved him with equal passion. All this happened in a matter of seconds. Once I saw what he was trying to tell me, I understood I'd lose him forever if I didn't hold him and kiss him, and then come what may.

But at that very moment, the people in the hall came to their senses, and thundering applause broke out calling him back to the stage. He was standing backstage right next to me, and his eyes were asking me what to do. My eyes filled up with tears because I suddenly understood how important he had become to me. I knew there were many days and nights still ahead of us. There is nothing more precious than moments of such wordless communication. Love is just one word, one look, and even silence. But the people in the hall were not ready to give up. It was close to midnight, but no one noticed. The Old Man appeared at the backstage entrance. The sound of the applause now resembled repeated explosions of thunder. I leaned into Romka, gently kissed him, and pushed him back to the stage. He then saw the tears in my eyes and understood everything that I was trying to communicate. Euphoric, fire burning in his heart and in his cheeks, he left the guitar behind and almost flew to the old black piano that stood in the corner of the stage. Jokingly, but like a real maestro, he threw back the tails of his coat, causing a sea of good-natured laughter and applause. He then opened the lid, and the gentle sounds of Strauss's waltz filled the hall. Everyone was enchanted by the melody, including the Old Man, who, after Roman's reentrance on the stage, managed to smile at me and show me that everything would be all right.

But that was not the end of it. The audience would not allow Roman to leave. He then winked, ran backstage, and put on the accordion that was prepared for the final performance of the night. In the blink of an eye, he was already back on the stage singing a traditional Russian song that made even the old officers leave their seats and start dancing. I lovingly watched him, fully entranced, but I also felt the fear that after this success he would be taken away from me.

As if he could read my mind, Romka finished his breathtaking performance and ran to me, removing the accordion on the way. Just like at the beginning of the concert, he pulled me aside and wrapped both of us in the heavy stage curtain. He kissed me until my head started spinning and the fear dissolved, and then he ran back to the stage to take the final bow. That was the end of the concert. Our dear Old Man started to remove the chairs and the benches and put the tables back in place. The only people who stayed to celebrate the New Year were the officers with their families and the soldiers who had participated in the performance.

We realised that we could no longer hide (at least for now), so we went out for a breath of fresh air. All the way people commended Romka for his talent and thanked him for the brilliant performance. Romka was completely relaxed and bowed to the right and to the left like a Hollywood star. Every once in a while he looked at me with a serious expression on his face to make me understand that he was doing it for us and that soon we would be alone with no one to interfere with our conversations, thoughts, and feelings. His smile grew mysterious, and I understood that he had prepared a surprise.

While we were waiting for the feast to begin, I stood next to my Romka under a big old fir tree, warmed by the coat he had brought, and greedily swallowed the cold night air in between the warm, soft, and gentle kisses bestowed upon me by the happy Romka. Carefully hidden by the huge fir branches that the generous giant had lowered almost to the ground, we watched the falling stars and made wishes, many of which would never come true. I didn't know it back then, and I didn't want to know. I felt that the other giant, the one standing next to me, was ready to give me the whole world, the stars in the sky, and himself, while asking for nothing in return. That is what true happiness feels like.

Then the bells started ringing. Romka pulled out a bottle of champagne and two glasses that were hidden under the tree. The glasses were carefully wrapped in cotton wool, and it made them look like the goblets of the Snow Queen. We started this brand-new year laughing and spilling champagne on our hands. Then Romka once again reached into the cotton wool and pulled out a razor blade to swiftly cut and peel a large, bright orange. In my excitement I dropped the jacket, and the pieces of the foreign fruit, handed to me by my very own magician, tasted like heaven. The last piece we ate together, each of us starting from the end, until our lips met in the first kiss of the year.

Then someone called us. It was the Old Man, who was coming toward our hiding place. In his hands he held glasses and a bottle of Old Tallinn (Oh! The sweetest memories of Estonia). We filled our glasses and raised them to toast the New Year. He carefully looked around (even though we hardly drew attention to ourselves, a lot of people had gathered in the yard) and hugged us in a warm and fatherly way, so that he was wedged between Romka and me. He pulled us in and said in a clear voice, "Happy New Year!" Then he added with a smile, "Run away, you two. The car is on the other side." Our dear, kindhearted Old Man! If only you knew how much we wanted to kiss your cheeks in front of everyone and show you our gratitude, to tell you everything, and after our confession, listen to your stories, because you surely had many to tell. I thank you from all my heart! Colonel, if you are still alive, I wish you health and many happy years ahead of you. If you are no longer with us, I will always honour your memory. You remained a mystery to us, but the truth is, we didn't try very hard to learn your secrets.

Tolik was already waiting for us. He didn't ask any questions but drove us straight to the flight house. Romka barely managed to take off his coat and jacket before falling asleep. A smile spread across his face from the liquor we had drunk, and he bestowed upon me one of his amazing kisses. I thankfully accepted it and also drifted off to sleep. When the daylight peeked into the flight house on the first morning of 1972, it saw two young and handsome men sleeping in each other's arms. Even in their sleep, both faces reflected happiness and peace. Let's not wake them from this bliss.

And then the days kept running like a frantic dream,
Down fell the walls and closer came the hour
When we would wake from the enchanting sleep…"

IV

Thus do I pine and surfeit day by day,
Or gluttoning on all, or all away.
William Shakespeare

I t was February. We were mercilessly exposed to the cold winds of
the month. If the Old Man hadn't helped us, it would have been
particularly hard. Every once in a while he took Romka and two or
three other pilots on army missions. While Romka was gone, I could
find no peace. Everything fell out of my hands, and only Romka's
phone calls brought me back to life. But often the pilots were sent
away and the Old Man remained at the base, and then, curiously
observing my impatience, he would try to cheer me up with expen-
sive chocolates. Funny Old Man! He knew how many good quality
chocolates I was getting from the pilots who tried to avoid their
fines. He also gave me permission slips for leave (my desk drawers
were full of them), but where would I go all alone? Sometimes in the
evenings he and Tolik would come to the flight house to chat about
Roman. It seemed that he loved Romka no less than I did. When
each mission was over, even if it was two o'clock in the morning
with a snowstorm raging outside—like that evening—the Old Man
always called for a car and went to meet his "young eagles." Dear
God! How many times I turned to you, asking you to protect them
(to protect him). And there was so much to fear. Nothing could stop
him from running straight to me.

It was two o'clock in the morning when the phone rang, and
the Old Man happily told me that Romka was on his way to see
me. I never went to sleep that night. I was waiting for him and kept
looking out the window, but even after the Old Man's phone call,

the car still wouldn't arrive. I was becoming increasing worried and wanted to call the Old Man, but all of a sudden a man covered in snow started to desperately bang on my window. I opened the door, and two huge snowballs fell inside, accompanied by the cold wind. I couldn't even tell them apart, so I quickly started removing their clothes. The bigger snowball immediately hugged me, and his eyes behind the slowly melting eyelashes were smiling. Romka! And the other one was Tolik!

The room was well-heated, so soon enough they warmed up and started telling me how the car had gotten stuck in the snow. They tried to move it for a long time, but when the car was becoming hopelessly snowed in, they decided to go the rest of the way on foot, since the base was not that far. I listened and nodded and couldn't take my eyes off Roman. We were never shy in Tolik's presence, but the emotions that had accumulated during our time apart asked for no witnesses.

Finally, the tow truck arrived, and Tolik, who only ever loved his car, went to salvage the abandoned vehicle. Romka immediately started to put on his coat, ready to help, but Tolik gave both of us a meaningful look, which made Romka raise his hands in surrender and stay. Finally, we were alone.

I tried to give Romka some hot tea and dinner, but it was becoming increasingly difficult. His hands pulled me down onto his lap, and he kept looking at me as if he were seeing me for the first time. I touched my lips to his forehead and felt that he had a slight fever, either from cold or from exhaustion. Eventually, I managed to persuade him to drink some hot tea with raspberry jam, and then I covered him with a warm blanket, lay down next to him, and held his hands in mine. I watched him as he fell asleep, so peaceful, so dear to me. Even though we tried to keep our eyes open and gaze at each other, soon enough sleep conquered us both, but our hands never let go.

I woke up in his arms and saw that the Old Man was standing on the doorstep and grumbling about the door that had been left open. "We are going to Tallinn," Romka and I shouted.

The Old Man nearly collapsed in our joyful embrace. He hadn't had the chance to tell us anything, just to show us the tickets. He now grunted in surprise and, not knowing how to free himself (even Tolik, usually so grim, smiled as he witnessed this scene) threatened to keep the tickets if we wouldn't release him.

Dear, dear Old Man! Tallinn would come later. We still had a lot to do, but at least we were together. Rejoicing in our reunion, we sat down at the breakfast table, and the Old Man raised his lemonade glass and offered a toast:

Smile on your face and white clothes,
Clear mind and bright hopes.
Let it all come true!

V

Fair, kind, and true, have often liv'd alone,
Which three, till now, never kept seat in one.
William Shakespeare

There are not many young lieutenants who soon after their promotion manage to gain the trust of their subordinates. I guess it took the approach of someone who had grown up in an orphanage to quickly establish himself as a successful pilot and befriend all the other soldiers, not by humouring them but rather by finding an approach that suited each individual. Therefore, it was not hard to understand that the new officer in command, fully immersed in the service, came to my dwelling in the evening (for an army base it was truly luxurious—two fully heated rooms with security and a direct telephone connection with the entire base) and relaxed himself to such an extent that I sometimes felt like a loving elder brother (the Old Man's comparison) despite being younger than him.

Sometimes Romka's behaviour was such that even I, used to shocking those around me, had no idea how to react. He immediately established that the flight house was the perfect hideaway from the unceasing attention of the ladies. To avoid the dormitories where the young pilots usually slept, he brought to the house a rudimentary couch which, after some adjustments, became the most comfortable bed I have ever slept in. On that February evening, he had just returned from the test flights. His break was just one hour long, but he came straight to me. Once we had properly greeted each other (we hadn't met for only forty-five minutes, but it made no difference), he lay down on the couch and questioningly looked in my direction. During the longer test flights I almost never had a break, but I did take a minute to bring him a tray with dinner that I had already warmed up. The mess hall was right next door, but even there the bothersome waitresses managed to give him longing looks instead of food. To spare Romka the unpleasant experience, I was the one who ordered his meals, and other pilots brought them to the flight house. Sometimes the Old Man himself brought the tray. I always found it amusing because, as a rule, he would keep looking at Romka and spill the drinks or break the dishes while muttering that there should be no waitresses younger than sixty working at an army base.

Romka would jokingly pretend that the Old Man's appearance with the tray made him so flustered he had no idea where to put it. He would walk around the two rooms and finally bump into the Old Man and let him have a long, admiring look. During this performance I would usually openly giggle and let the Old Man enjoy himself. Then I would take away the tray and sit Roman down so that he could finish his meal. Once the Old Man had regained his composure, he would wish Romka a pleasant meal and, grumbling kindheartedly, take his leave.

On the days when he thought I took the tray away too quickly, he would playfully slap the back of my head and admonish me for my heartlessness. That day, after having a hearty meal and finally warming up, Roman put a bag full of old clothes that served us as a pillow underneath his head and lay down with his eyes open. I was working and pretended not to notice his presence, but his endless sighs finally made me get up and look behind the curtain. He then became still, and while my eyes tried to adjust to the darkness so that I could try to understand the reason for his preoccupation, his strong arms pulled me close to his body, and his powerful yet gentle kiss answered all my questions. The kiss consumed me to such a degree that I only came to my senses when I heard his light snoring. In less than an hour, I would wake him up and send him off to the next flight, and I would worry and yet again wait for his return. That's what my Romka was like—he could fall asleep in an instant, knowing that I was close and lulled to sleep by my kiss. Here is another story.

Once, having just finished my eighteen-hour-long working day, I dejectedly looked around the room trying to find my pillow. I was so tired I could no longer see straight. Romka was late, and I could not manage to stay awake until his return, though I had no doubt that he would come. Disregarding all the safety regulations, I left the front door unlocked. The last thing I remember before drifting off to sleep was Romka's head in the doorway, his smile, the sympathetic look in his eyes, and his hands that scooped me up and held me close. He put our coats on the couch, laid me down, and, after unsuccessfully trying to find the pillow, placed my head on his outstretched arm. He pulled me close like a baby and started humming something that resembled a lullaby. That was how I fell asleep—smiling blissfully and quietly wheezing. I woke up six hours later (the national anthem was playing on the radio), and my first thought was, "What am I sleeping on?" Romka was already awake. It was still dark outside, but his eyes were burning with such happiness and delight that all the lights in the world would fade in comparison. His lips wished me a good morning and immediately gave me the first kiss of the day, while his free hand tried to smooth out my wild hair. I raised myself slightly and discovered that he had not moved all night. His arm supported my head, and he had done everything in his power not to disturb my sleep. His arm had lost all feeling, so I started to massage it, angry at myself for causing my love discomfort. An embarrassed smile appeared on Romka's face, and he kept telling me that his arm would be all right before the first flight. To prove that he was right, he tried to put his arm around me, and indeed, it had regained its strength. He then gently placed me back down on the couch, and my head rested on (Oh, God!) the pillow that had suddenly made its appearance. And that was what Roman was like.

My Roman!

VI

*Love is the only passion that is repaid
with the same coins it mints.*
Stendhal

With my heart trembling, I keep returning to those days and remembering him—my joy, my sorrow, my sweet torture— my Roman.

The March air was cold and dank. We repeatedly had to cancel the flights, and the days dragged on like the never-ending freight cars of a train. The base was wrought with confusion. It was a long drive to the nearest town, and the base was surrounded by the Finns and the Swedes. But I almost didn't notice any of it. Roman and I were getting to know each other and discovering the beauty of nature (as much as we could in the given circumstances). Once our working day was over, we had dinner and then immediately headed off to the surrounding fields and woods to forget about everything else. Even if the spring was not glorious, it was still spring. Our hearts and souls longed for the mystery and newness of the season that had just started both in ourselves and in nature.

And again I keep talking in circles…Back then we could not understand what was tormenting us and not letting us enjoy the coming of spring. We resembled millions of young lovers who felt the same way, but we were still unaware of it. Inside us something was stirring and building. We felt our hearts bubbling like the spring sap trapped inside the birch trees.

The resolution of these feelings was once again unexpected. During one of our walks (it was still raining, and even the most optimistic soldiers had lost all hope, but not us), we started a silly game of outstaring each other without blinking or smiling. (My God! We were like little kids.) How could I not smile looking at his handsome face? We got so carried away that we didn't notice how far we had gone. It was time to return, but we had no strength to go back. In front of us stood an abandoned barn, and it became our shelter. The game still continued, but then, all of a sudden, because of our tiredness or maybe because of something else, we both started laughing. Sitting on a pile of old hay, we kept laughing for at least five minutes. Tears started running down my face. I wanted to say something but couldn't, just like Roman.

Once we stopped laughing, I helplessly laid my head on his shoulder. I couldn't see his eyes, but I felt that something was about to happen. When I raised my head, I knew I was not mistaken. His clear-blue eyes, surrounded by a thousand beautiful eyelashes, were trying to ask me something…oh no…It was no longer a game. The game was long forgotten. His eyes burned with youth and passion, awareness and love. He held me in his arms for a moment longer and then, still not saying anything, carefully and gently, almost without touching, laid me down next to him. And then, just like the sap that finally finds release from the trunk of the tree where it's imprisoned, he moaned in delight and covered me with kisses…

I thought I would choke, but I had no strength or desire to stop him. I was floating on cloud nine—no, higher! And he, used to heights and flying, was taking me higher and farther away from the ground. The spring had finally started!

VII

He does not know how Love yields and denies;
He only knows, who knows how sweetly she
Can talk and laugh, the sweetness of her sighs.
Petrarch

Three days earlier the dark clouds that had gathered over the base exploded in thunder, lightning, and the first rain. Almost immediately the bare branches of the trees were covered in tiny buds, and bright-green strands of grass were bursting out of the ground and reaching toward the sun. The first flowers were blooming, and so were our feelings. Most of the people on the base walked around alone, but we were always together.

During one of our walks, Roman pulled a puppy out of the water. Once its fur was dry, we realised that it was almost impossibly fluffy. Here's how it happened: We were looking at the waves beating against a fallen log and a pair of ducks swimming past, and then we noticed that on the other side, something dirty was desperately moving and whimpering. Roman immediately waded into the water, took a long stick, and started to pull the log toward the shore. The sleepy ducks angrily withdrew. The puppy, feeling the hope of getting out, held on to the log and safely reached the shore.

Once it got out of the water, it shook the moisture and dirt out of its fur. It immediately started whimpering, wanting to get warm. I wrapped the puppy in a bag I had brought in case we decided to walk to the store and put it under my arm. It stayed there and watched as we walked around, and once it was warm enough, it fell asleep.

Live beings are drawn to one another, just like seeds are drawn to the earth. It was April—the middle of spring. My every minute, every hour, every day was filled with Roman. Despite the fact that we were very busy and very tired, I still loved the days of the test flights because then I could see him more often. On other days I could hardly wait for the evening and excitedly ran back to the flight house, informing the responsible officer that I would be working there. That way no one would interfere with our evening by calling or coming over for an inspection.

No! I can't seem to escape long introductions. But on the other hand, how can I just tell you what happened that night? No, not happened but occurred. No, came true…oh God! I don't even know what to call it. There were no flights that day, and I went to the house before dinner with the intention to prepare for the flights of the next day. The day was filled with petty administrative tasks, so once I got back, I immediately took a shower (another one of Romka's constructions) to wash off the dirt and tiredness of the day. I knew that Romka would come as soon as his twenty-four-hour shift ended, so I forgot about my intention to work, lit the stove, and started to cook.

We called the rescued puppy Pilot and secretly let him stay at the flight house. Several times he found a way to get up on my desk and then fall down, spreading his paws as if he really intended to fly. During the day he always missed our company. I came to feed him but then, despite his insistent whimpers, always locked him up again.

That night he was very happy about my return and watched my movements from the side of the warm stove. He was particularly interested in the smell of the meatballs that I was warming up. Given his young age, he was always the first one to eat, and once he had filled his tummy and enjoyed my company, he fell asleep in his usual place—in a vacuum-cleaner box lined with leftovers of an old parachute.

Soon I could hear a car approaching, and the silent and morose, yet unbelievably kind and faithful, Buryat with the Russian name Tolik brought in the tired and hungry but still smiling Roman, who obviously had no intention to sleep. It was not the first time that Tolik came to visit us, and his direct superior, the commander of the regiment (our Old Man) was also a regular guest, so I was not at all surprised to see the three of them arriving at my door.

The first thing that Romka did was kiss me (which deepened Tolik's frown and made the Old Man smile), and then he went to the box and took out the sleeping Pilot. The dog started to whimper but then smelled Romka and licked his face. Once Romka placed him on the floor, Pilot started wagging his tail and sniffed Tolik, but the strong smell of petrol made him move on to the Old Man. Seeing Pilot, the Old Man tried to look reproachful, but the puppy's innocent and trusting look in combination with his attempt to lick the Old Man's face immediately won him over.

Soon all four of us (I'm not counting the dog) washed our hands and sat down at the table. Pilot was not happy with the arrangement and demanded another portion of food, even though the previous one had made his tiny tummy blow up like a balloon. I had no choice but to take him back to his box, where he soon settled down and fell asleep.

Meanwhile, our dinner was in full swing. The Old Man loved the fried potatoes and the sauce I had made, but he showed no interest in the meatballs. When he found out that I had gotten them at the officers' mess hall, he once again threatened to get rid of the chef. However, he soon forgot all about food and, looking at Roman and me, told us stories about war and his years in the service, and he pointed out how important it is to have a friend by your side whom you can fully trust. We nodded our heads in agreement and dreamed about the time when we'd be able to go to sleep, but the Old Man was clearly in need of communication and, despite Tolik's subtle hints, showed no intention to leave. While he possessed the character of a true commander and never tried to hide it during service hours, once he found himself in an informal setting, he became gentle and vulnerable, which made us feel like helping him. We felt that he really didn't want to leave, so we made his favourite peppermint tea, using the fresh mint that grew on our windowsill.

During our late evenings with the Old Man, Romka would always start singing, and I would read poetry. This time was no exception, and we all stayed together till midnight. Tolik probably thought that the Old Man was not planning to go back at all and kept reminding him about the morning test flights.

Why am I remembering all this? I guess it confirms something that I once read—every person has a special place that seems calm and unchangeable, just like childhood. For me that place is my tiny room and the evening that warmed us and allowed us to say everything we thought and felt. What can be more beautiful? While Roman and the Old Man were saying good night and discussing the last details of the upcoming flights, I cleared the table and even washed the dishes.

As I was about to reenter the room, I heard the words of the Old Man: "Take care of him. He is worth everything."

And Romka replied, "I know. That's why we are together. Everything will be all right."

The sound of the car engine slowly grew quieter and finally disappeared completely. While Romka was taking a shower, I took Pilot outside, then made our bed (oh, the wonderful couch!) and aired the room. Finally, I heard him turn off the water. I let the wet dog back into the house (it had started raining) and closed the door but found myself in complete darkness.

"Romka…"

"Don't worry; I turned it off."

"I can't see anything. Turn it back on."

He didn't reply. The only sound I could hear was the breathing of Pilot, who tried to make himself comfortable inside his box. It was not hard to reach the couch. I tried to feel my way in the darkness, at the same time removing my clothes. I thought that Romka was already asleep. But then in a flash of lightning (a storm had started outside), I saw his strong body covered with nothing more than a sheet. I finally understood why he had turned off the light—for the first time he was completely naked. I stood dumbfounded. I was almost next to the couch, but I couldn't move. I heard Romka's voice—quiet, soft like silk, and partly amused but with impatient undertones—and it brought me out of my trance.

"What's wrong? Come here! Don't be afraid."

As the next bolt of lightning struck, I saw his hands reaching for me. I touched them with my fingertips. He grabbed me—possessively but carefully—and just as I removed my underwear, he laid me down next to him under the cold sheet. For a while we just lay there, not talking, not moving, just getting used to this new situation. I was barely breathing. I didn't know what Romka wanted. I could not imagine how and what would happen between us. I was also afraid to frighten him. Underneath his strong masculinity and confident bearing was hiding, at times, a shy and vulnerable person. I mostly saw him as a leader, so it was easy to forget about his gentler side.

For the next five minutes we lay still, not moving. Then his hands, so used to bending the heavy pieces of machinery to his will, tenderly started to caress my body, touching everything he finally had access to. I could no longer breathe. There was music in my soul that made me feel like crying and singing at the same time. It was obvious that the same was happening to him.

When his loving hands and lips reached my waist, he suddenly stopped and lay down on his back. I found the strength to raise my body and look at him. He timidly reached for my lips, and I took over. I wrapped my hands around his face and kept kissing him, feeling how every kiss gave him more confidence and strength. Changing his position, Romka once again hovered over me, and this movement fully revealed his burning desire.

Just then Pilot whimpered in his sleep, and Roman once again froze and lay down, feeling embarrassed. I called Pilot's name. The dog whimpered and then became quiet.

Roman raised his hand and with one swift movement did what I hadn't dared. The sheet slipped off and revealed to me this beautiful creation of nature. A divine prototype made long ago but never released to the world. He was lying there completely naked. I could finally see everything that had been hidden from me yet constantly present in my dreams and fantasies. I let my eyes slide over his expansive but well-sculpted chest and moved them lower when…oh dear!

At the bottom of his navel, there was a birthmark in the shape of a star. Underneath it, a light dusting of hair led all the way down to his groin—also strong and expansive and beautiful in its primeval masculinity. The hair that covered it reminded me of soft and silky grass. It caressed my tongue and tickled my nose. I felt a wild desire to bury my head right in it. The peak of this creation was his impressive member. Just a single touch made my body shiver in delight. Awakened by my gentle tongue, it grew and opened like a midnight flower and then dove into the abyss of my mouth, filling me with happiness and realization that my dream was coming true.

Some invisible force made Roman move, and now we were lying sideways across the bed. My mouth greedily engulfed his member while my hands caressed, pulled, rubbed, and kneaded his magnificent nipples, tickled his hips and calves, and then once again moved upward. My mouth and my tongue briefly let go of the long-desired prize and joined my hands.

Starting from horsehead and moving downward, I kissed and caressed this blissful giant, waiting for the moment when he would beg for mercy and then, no longer able to contain his desire, give me the nectar of his flower.

But Roman was trying to make this pleasure last, and only when I yet again traveled the length of his body, the moment finally came— he moaned, his body tensed, and his breath hitched. Then I greedily returned to the flower, pressed my lips around it, and started to gather up the nectar that gushed out in a powerful stream.

Oh, what a miracle it was! Our moans became a new language and flew up into the sky. Our bodies melted together and then fell apart. We were lying next to each other, not able to move. The night of love had finally come. Its glorious aftertaste would stay with us for a long time, surprising and scaring, enchanting and blessing us. We were greeted by the spring storm raging outside the window, and we let the first warmth of April float into the room.

VIII

*Love is the strongest of all the passions
because it attacks at once
the head, the heart, and the body.*
Voltaire

Gently falling poplar puffs and cold wind playing in my hair. In the balmy May weather, the military base seemed to come alive. The sunlight was warming the walls of the buildings, and the velvety earth spread under our feet like a carpet. Our hearts were waking up. A lot can change on a May afternoon. All the bad things disappear and are replaced by something good, kind, and pure. It is then that happiness quietly comes into our lives. It's a simple and worldly joy of loving, breathing in the tangy smell of bursting buds, and touching the bark of the birch trees. All this I could experience with Roman. Our days and nights were a constant feast for body and soul. We could not imagine being apart and ran to each other whenever we could, as if we were afraid not to have enough time to enjoy each other's company.

As always, May was hectic: there were a lot of festivities, a lot of errands to run, and many night shifts, and I was constantly worried about Roman, who tried to achieve justice in situations that had no chance of just resolutions. Nothing bad had happened, but success often makes enemies, and envy makes people pay too close attention to others. When that happened, Roman usually blamed himself and came to me preoccupied (a state that didn't suit him at all). His eyes were looking for answers in the corners of the room, on the floor, and on the ceiling, and then, not finding what they were looking for, turned dark and disinterested. In moments like these even our ever-growing puppy, Pilot, could not change his mood, no matter how hard he tried. Romka automatically caressed the dog's back and handed him delicious sugar cubes, but Pilot knew that he felt bad. Then Pilot came to me, as if to tell me that his attempts at cheering Romka up were futile.

I usually made the dog go outside and departed myself, or found something to occupy myself with, for I knew that in these moments it was better for Romka to be alone. It always ended the same way— when some hours had passed, he came to find me and Pilot, kissed both of us, and silently apologized for the hours of morose silence. Of course, we always forgave him and went to have dinner without asking any questions. After we had eaten, we always went for a walk, during which Romka seemed to let go of the heavy burden of the day and told me about what had transpired.

That evening was no different. I sent him to take a shower so that he could wash off the tiredness and return to his good spirits. Meanwhile, dressed in athletic pants and a T-shirt, I busied myself at the stove, trying to figure out the best way to prepare a chicken that Romka had brought in that morning. Pilot was attentively watching my attempts to cut the chicken and requested a piece, but not raw—it had to at least be boiled.

Then, through the sound of running water, I heard another voice asking for something (or so I thought). I couldn't make out what he wanted, so I put down the chicken, washed my hands, took the large towel that he had left behind, went to the shower, and extended my arm, fully convinced that he would take it. Romka's arm extended as well and took hold of me. It all happened in an instant, and no matter how hard I tried to free myself and return to the preparation of our dinner, soon enough large drops of water had made me soaking wet from head to toe. The wet clothes clung to my body, and realizing that I would have to take a shower after all, I tried to remove them.

Romka, who after that night in April was undressing in my presence more often, started to help me. It gave him real pleasure, and he watched me with open curiosity, gradually exposing my flesh. He took off my wet shirt and then knelt down to pull off my pants and underwear. He then got up and took a bar of Finnish soap that smelled of cherries. He angled me away from the spray of water and started washing me. After a while, he washed away the suds and leaned down to kiss my skin with obvious enjoyment.

In another soap dish, we had a bar of Swedish soap with the aroma of nutmeg, and the smell mixed with that of cherries. I joined the game and started washing Romka. We squealed and splashed in the water like children, trying to compete in the number of kisses we could bestow on each other's bodies.

Once our hands moved below the waist, the laughter stopped. With our lips interlocked, Romka brought both of us under the strong and cool spray of water. While the water caressed both of us, his hands caressed my body. I could no longer contain my desire. Romka felt it and slowly started to sink to the floor, kissing every centimetre of my skin as he went down. Soon he reached his destination, but instead of doing what my body was begging for, he languidly caressed my stomach and hips, making my skin burn with heat despite the cold water that cascaded over it.

I almost couldn't take it. The first touch of his lips made me arch my back, and I could no longer stand up straight. The sensations that he was giving me took away any strength I had left. Letting me catch my breath without stopping this sweet torture, he started to kiss his way up my body. Once our lips connected, two magnificent members also reached out toward each other and gently touched. Our clean skin rubbed together for the longest time and gave us such pleasure that just a minute later my nectar flowed out like the stream of a fountain. Romka put his neck, chest, stomach, and legs under it, then gathered it up in his palms and greedily licked it up. As he was doing it, he felt like a part of me was entering his body.

The pleasure had drained me of my last shreds of strength. I could barely stand on my feet. Romka once again gently washed me, wrapped me in the towel, which by some miracle was still dry, and took me to bed. Seeing this, Pilot showed his excitement, since he obviously had been waiting for us to reemerge. Romka laid me down and dried both of us with a clean sheet. He then opened his bag and took out two wonderful bright-green terry robes. With a festive smile on his lips, he dressed both of us while still managing to kiss me and sing melodies from old operettas.

Poor Pilot! As we fell asleep, we could hear his dissatisfied growls and the sound of him gnawing the raw chicken. I'm sorry, my friend. It was spring.

IX

When you're not near me, I love you even more,
But when you are, I miss you like never before.
Marina Tsvetaeva

The evening was slowly fading into one of the short nights of June. It was finally becoming slightly cooler. The air was infused with the smell of freshly cut grass, the recent thunderstorm, mushrooms, pines, and the surrounding bogs. Something strange and inexplicable called everyone out of the barracks. To tell the truth, there were no barracks. We were in the middle of a training session and slept in tents next to a forest. Our bodies, heated by the daily "battles" and bundled in layers of clothing, could not cool down even in the evening, and we had no energy to look for a place to swim. I had not seen Roman for twenty-four hours. I tried to talk myself into falling asleep. Our regiments were supposed to meet the day after, and then…there were two of us in the tent. My tentmate was already asleep, but I was still tossing and turning, trying to picture our meeting. Suddenly a shadow crossed my tent. My heart jumped in excitement, and it was not mistaken. A voice I knew so well was calling me.

"Roman! You found me!"

His eyes were burning feverishly, and his hands were playing with the stalk of a flower he had just picked up. With the speed of an arrow flying out of a bow, he dragged me into the forest. It was useless to try to resist him, and I was blissfully happy to be with him after all this time. We stopped at a small lake. I have no idea how it happened to be in the middle of the forest, but the moonlight made this place so beautiful that even Roman stopped and stood still.

I was starting to come to my senses after our frantic walk and wanted to ask how he had come to be there, but he kissed me, put a finger on my lips, turned me away from him, put his arms around my chest, and stood still, enjoying the view. The sparse and mixed forest made up of pines, firs, and small birches that surrounded this lake of mysterious origin almost seemed alive. It looked like an assembly of giants and midgets who had gathered here for a swim but didn't dare enter the water. I don't know if it was their doing or someone else's, but one side of the lake was cleared of stones, and a rudimentary hut stood close to the water. There was long grass on both sides and clean sand in the middle. In the moonlight the outlines of this strange creation almost reminded me of a small castle inhabited by trolls. It was light and quiet where we stood.

I was still for a while, but just as I was about to free myself from Roman's embrace and talk to him, something moved in the bushes and made me cling to him even closer. And then I understood what it was. Pilot, who also seemed to enjoy this enchanting silence, ran up to us barking soundlessly. We both leaned down to greet our friend who had been looking for us. We gave him some sugar cubes I found in my pocket, and without saying a word, enjoyed the breathtaking scenery. Almost transparent fog was rising from the surface of the water, and the clear-blue colour of the water told us it was clean.

As always, Romka started undressing first, still in complete silence. To tell the truth, I didn't feel like swimming, but then Pilot understood his intentions and ran into the water, followed by the gloriously naked Roman, whose skin was bathed in serene moonlight. I had no choice but to follow their example. The three of us entered the water. Soft like velvet, it covered our nakedness and brought us closer to each other, encouraging us to play in the moonlight. At first I felt slightly uncomfortable, but then strong and gentle arms took hold of me, and guided by their support, I was soon able to fully join the two happy creatures in their excitement.

Every once in a while Romka dove under the water, positioned himself right under my body, and carried me like a dolphin above the surface. Then he suddenly hid in the depth and later reemerged on the other side, calling out like an owl and scaring both Pilot and me. He rested on a large log that was partly covered by the water. In the pale moonlight, covered with seaweeds, he looked like an alien who had come down to earth for a swim.

When Roman saw his reflection in the water, he became even more excited. He started to wave his hands and shout in a language I didn't understand. He threw a stick ashore for Pilot to follow, but the dog was in no hurry to return. Then Roman gracefully jumped into the water and found himself next to me. His endless caresses calmed me and gave me confidence. Out of envy or jealousy, the moon hid its face, leaving us in almost complete darkness. It made me shiver, but Roman's gentle hands pressed me closer to his body.

We then swam to the shore like habitual swimmers no longer lost in the magic of the moment. Coming out of the water, we found Pilot, who had made himself comfortable on our discarded clothes. As soon as he saw us, he jumped up and ran toward the hut, as if knowing we would be headed there. He was barking happily and kept stopping to look at our lingering forms.

Romka saw that I was cold and started to rub my body. His hands, confident like those of a professional masseur, traveled the length of my body, and soon enough I felt warmth spreading all over my skin. The combination of tiredness, excitement, and longing for these sensations to continue forever made me lie down on the blanket that was spread on the ground.

Roman, not expecting this move, fell down and found himself on top of me. His body fully covered mine, and he froze, too afraid to move. At this moment the curious moon appeared from behind the clouds, and I could once again see the eyes of my beloved. A thousand blue and velvet-soft lakes seemed to reflect from them. Oh! I had seen those eyes so many times, yet every time I had to take a moment to show respect to nature, who had created them. His eyes always told me everything that he could not find the words to say. In different situations in our lives, I could read in them the whole variety of emotions—anger and tenderness, indifference and unstoppable desire. Even when he pretended to keep his calm, those beautiful eyes always told me the truth. And once I had read him without any words, he started a new game that only I knew but never fully understood. But that story I will tell you later.

At that moment his eyes seemed to apologize for the clumsiness of their owner, who was trying to raise himself from the awkward position. They were smiling and reflecting the gentle moonlit night and asking me if they had understood me correctly. Yes, my love. Yes! You did understand me correctly. I wanted to repeat the experience of that April night. I wanted you. Ever since your first kiss, I was hungry for you. Only you could give me everything that the loving heart of a young man needs. I knew you understood because your body shivered on my heated skin and made my desire burn with an even brighter flame. You were like a breeze, a storm, a hurricane—but not at first. Some invisible inner force stopped you from letting go of your shame and acting upon your desire. Or maybe I was too weak and gave up too easily. Who knows…your body became tense, and you covered me with kisses, drawing me closer and closer…and then we felt that someone was pulling the corner of the blanket. It was Pilot, who could no longer wait for us and had decided to show his impatience at the least appropriate moment. And then the moon hid its face behind a cloud. We lay still and quiet for a moment longer but then, driven by the apologetic nudges of the dog and the light rain that had started to fall, we slowly moved toward the hut.

X

And while the candle is lighting the dark
I want to talk about love...
Omar Khayyám

The door of the hut was secured by the enormous branches of a fir. They were so heavy that even Pilot could not move them. He started growling and waited for our assistance. Moving the branches aside, I followed the dog into the hut. Once again I was enchanted by what I saw: the floor was covered with fir branches and small bunches of dried plants that gave the room a pleasant smell. To soften the prickliness of the fir branches, someone had thrown grass on top of them. It was partly dry but still infused with a divine smell. The hut was made out of thin and flexible branches tied together with brittle-looking twigs that, surprisingly, were strong enough to keep the construction together. The roof was made of fir branches through the gaps of which we could see small patches of the sky.

Pilot didn't approve of the place. He was growling and sniffing the corners, unsure where to position himself. Romka, having entered after me, yelled for the dog to stop but then, after seeing my surprise at such behaviour, put a blanket in front of the entrance and told him to guard it. The dog obeyed. He stretched out on the blanket, placed his head on his paws, and from time to time threw sideways glances in our direction.

I understood Romka's previous reaction and wanted to help him return to the state we were both in by the lake. I spread the dry grass and covered it with our clothes, on top of which I put a sheet that I had taken from my tent (as if somehow sensing what would happen).

We both lay down and covered ourselves with another sheet. Oh God, how amazing it was! The smell of the grass and flowers and the experience of that night cannot be described. It was still dark, but we didn't want to sleep. I was freezing, and Romka held me so close I could barely breathe. The large fir branch that was standing next to our improvised bed started to slowly sink down until it spread over us like a blanket. Oh, God! I can still feel the smell of the branch and the tenderness of Romka's caresses, which were becoming more and more insistent. The burning heat of love diminished our chills, probably created by the newness of the circumstances rather than the cold. Our desire lit up like a flame, and the spirit of the benevolent old tree made our bodies pliable and open to love. Romka was always excited by new experiences. Trembling no less than I, he slowly entered my body and drank in the excitement of the unknown, yet he was ready to stop at any moment and ask for my forgiveness. Feeling how easily I yielded to his body, he continued pushing on and filling my body with delicious pain, all the while covering me with kisses and gentle caresses and whispering soothing words of love.

The darkness that engulfed us and was dimly illuminated by starlight (or maybe it was the light of love burning in his eyes) made me feel like we were on another planet. Only the sparse raindrops echoing the music of our souls reminded us that we were on earth. Our bodies spread through the breadth of the hut and then joined again. They sang an anthem to the love scorned by everyone else but given to us by a higher power that kept us under its spell.

Roman was so gentle! His arms were lifting me and laying me back down. His lips were like the red flowers of the night that was slowly coming to an end—they nourished me in my thirst. His body sang to me like a nightingale, a melody that was flowing and ebbing inside me and taking us closer and closer to the sunrise.

Finally, with one last moan of pleasure, the music stopped and the air around us became perfectly still. Our bodies separated, but Romka immediately took me in his arms and held me close with unparalleled tenderness, thanking me for the night I had given him, for being there, for being with him, for everything.

My love! I was the one who desperately wanted to thank you and the whole world for the fact that you were in my life and that I belonged to you and no one else. Many years later (and what years those were!) I can still repeat that you always stood out among every-one I ever met in my life. Only you could make my heart beat with the sound of galloping hooves of wild horses. Only you could let go of reason and dive headfirst into the abyss of love. I have kept your tenderness inside me for all these years.

Then we fell asleep, but later, warmed by the breath of love, we dove back into its gentle waters.

XI

Look, what is best, that best I wish in thee:
This wish I have; then ten times happy me!
William Shakespeare

Then came the moment that I loved the most and impatiently waited for: Romka, blissfully tired after swimming, finally allowed himself to fully relax. He noisily waded out of the lake and seemed to bring half of its water with him. He fell down onto the sand and sprawled his beautiful body for the early-morning sun to admire. And admire it did! It tangled its rays in Romka's dark and wet curls, then looked into his blue eyes and was surprised to discover that the sky was so close to the ground. Slowly waking up, the sun marvelled at this beautiful creation of nature lying there almost naked. Its rays became stronger and bolder. They engulfed his wide and tanned chest, playing in the dark hair and running over his nipples, then moving lower down his torso. Like a greedy moneylender wishing to get his hands on the desired object before even seeing it, the sun moved lower still. Romka's wet swimming trunks, clinging to his body, left little to the imagination, and the sun suddenly grew shy, timidly apologized, and like a faithful dog, started licking his legs with comforting warmth. Finally, it reached its peak up in the sky and unwillingly became the witness of our restful morning. It blushed and burned with jealousy and tried to hide its face behind every passing cloud. However, it was a hopeless rivalry—I had already won the heart of its object. The Greek god lying next to me welcomed each return of the sun but welcomed the touch of my hands even more.

And he didn't need to wait for long. We both longed to continue what we had started in the moonlight, just this time under the
warm and welcoming sun. However, something strange happened.
There came a moment when Roman suddenly tensed up and seemed
to move away from me. The idea that he wouldn't see how much I
wanted to belong to him made me shiver, my warm skin broke out
in goose bumps, and my teeth started chattering.

But that didn't last long. His arms lifted me like a feather (even
though my frame was certainly not slight) and firmly pressed me to
his body. His warm, soft, and moist lips reached toward mine. As
soon as I felt their touch, I was surrounded by his tender love and no
longer felt scared or alone. His strong and wet body had absorbed
the freshness of the morning and the smell of the sand and seaweed.
It made me forget all my worries and encouraged me to smile with
desire, the memories of which make my head spin even now.

In between his kisses and caresses, I was frantically gulping the
air, trying to survive the onslaught of the powerful emotions that
threatened to consume me. Oh, those blissful moments of joy! When
Roman had had his fill, he relaxed his body but still held me close.
The coolness of the morning air still had not dissipated, but his body
kept me warm.

I felt an overwhelming thirst. While I was thinking about where
to find some water (even though we were lying next to a lake), Romka
managed to once again plunge into the lake and return to my side.
Overpowered by thirst, I playfully started to collect the droplets of
water pooling on his body with my tongue. He raised his eyebrows
in surprise and even tried to get up but then almost growled and sank
back onto the sand. I collected the nectar from his forehead, eyes,
nose, ears, and lips, and I finally reached his chin, but as soon as my
tongue touched it, Romka started shivering, slightly raised himself,
and started breathing so frantically that I had to stop and look at him.

His eyes were half-closed, his chest was rising and falling like
bellows, his whole body tensed up, and his heart was beating so fast

and loud that my ear, now firmly pressed to his chest, almost went deaf. It seemed that one more movement, and his heart would burst.

I was scared. It was sometime later that I (and he as well) learned what had caused it. When Romka noticed that I had stopped, he quickly regained his senses. Only the surprise that his eyes couldn't hide told me that he was still worried. Then our bodies entwined, and we rolled down the sand till we found ourselves in the clear-blue water of the lake. Not a single cloud was visible in the sky. It was as bright and spotless as our love. Nothing suggested that there would ever be sorrow in our lives.

PART II

I

And once again the late evening is slowly drifting into the night. Outside the window there is only darkness and cold rain. My thoughts, scattered and frantic, refuse to form a chronological sequence of memories. It's almost hard to move. The slightest tension in the body results in dull pain. My soul is straining against my chest and begging for mercy. There is a picture on my table—two young men with their heads together, lost in a blissful moment of forgetfulness, but their eyes are full of sorrow, their bodies tense and their future unpredictable. Unfortunately, it is not a picture of Roman and me. The fate of our pictures was decided by a force we couldn't control. These are just two out of millions of hearts full of love. The purpose of love is to bring people together, but I am alone in the darkness of the night.

"Roman! Roma…" I scream. I whisper your name, calling you to my side. The tears are falling, then stop, then once again fill my eyes. My breathing keeps getting faster but then slows down. Already for many years, your only reply is silence…oh, Roman! How I long to see the love in your eyes, to feel your warm hands, your gentle lips, your burning skin. The young men in the picture are watching me, but there is nothing they can do. They are frozen in timeless desire to love and to be loved, to rest in the arms of hope. I have no choice but to open the door of my heart and let the memories in. How strange! I promised myself not to follow the events chronologically, yet I stubbornly do, since that is the only way I can be fully honest in this confession of love—the story that can be experienced only once and never repeated.

II

July, the crown jewel of summer. The hot air was all tremor and vibration. The long forest grass reached my waist. Mushrooms were shyly peeking through its green and luscious blades. Every drop of morning dew reflected the golden sunlight. The birds were singing their hearts out, and the linden trees were in full bloom and tirelessly feeding the buzzing bees with their nectar. Our souls were full of music and harmony, just like in the beautiful lines of Fyodor Tyutchev's poem:

The sun is shining and the water shimmers,
The world is full of smiles, life full of glimmer.

The training continued. Due to some technical issues at the tank company, we had an entire week to ourselves. We had time to swim and sunbathe and even to learn something useful—to work with a scythe. Actually, for Roman it was not a new skill, but I had no idea how to manipulate the impressive tool. However, I should not run ahead of the events.

Tirma was the remotest and the most sparsely populated village in the whole area. You can, therefore, imagine our surprise when during one of our countless walks, we found two dilapidated houses inhabited by two Russian women—Alekseyevna and Zaharyevna. They used to live in Leningrad but came to visit the graves of their relatives, who lost their lives during the war, and ended up staying. They lived and worked together, and as we entered the property asking for a cup of water, we didn't even notice the empty sheepfold. While we helped the tiny and fragile-looking Alekseyevna to fill the cups with water from the nearby well, Zaharyevna returned with their flock of sheep. She was a tall, large-breasted, and strong woman with a sonorous voice. Once all the sheep were securely locked inside the sheepfold and fed, and when the chickens had received their fill of grains, the women offered us dinner in the shade of their tiny garden and told us the stories of their lives. The meal was frugal, but we had lived on army food for too long, so the fresh milk and still-warm and soft bread kept disappearing so fast that the old ladies just smiled with curiosity and kept renewing the delicious supplies of food. Pilot had earlier prevented one of the sheep from escaping, so he was rewarded with milk and a big bone that he shamelessly chewed right in front of the household guard dog. He was not afraid of competition but didn't think of sharing his prize either.

It was getting late. As we were getting ready to leave, Zaharyevna, the more forward of the two ladies, looked at Roman's strong and tanned arms and asked if we knew how to scythe. All I could do was smile and shrug in apology, but Roman's eyes burned with interest. It was clear that he knew how to do it but hadn't had the chance to use his skills in a long time. He quickly overcame his doubts and asked to see the scythe. Alekseyevna soon brought the large tool, and Roman swiftly took it out of her hands and set to test it on a patch of wild grass that once used to be a flower bed. He surprised Alekseyevna by bending down, picking three stray flowers from amid the grass, and presenting them to her with a courteous bow.

Meanwhile, Zaharyevna, surprisingly quickly for her age, climbed the stairs leading to the top of the shed, put her head out of the window, adjusted her kerchief, and asked without the slightest hesitation, "Can you do it with this one as well?" She pulled out an even bigger scythe and a whetstone. The scythe was too big for either of the women, so it obviously had not been used for a long time. Roman took the scythe, helped the blushing woman descend, and attempted to sharpen the scythe, but then, noticing my impatience, agreed to postpone it till the next day.

We wished the women good night and called Pilot, who had finally given up on his bone and apparently offered it to the other dog, since it was now lying in his bowl. Remembering how he got the bone in the first place, Pilot was now carefully watching the sheepfold. He was unconvinced by my promises of a return, and only Romka's strict order made him obey. Then we finally rushed to the camp, hoping to get there in time for the evening inspection.

When we finally reached the tent, we found our dinner and a note from the Old Man, who was worried about our long absence. We gave in to our tiredness but soon heard someone approaching the tent and saw the Old Man, who was grumbling that we hadn't even touched our dinner. We wanted to apologize for making him worry but couldn't keep our eyes open, so the words came out in a stream of unrecognizable sounds. Then Pilot followed our example. He stretched out next to our legs and also fell asleep without touching his food. The Old Man could take no more, and as he was leaving, we heard his final words: "What a family!"

Golden stars were quietly walking across the sky. The night guards shouted commands to each other. Pilot was breathing loudly and every once in a while growled in his sleep. Roman's strong arms held me tight to his body; his even breathing raised the hair at the base of my neck. His enlivening warmth made our lips meet. Thus, under the whispering stars, sleep finally overtook us, and we surrendered ourselves to the enchanting summer night.

The first person we saw in the morning was the Old Man. He woke us earlier than everyone else and, having finally received information about the reason for our disappearance, calmed down and encouraged us to ask the old ladies if any other assistance was needed. He then sent us on our way, instructing Tolik to accompany us. When we pulled up to their house, the women were already awake and ready to work. They offered us a breakfast of bread and milk, and I noticed that even Tolik was smiling from delight at obtaining such delicacies. Soon he said goodbye to the women, promised to bring them all the necessary supplies, and left us there till the evening.

We took our tools, grabbed an extra scythe, and went to the field. All three scythes were already sharpened. As always, Alekseyevna stayed at home to take care of lunch and dinner, and Zaharyevna took their flock of sheep to the field. She was going in the opposite direction from where we were heading, so Pilot confusedly waited for a command, not knowing whom to follow, torn between his duty and desires. His relationship with the owners' dog was settled, so Roman allowed him to leave, and Pilot started following the sheep with a happy bark. All this happened in front of my eyes, still heavy from sleep.

We finally reached the meadow. I had always lived in a city, so the abundance of grass and flowers was a true assault on my senses. The soft and luscious grass at times reached up all the way to our waists. Like a magic carpet under our feet, it was begging to be scythed.

I often stopped my endeavours to look at Roman. The long and sure strokes of his scythe left the freshly cut grass in even rows. Roman was smiling, happy to enjoy the morning, the smell of the grass, the sunlight, and the possibility to be free from all the worries.

We worked on. I was finally fully awake and dedicated all my attention to the grass. I was neither as fast nor as neat as Roman, and every once in a while he had to encourage and support me, but I was still enjoying this delicious labour. I tried my best to keep up with him and increased the speed of my endeavours, but my scythe ended up hitting a stone that was lying hidden in the grass. I yelled out in surprise and bent down, not sure what to do, but Roman was already next to me and tried to draw my attention to a little spring that started gushing out from the place where the stone once stood. We watched in awe as the tiny crater filled up with clear and fresh water, inviting us the quench our thirst. We lay down on opposite sides and started drinking but soon enough noticed that the spring was so small the water quickly turned muddy.

I had finished most of the water we had taken with us, so the thirst became almost unbearable. I also felt pain in my leg where the scythe had lightly grazed the flesh. My eyes started filling up with tears. I tried to hold them back, but the thirst and the unfortunate incident with the scythe made it increasingly harder to do. I finally fell back onto the grass, which covered me like a green curtain, and hid my tears.

Meanwhile, Roman was busy at the spring. I slightly raised myself and wanted to call him, but then I noticed that he was trying to enlarge the mouth of the spring with the hard stem of a thistle. The stream increased. He gathered the water in his palms and was immediately by my side. I buried my face in his palms, and the cold nectar of love revived me. The tears in my eyes immediately dried up. I smiled at him and whispered, "More…" We repeated this ritual several times until my thirst was finally quenched, and I once again fell back on the grass, happily drawing its scent into my lungs.

I heard Romka down by the spring getting his fill of the cool water, splashing and puffing like a giant fish. He then became quiet, and our love surprised me yet again. He bent down over me, engulfed me in his embrace, raised my head, and let the water from his mouth run into mine during our passionate kiss. All the while his eyes were shining in delight. When our lips finally parted, I softly whispered, "Again…just like that…" We both bent down over the spring and drank and kissed and laughed…oh, God! Was it just a dream? No! I can still feel the taste of the water, the smell of Romka's palms, the warmth of his lips. These memories still live inside me despite all the years of separation.

The day was becoming warmer, and we decided to take a swim in a nearby river. We hid the scythes, joined our hands, and ran over the soft grass all the way to the river. Roman took off his pants and wanted to enter the water in his underwear but then changed his mind and removed it. I had barely managed to undress when he pulled me toward the water. There is nothing better than the feeling of cool water on overheated skin. It doesn't matter if you immerse yourself in an ocean, a sea, a lake, or a bog. The body comes to life under the gentle caresses of water, and you instantly revive from the heat and stuffiness of the day.

We didn't stay long, but these precious minutes seemed like hours. Not a second is wasted when you are together with the one you love, the one you belong to, the one who makes you happy just by being near. The water that had cooled our skin suddenly lit the fire of pure desire in our hearts. Romka swam up to me, embraced me, and started kissing my hair, my eyelashes, my eyes, my chest, the palms of my hands, and finally my lips till we were almost drowning. The river was not very deep, but his love made me feel like I was sinking to the bottom of the sea. His strong and gentle hands held me up and moved me toward the surface, where he continued to assault my senses. We were both happy that just for a day the world was ours, and we loved each other with equal passion and desperation. He carried me out of the water, and we once again found ourselves in the kingdom of the green grass, where we succumbed to the burning flames of love. We were lying in each other's arms amid the freshly cut grass, and the spring was singing a gentle lullaby. The flowers surrounded us and watched us curiously. Our hands and bodies entwined, our breathing mixed into a single breath, and this moment became the reflection of our magical days, the enchanting summer, and our love. At that moment I was scared to even imagine that there was someone else in this world apart from Roman. My Roman…

III

Finally, the last recollection from July—the month that gave me so much happiness that I could never forget it. July 1972 would not have been complete if we didn't experience another surprising and beautiful night of closeness. It was a gift given to us by Tinu.

We had heard that sometimes during the summer he went to the old house of his now-deceased parents. The house stood on the other side of the river we had chosen for our refreshing swims. Sometimes in late evening, he crossed the little bridge and came to the house of the old ladies to buy bread and milk. He was always polite but never talked much and never agreed to stay for dinner. Sometimes his friends came to visit, and then all the young men, completely nude, ran around on the opposite side of the river, laughing, talking, and slightly embarrassing those who happened to be around. Most of the time, however, he was alone. The old ladies told us that our appearance made him a bit more talkative, but until that night, we were never officially introduced. By that time the grass in the field was almost fully cut. The Old Man visited the ladies and later sent over two scythemen, who, with Romka's help, managed to cut so much grass that the women in their gratitude organised a veritable feast.

Our days of rest were over. It was time to move and continue the training. Once the dinner was over, the Old Man told us it was time to depart. We begged him to let us stay another day, but he firmly refused. Eventually, Alekseyevna's tears and Zaharyevna's lamentations made him give in. He told us to return no later than midday, got into his car, and drove away. "Oh, sweetest guest, the sacred memories!" It now seems almost amusing that we felt so sad that night. I was suddenly overcome by jealousy toward the departed scythemen. I realised that I unintentionally prevented Roman from interacting with other people and thus kept our love away from the support that it needed. Yes, we had experienced so much. We had seen the different faces of love yet tried to preserve it, pure and beautiful, by rejecting everything that could separate us. Roman had never said that he was unhappy with me, even though I was clearly no angel. But my inner voice kept saying, "Remember how he looked at the young and strong scythemen. Remember how he asked you to stay home and help the old women, but when you went over to bring him dinner, they were lying on the ground and laughing, and he…"

"No," I tried to calm myself. "I can't scythe anyway. It made no sense for me to join them. I know that he was different with them. So natural and relaxed, the way he never is with me, but…"

"You are losing him. You are losing him," whispered the evil voice of jealousy, appearing and disappearing like a ghost.

"No," I screamed. "We can't live without each other."

Maybe Roman could also feel the inner struggle that was raging in my heart. The balmy evening of July was slowly drifting into the night. Once the loud and joyous dinner was over and the singing and dancing had stopped (the Old Man and the old ladies recalled their youth), we didn't go to sleep but in silent agreement started heading toward the river. During the dinner I was loud and happy, but when it ended, it seemed that a dark cloud had gathered above my head and kept enveloping me in ever-growing darkness.

Romka could no longer stand it, so he stopped in the middle of a field. The air was saturated with the intoxicating smell of grass and flowers. He put his hands on either side of my face, carefully studied it, and then started kissing me. When we once again started moving toward the river, I wanted to say something, but the words seemed so strange and heavy. I was choking with the tears that threatened to spill, and finally I crashed my head into Romka's chest and let them fall. We had reached the end of the field and could see the river from where we were standing. Its smooth and glittering surface seemed dark and unfamiliar.

Roman sat down by the water, put my head in his lap, and dried my tears with his warm breath. His touch was so earnest that I finally felt hopeful and able to smile. His eyes were also smiling, and his lips kissed away the last remnants of my tears. That night I had found him anew. I understood that and felt immeasurable gratitude. I wanted to find a way to show him that he was my breath, my heart, my life, and my only true love. Our trembling hands touched, and their warmth helped us express our love for each other.

Lost in our wordless communication, we didn't notice that the previously still surface of the water was broken up by a multitude of tiny waves that caressed our feet. We raised our heads and saw that through the dark water, a man with a shy but benevolent smile on his face was coming in our direction. The moon—the tireless companion of young lovers—allowed us to observe him from the distance. He was tall, handsome, and flaxen-haired, like most Estonians. His pleasant smile revealed white and strong teeth, and his tanned body was well defined and athletic. He was not wearing swimming trunks; instead, his hips were barely covered by something that resembled a loincloth.

His sudden and noisy appearance bewildered us. I immediately forgot about my previous worries and clung closer to Roman's chest. He, however, quickly stood up and pulled me to my feet. Finally, the young man came close enough for us to see his eyes, and we were surprised to discover that they were dark violet. He spread out both arms and spoke with a strong accent, yet trying to pronounce the words as clearly as possible, "Good evening! My name is Tinu." After a moment's hesitation, he added, "Can I join you?"

Even if he had spoken to us in Estonian and we wouldn't understand a word, his expressive face and smile in combination with his outstretched arms explained everything he was trying to say. We reached out our hands in greeting, and once I felt his cool palm and looked into his unusual eyes, I immediately thought that fate itself had sent him to us. Tinu couldn't have known what had happened between Roman and me right before his arrival, but it was almost as if he could sense it.

Despite our smiles and the easy conversation that had started between the three of us, he suddenly asked, "Is this a bad time?" His stance was apologetic, yet his face clearly showed how much he wanted to stay.

For a second Roman and I stopped looking at Tinu and turned to each other, but then we heard his calm and clear voice. "Thank you! I will be happy to stay." He sat down between us, put his arms around our shoulders, and asked, "So, how is it going?" His question made us laugh, and we finally freed ourselves from the mesmerizing power of his eyes. It seemed that at that very moment we also lost all our doubts and fears.

We leisurely lay down on our backs. Our heads were all on the same level, and something seemed to pull them closer to one another. Our eyes sent out unfamiliar signals, which were absorbed by Tinu's face and grew into desire.

He swiftly got up, took off his loincloth, and, completely naked, stepped into the water, asking us to join him. What kind of evening was that? Roman and I seemed to find ourselves and then lose each other again. Our mysterious guest pushed us apart and joined us together, always staying in the dark but at the same time pulling us to him with inexplicable force. Seeing our hesitation, he once again spread out his arms and called us to join him, quietly repeating, "Everything will be all right…"

Our bodies seemed to respond to his call. We immediately started removing our clothes, but Tinu came out of the water, took each of us by the hand, and impatiently dragged us toward the water, eyeing Roman with pure desire and softly smiling at me. Only when we finally entered the water did we feel relief.

We swam to the middle of the river, trying to keep up with one another. We were finally equal in our rights and desires. From all the tension of the evening, I felt a cramp in my leg but continued swimming toward the sandbar in the middle of the river, where we could all rest.

Roman was so taken with Tinu's presence that for the first time he didn't notice I was not near. The suffocating jealousy that I had felt so many times over the past months, in combination with the cramping leg, almost pulled me down to the bottom of the river. Just when I could no longer see through my tears, his familiar hands took hold of me and placed me on his chest. Supported by Roman and Tinu, I finally reached the sandbar. They carefully placed me on the sand, lay down, and leaned over me. Roman's clear-blue eyes seemed to mix with the violet shades of Tinu's irises, and right in front of my eyes, love started painting an enchanting and everlasting picture of perfection. Lost in our longing for something new and unreachable, overcome by our worries and sorrow, we sometimes lose that which we already own. When the invisible pull of unseen happiness finally disappears, we remain lonely and filled with sadness. Oh, love! You are our best friend and our fiercest enemy. You are our salvation and damnation. Love, what are you?

I smiled at both of them and felt that the burning jealously was leaving my body, dissolving in the bliss of their gentle kisses and caresses. I was free of everything that could stop me from caressing Tinu while I was kissing Roman or prevent me from kissing Tinu while Roman was touching my body. And all the while, Tinu kept whispering that everything would be all right.

But when he reached out to touch Roman, he couldn't overcome the inner fear that prevented him from reaching his goal. Feeling overwhelming gratitude toward both of them, I touched their heads, turned them toward each other, and made them join their lips in a kiss while I lay down on my back and watched them with great pleasure.

I felt that Roman would absorb Tinu's exceptional ease, while Tinu would soak up the depth and tenderness of Roman's feelings.

For a moment they were both lost in their desire but then suddenly stopped. When they saw my smiling eyes, which I wanted to hide from them, they once again returned to me and covered my body with grateful kisses. Our bodies gradually filled up with a new kind of energy. It seemed that the sandbar was becoming too small for us to express what the god of love, now in full control of our bodies, wanted us to show one another. The fire burning in our bodies prevented us from feeling the cold air. The cool droplets of dew, the first glimmer of the morning light, and the awakening voices of the birds told us to hurry but at the same time gave us the chance to fully submerge into the feeling of boundless love. It entered our hearts like a bolt of lightning.

Tinu pulled himself up to Roman's magnificent groin and swallowed his burning flesh like the earth swallows everything that surrounds it, drawing strength from his body. Oh, the fleeting moment of love! You make your own laws. Roman and I were lying head to head. His hands gripped me tight, lifted me, and placed me next to him. Tinu, feeling my heartbeat, succumbed to his endless desire to love and joined us together. Moaning from pleasure, the three of us were tied into a knot that only Tinu could untie.

As the first whirlwind of desire slowly subsided and I was lying on Roman's chest, trying to steady my breathing by inhaling the scent of his skin, I once again realised that Tinu had been sent to us by fate and that we should not try to fight against it. I looked deep into Roman's eyes. We raised ourselves and reached for Tinu, who was still lost in the torturous depth of desire and desperately willing to succumb to its power. His body asked for nothing. He felt us move and once again was ready to give us pleasure, but this time we didn't let him. Now his body became ours, and as the light of the morning finally broke through the darkness, he got to experience the same pleasure he had given both of us.

"Love…" whispered the faraway trees.

"Love…" sang the grass and the flowers in the meadow.

"Love…" screamed our burning lips.

"Love…" sighed the wind.

Oh, how sweet was the pull of love! How welcome the cool morning air! How beautiful the slowly dimming stars!

"Love! Love! Love like it's the last time you will get to do it," the eyes of our

unearthly yet dear guest Tinu told us.

"Why would it be the last time?" we were asking him, but he didn't say a word. The

pleasure he received made his eyes change colour. His only reply was a mysterious smile.

We came out of the water still holding hands. We crossed the field and entered the hayloft, where we fell back on the soft hay. Tinu, it wouldn't be long until we discovered your secret. When we woke up in the morning, we still felt his presence with every cell in our bodies, but all that was left of him was his loincloth—the only proof of his existence.

IV

"Seryozha…Seryozhenka…Serzhyk…Wake up!"
I was woken up by the bright August sun that shone through the window of the hotel, the strong smell of coffee, the sweet aroma of roses, and Romka's velvety baritone. Oh, God! I was twenty years old. Roman was twenty-five. I immediately opened my eyes and saw the smiling face of Roman as he leaned down to kiss me. "Happy birthday! Happy birthday! My love, my life, my baby…"

I tried not to get lost in the sweet sensations caused by his lips, but as always, it was futile to resist. His love for me was like a burning fire and a gulp of fresh water. That was how my day started on August 12, 1972. A beautiful tray stood on the nightstand with two steaming cups of coffee, roses, and something that was wrapped in silvery paper. Roman congratulated me once again and reached for the parcel.

"Wait!" I screamed. "Wait!"

I jumped out of the bed and, completely naked, ran to the other room. The night before, I had hidden my gift for Roman in the little TV table. Seeing the blue paper, he raised his eyebrows in surprise. Like a playful kitten, I jumped back into the bed, kissed and congratulated him, and waited for the moment when he would open the present. Of course, I was no less eager to see what he had prepared for me. We untied the ribbons and burst out in amused giggles. We had bought each other exactly the same shirts, selected the night before in the only nearby store.

But soon enough, the shirts were forgotten. Roman leaned over me and tried to get me out of the bed by tickling my nose, cheeks, and lips with the belt of his robe. Just like Pilot (poor dog—how much he wanted to come with us to Tallinn…), I snatched the end of the belt with my teeth and with a playful growl tried to pull the knot lose. Romka didn't have time to stop me. His robe opened and revealed to me the world of delight that I could never get enough of. With my lips and chin, I tried to free him from the soft fabric that still engulfed his body.

Surprised at my assault, for a moment he stood still, but then his desire pulled him closer to me. Through the waterfall of his kisses I heard the music of his words: "I love you. I love you…only you."

Oh, Roman! Do I have to tell you how much I loved you? Even when we were next to each other, I was wrought with longing and worry. My love for you made me forget that anything else existed in this world. I always loved you, and I always will. The sweetness of love that we first learned in the moonlight was now lit by the bright rays of the morning sun, and once again we drank from the blissful cup of desire.

At first Roman was slightly reluctant, but I could see and feel all the love and desire welling up in his body, so I told him to hurry while my body was trembling with impatience. The touch of his hands and the softness of his lips had started a wave of longing that demanded release. I was riding this rolling wave and whispering sweet words of love to spur him on. These words always moved my Roman, and soon enough he was also engulfed by the storm of passion, screaming, whispering, and singing out his own feeling for me. I was drowning in this heavenly bliss, and the sunlight gave us hope that it would never end. It tied us to the entire world and to each other.

The force of our feelings was not lost even upon the maid who entered the room to wake us. Our desire was so strong that neither of us felt how the two single beds, moved together the night before, started sliding apart. At first we were half suspended in the air but eventually slid down onto the floor, covering each other's bodies. I felt Roman as close to me as was humanly possible, and this first hour of our morning ended in sweet moans that surprised the maid, who was still standing in the room. She never saw us in our cover.

Roman loudly thanked her and pulled a blanket over our heads, separating us from the rest of the world. His calming breath was gently washing over me. I revelled in the weight of his body on top of mine and languidly kissed his nipples. Despite my having satisfied his desire, he gratefully accepted my tenderness and continued caressing my body. Roman! How bittersweet is this return to the past. My heart still clenches with the realization that during those days of love, I never fully managed to express how much I loved you. That morning was Tinu's gift to us. We saw his reflection in each other's eyes and smiled as if he were near. A bright ray of sun shone into our hiding place. It finally made us get up and take a bath—a luxury afforded by the suite that the Old Man had organized for us. We were planning to meet him for dinner.

V

"Roman! Romka! Romchik…" I screeched in his arms under the stream of the cold water.

He laughed but didn't let me go. His gentle fingers kept exploring my body, his lips kissed my skin, and in between the kisses, he even managed to sing a cheerful tune. Finally, he started filling the large round bath with hot water. I slipped out of his arms and sat down in the bath. He jumped in right after me, causing a lot of noise, spilling water all over the floor and laughing. The open bottle of liquid soap fell into the water, but we didn't even notice it since once again we were in each other's arms. The water kept spilling over the sides of the bath, but we were oblivious to our surroundings. We were possessed by desire. Cupid, flying high above our heads, shot a string of arrows straight into our hearts, and we did nothing to hide from them. We were surrounded by soft and pink foam and let ourselves get lost in our feelings. I felt so warm, so happy, so blissful…time stood still, and so did I, sitting down in between Romka's legs. I slid up to the level of his chest, where my head, covered in suds, could finally rest.

He reached out and turned on the showerhead, and the cold water cooled down our burning bodies and almost lulled us to sleep. After a while Roman turned my body so that I was facing him and pulled out the plug. While we were kissing, the water slowly drained out of the bath, leaving traces of airy suds on the edges of the bath and our bodies. We then got up and once again surrendered to the stream of water flowing out of the showerhead. It was almost at the level of Romka's head. Standing in front of him, I threw my head back, wrapped my arms around his neck, and pulled him closer to me. The cool water caressed our lips and cascaded down our tense bodies. I kept drowning in Romka's blue eyes, and I never wanted to be saved.

"Romka! Romochka! Rom…"

He didn't answer, but I felt new strength rising in his body. His lips were no longer kissing but rather devouring me.

"Roman…Romka! Romashka…"

He straightened his back, and I almost fell in his arms. He then carried me into the bedroom to continue enjoying this day of love that didn't seem to end. Some time passed in blissful forgetfulness. I felt his warm breath on my skin. I had no strength to get out of the bed, but there was no need—he was near me. I looked at him, and as our eyes met, I discovered that we were both feeling a degree of discomfort. But why?

"Roman?"

We were no longer laughing, just smiling at the discovery we had made. During the passionate hours of our morning, we had forgotten to eat. Of course! Where were the sandwiches? Where was our coffee? Oh, how little it all seemed. But we had ordered breakfast. All we had to do was to call and ask for it to be delivered.

"Roman…" I didn't have to wait for long; he was still right beside me. He was mine! He loved me! Oh! Once again we longed to be consumed by love. Oh, God! What was happening to us that morning?

"Seryozhenka…Seryozha…"

I took a deep breath and opened my eyes. Roman was already dressed in his robe and busied himself by the table on which the breakfast was waiting for us. We ate our sandwiches and drank our coffee, then got dressed in civilian clothes (another gift of the Old Man) and started making plans for our day in Tallinn. The day of love continued.

VI

"Hello, birthday boys!" The Old Man's voice on the other end of the line sounded almost too cheerful. "How are you doing? Have you woken up? I will be a bit late, but I will be there. Wait for me."

"Will there be a surprise?" I asked him.

"Not one but three." The Old Man was laughing.

"Then hurry up!"

As soon as the conversation was over and we were about to leave, there was a knock on the door. On the other side stood the same maid who had walked in on us earlier. She smiled, curiously looked at us, and asked if she could clean our room. There was no need to answer. She made it clear that she only asked the question out of courtesy.

We stood still, and the maid, called Itta, couldn't take her eyes off Roman. Oh, God! Wherever I went with him, both men and women were unable to hide their feelings. Everyone had a different way of showing them, but no one could hide them completely. Itta was whispering something in Estonian. I was not sure if she was praying at the altar of Roman's beauty or just trying to find the right words to express what she was feeling. Roman always told me that he didn't do anything to provoke these extreme reactions.

He smiled, held me in his arms, looked at Itta, and gave her the possibility to take both us of in. However, she saw only him. His dark hair and clear-blue eyes looked even brighter because of the yellow shirt he was wearing. The Old Man had bought him a pair of tan trousers and light-brown shoes with adorable old-fashioned tassels, which Romka called "the Old Man's ribbons." Whenever he put the shoes on, he said that he felt like an old alchemist.

Finally, Itta came back to her senses and left the room with an exasperated sigh. Roman smiled at me and put his hands on my shoulders as if saying, "Well, you saw what happened. What can I do?"

I sighed my answer: "Yes, I did see."

We both started laughing at our soundless dialogue, and he kissed me so tenderly that my head started spinning, and I fell down on the sofa, pulling him along. "Roma, let's not go anywhere."

"If you want to stay, we will stay." He put one of his arms around me, and I placed my head on his shoulder. We didn't need to talk—we could understand each other without words. He made me raise my head, and for a second I saw that his eyes were filled with sorrow, but it was immediately replaced by a smile that radiated boundless and unrestrained love. This love had been burning inside my heart all this time, but on this very day, I suddenly felt something inexplicable and dangerous that threatened both of us.

"Oh, God!" I once again caught myself thinking. "What will happen to us?"

But no one could answer my question. Roman was still smiling, his lips gently pressed together. He always knew what I was thinking and probably tried to answer my question, but his lips would not let him. Instead, they caught mine in a delightful kiss, which was followed by silence. All we could hear was the ticking of the clock. Our hearts screamed "Yes," but our minds told us "No."

Our eyes met, and I heard (or at least I thought I did) him quietly say, "Forgive me." He read in my eyes that everything was forgiven—I didn't even know what exactly—and slowly raised his body. There was nothing he could have told me that day. He was not ready. Neither of us could answer the question that was gathering over our heads like dark clouds before a storm.

Itta once again entered our room with a big crystal vase in her hands. It was filled with beautiful roses of all imaginable colours. It suddenly seemed that a benevolent breeze had blown away all the threatening clouds that hung over our love. She saw our questioning looks, placed the vase on the table, arranged the flowers in a way that made them look even more spectacular, and said, "The flowers are from your loving grandfather. He will be here for dinner."

Her words made us burst into laughter. We laughed so hard that we ended up falling off the sofa and found ourselves on the floor. Itta waited for us to quiet down and said, "All grandsons are the same." Then she turned around and left the room.

VII

Before our departure for Tallinn, I received a letter from home asking me to buy a gift for the newborn daughter of our acquaintances. For some reason I wanted to do it as soon as possible and without Roman's presence; however, I never had the chance. Eventually, Roman and I went to a children's store. Four of the six shop assistants immediately tried to help us by showing us different onesies, cardigans, shirts, nappies, dresses, and even socks. They placed all these items wherever they could so that the store soon looked like a colourful pavilion in the centre of which stood two bewildered "young fathers" (as we heard someone say) trying to pick out gifts for their newborn children.

Of course, Roman was the centre of attention, and looking at him, I couldn't hide my smile. The two trainee shop assistants who were told to take care of other customers couldn't stop looking at him. They handed their customers whatever happened to be nearby and didn't listen to their questions, so soon enough they left, throwing angry glances in our direction. The two young shop assistants disappeared for a while. While they were gone, the employees from other sections of the store kept appearing near us and lingering until they were called away. One of the girls brought in a doll of a newborn child and started showing us how to use the items we were about to purchase, never ceasing to ask probing questions.

Roman showed impressive abilities in storytelling. He didn't know anything about the little girl (neither did I) but kept making up stories that, at the same time, revealed nothing of any importance. All the people in the shop were amused, and the whole situation started to seem rather entertaining.

But then came a moment when Roman could take it no longer. The shop was full of curious shop assistants, and it started to remind me of a conference hall. He suddenly sat down on the floor and looked at me, pleading for help. That was when the manager of the department—a beautiful forty-year-old Estonian woman called Regina, who had been present the whole time but didn't join in—decided to restore order and made all the shop assistants return to their posts. When she noticed that there were no other customers in the store, she started asking us questions.

Neither Roman nor I were ready to admit the deceit. The quiet environment of the store allowed me to continue observing Roman. I saw that his fantasy had started to become real. He carefully looked at every item of clothing and measured it against the doll. His eyes were burning with inexplicable love for the child he had never seen, and my blood froze with the thought, "What will happen next?"

Apparently, the expression on my face changed, because Roma turned to me with a smile on his face and pretended to show me one of the items but in fact covered our faces with it and gave me a soft kiss to show that he was near me. Still, I saw in his eyes the shadow of a child that would once take Roman away from me. In my despair I leaned against the counter and tried to come to terms with the frightening thought that he needed a family, a wife and children…

To make sure he wouldn't see the tears in my eyes (God, I really cried a lot in those days), I turned around as if to look at some of the items that were still lying around. I tried to steady myself, but some treacherous drops of moisture still managed to escape and fall on the shirt I was holding in my hands. I quickly looked up and saw the eyes of Regina, which almost made me cover my face. Her dark-green eyes were not malicious. They even seemed sympathetic, but in their depth I could see the flickering fire of a strange joy at my suffering. It almost seemed that she would start laughing and tell everyone about her discovery. She challenged me with her eyes, and just when I felt I could no longer take it, I quietly prayed to God to be released from this torture.

And he (or maybe it was something else) helped me: I felt Roman's hands on my shoulders. I fell back against his chest and tried to smile, and at that moment I saw the ice in Regina's eyes start to melt. They slowly became velvety soft like the August day that surrounded us, and only tiny flickers of darkness still reminded me of the coming autumn.

Two or three of the shop assistants who had relentlessly tried to get Roman's attention expressed their curiosity at what was happening but then decided that it had nothing to do with them and turned away.

Finally, Regina's eyes softened to summery warmth, and she carefully packed all the items that we had selected. We paid for our purchases and left the store feeling many pairs of eyes following our departure. We were desperately looking for a change of scenery, which was offered by a tiny, red-haired trainee shop assistant who appeared in the doorway like an angel from heaven. She looked at our gloomy faces with a bright smile, removed a sign from the other side of the door that said "Inventory" and asked, "Have you finished? Because we need to…I'll take it."

The store broke out in laughter, and we heard something fall. Regina questioningly looked at the girl, then at the sign, and finally turned her eyes in our direction, but we were already gone.

"Oh, God! It's all over," I thought when we were finally out in the street.

But Roman abruptly stopped, dropped all our bags on the pavement, took my face in his hands, and gently smiled at me. I pressed myself closer to his body, as if I was trying to absorb all the love that radiated from his being. At that moment I understood that, as long as we were together, I was not afraid of anything. "That's better," he said.

To cast off the last shadows of this unpleasant incident, we went to the post office and sent all our purchases to the little girl, Irina. Her name means "peace."

VIII

Already, for many years, I have been looking to find Roman's features in the faces of passing, running, calmly sitting, and even sleeping people, but apparently nature has its own plans for creating miracles. It is in no rush to bestow them upon our sinful souls. Then why was time in such a hurry to shorten our stay at the beautiful and enchanting Tallinn?

The Old Man was supposed to arrive in an hour or an hour and a half, but we were still walking around the narrow streets, enchanted by the inviting atmosphere. In all my twenty years of life, I had not seen as much as I saw that day. We visited the oldest pharmacy in the country and a castle harbouring the ghost of the Lady in White—a girl who was once walled in alive. We saw countless towers with names like the Tall German and the Fat Elza and also a weather vane called the Old Thomas—the timeless guard of the old town. I can't even describe everything. We were surrounded by life itself and revelled in its colours and energy but then retreated back into our own world, where we felt completely isolated and sheltered from everyone and everything else. It seemed that nothing would ever break the spell. However, I have to mention two brief and significant encounters that became the closing scenes of the eventful August, or maybe the opening scenes of the chilling and torturous September.

We sat down in a comfortable summer café and slowly sipped our milkshakes. Suddenly, we noticed a wedding party that had gathered on the doorstep of an ancient church. On the other side of the park in which were sitting stood several brightly decorated carriages. The people who were sitting in the café immediately got up to see the wedding party closer.

The traditional dark suit of the groom and the cream-coloured dress of the bride stood out amid the bright national costumes of the wedding guests. The newlyweds looked happy and slightly embarrassed by all the attention. Holding small bouquets of flowers, they started to move through the park accompanied by the blissful sound of music. The little ringbearers—a boy and a girl of five who both looked alike in their bright costumes and resembled little fairy-tale gnomes—barely had time to pick up the long trailing end of the bride's veil. When the groom turned toward us, I noticed something familiar about his features. I touched Roman's hand, and his eyes told me that he noticed it as well. While we were smiling at each other and trying to understand who it could be, the crowd turned in our direction. The reaction of the crowd soon became clear. We turned around and gasped in surprise: the groom had left the side of his bride and was running toward us with his jacket open, jumping over flower beds and smiling in unrestrained delight. It was then that we understood—the groom was Tinu. He stopped a couple of metres in front of us and seemed to evaluate his impulsive reaction, but hearing our shouts of joy, he immediately flew into our open arms.

A group of foreigners who were watching the whole scene unfold in front of their eyes suddenly started clapping their hands. The rest of the onlookers were still puzzled by what had transpired and tried to draw their own conclusions. Finally, three young men from the wedding party started moving in our direction.

Tinu kept kissing our cheeks with tears in his eyes, but seeing the approach of his friends, whispered, "Thank you for the stag night! I love you! Please, don't forget me. You are my brothers. I love you!" As he said the last words, his voice started trembling. He put his hands on our necks and pulled our heads together so that our lips joined in possibly the last truly desired kiss in his life.

We were bewildered and couldn't say a word. But were words really necessary? All the magical minutes that we had spent together were forever committed to our memory.

Many years later a brown and brittle flower fell out of my notebook, and I remembered how suddenly Tinu came into our lives and how suddenly he disappeared. All that was left was the rose from the lapel of his jacket.

The second encounter of the day was even more fleeting. The carriages took away Tinu and his wedding party. The curious crowd started to disperse, but we were still standing there, unable to move. Our legs, our minds, and our hearts were paralyzed. The overwhelming joy that we had felt just a minute before had completely disappeared. The warmth that had spread between the three of us was suddenly gone.

The wind became stronger, dark clouds started to gather, and their shadows, having blocked out the sun, filled us with sadness. Suddenly we felt exhausted and lost. Amid this darkness we heard the laughter of a child. We turned around and saw a young man in glasses running after a four-year-old boy. They wanted to hide from the approaching storm and were running toward the café.

When the boy was running past us, he suddenly stopped, waited for his father to catch up, and said, "Daddy, you see? Grown-up men also get lost. I am still a child, but you were angry with me." He then turned to us and added, "Don't worry; someone will find you. Just like my daddy found me."

His grey eyes seemed to blink at us in secret understanding. The joy that radiated from the boy made us reply, "Thank you, little one. We are no longer lost." We then ran to the taxi holding hands.

IX

All the way to the hotel, we sat in silence. Our eyes communicated that the events of the afternoon had left such a strong impression that everything else would seem calm and relaxing in comparison. We were so quiet that the taxi driver turned around several times just to make sure we hadn't fallen asleep. Seeing our happy but thoughtful faces, he shrugged and continued driving. However, he was not able to restrain his curiosity. When my head rested on Romka's shoulder and I really started to fall asleep, he gestured toward me and asked, "Your brother?"

Roman adjusted my head and leaned closer into my body, still not giving away the true nature of our relationship. Through my half-closed eyes, I saw the happy expression on his face and felt his happiness seep into my body. Forgetting that we were not alone, my lips reached toward his, and he answered my kiss. That one day nothing could stand between us.

The car abruptly stopped, and we realised that we had reached the hotel. The unwilling witness of our tender moment looked at us with surprise and a degree of jealousy in his eyes but didn't say a word. Only when we tried to pay, he suddenly said, "No need. I'm happy you enjoyed the ride." He paused and then added, "I am all alone." And with those words, he sped away.

Very slowly and gradually, gentle drops of rain started falling from the sky. We greedily inhaled the cool air and thought that not all clouds are the harbingers of sorrow. We never said it out loud and didn't have the chance to do it—the Old Man was already coming toward us through the door of the hotel. His face radiated understanding; he was not angry about our late arrival. We were quiet but happy, and all we could do was smile.

When we came into our room, we saw that Itta had just finished setting the table. She greeted us quietly, grumbling "Finally!" but her smile was kind and gentle. We leaned against the Old Man's shoulders and almost felt like crying from joy. Seeing our emotional state, Itta also wiped away her tears and whispered, "Oh well…"

But the Old Man, hardened in his behaviour by the army rules, immediately told us to stop. He then smiled at us and said in the theatrical voice of a ringmaster, "The first surprise—appear!"

The door suddenly opened, and Pilot burst into the room followed by Tolik. Pilot's paws slid in all directions on the freshly polished parquet, and he clumsily bumped into our knees.

"Up!" urged the Old Man, and Pilot stood up on his hind paws to lick our faces in greeting. Overjoyed at the reunion, he finally lay down on the floor and kept wagging his tail and enjoying our smiles. The Old Man leaned down and gave the dog a sugar cube. At that moment, for the first time, we looked at the Old Man, who was always so kind and considerate, and a nagging thought came into our heads. Why was he doing it? What would he eventually ask in return? Why did he choose us among the hundreds of lives that were entrusted to his care? And how long would it last?

"Old Man, who are you?" we wanted to ask as he was fulfilling his promise of another surprise and putting on the table various parcels, boxes, and books. He took two bottles of champagne out of his bag, happily rubbed his palms together, and proceeded to open one of them. The cork noisily flew into the ceiling, and the clear ringing of the crystal lamp announced to everyone that the celebration had started. We returned to the table, where the glasses were already filled and overspilling with the bubbling drink. The Old Man noticed the change in us, but the noise and the elation spreading through the room prevented him from asking any questions. His toast was brief. Just like Roman, he never liked to give long speeches. He congratulated us and proceeded to hand us presents. He gave Roman a compass watch that was such an advanced piece of technology that the only thing missing was a built-in TV screen. Roman usually tried not show his emotions, but this time he wasn't able to hide his joy, especially since he realised where the Old Man had bought the watch. Roman had noticed it in the window of a pawn shop where foreign sailors pawned their possessions, and the Old Man clearly recalled his interest. Roman showed so much gratitude that the Old Man started protesting. "Leave a little bit of me also for the others." He touched Pilot's hair and sat down. The dog decided that it was his turn to show gratitude and started licking the Old Man's hands.

"Is it your birthday as well?"

Pilot let out a bark and didn't leave the Old Man's side until he had received all the food that he desired. I was so carried away by Roman's happiness that I didn't even hear the Old Man saying that my gift would be of a different kind. To finally get my attention, he threw at me the bloom of the rose, and my empty plate was filled with rose petals.

"It's time for our other birthday boy to receive his gift," the Old Man said.

Roman was holding my hand, and at that moment he pressed it so hard that I really couldn't imagine what my gift would be. Then the Old Man ceremoniously handed me a leave of absence to visit my family—ten days and the extra time needed for the trip. Oh, God! I keep calling out your name. I still don't understand what possessed me that day. I immediately pictured the surprised face of my mother on the day of my unexpected return. I was so overjoyed that I immediately ran to the Old Man to thank him for this wonderful gift. But at that very moment, I was suddenly paralyzed by the thought (Mother, forgive me!) that I wouldn't see Roman for ten—no, thirteen or even fifteen—days. I would be away from his eyes, his hands, and his lips…

"No! No!" I started shaking my head.

The Old Man, Itta, and Tolik decided that I was expressing my happiness and started to talk about the joy that my mother would feel upon seeing me. I looked at Roman. I knew that he had fully grasped my meaning and was desperately trying to think of a solution. One look at his face was enough for me to seek shelter in his arms and keep repeating, "No!"

The others finally understood my meaning as well and stopped their conversation. Itta put her palms together as if she were going to pray and then stopped moving altogether. The Old Man's countenance became gloomy. Tolik started nervously playing with the pack of cigarettes that was lying on the table. Even Pilot suspiciously moved his ears. Everyone looked at Roman, who was now clearly the one to decide my destiny. My love, please, forgive me! All our guests, forgive me for almost ruining the celebration. I was only twenty years old and loved him with a blinding passion. Some people say that it is not age that makes us wise but the experiences we have had. Roman's eyes were all alight with love and tenderness. He kissed me, held me closer to his body, took the paper that the Old Man was still holding in his hands, and gave it to me. He made sure that Old Man understood how precious his gift was. Then he said, "You will go home. There is no doubt about that. And we will be waiting for you."

He saw that I was not able to reply, so he smiled and offered to light the candles. Roman was always able to persuade people to follow his suggestions. He started to clear the table, and everyone else quickly joined in. Itta and Tolik closed the curtains. The room was suddenly bathed in soft twilight and only rarely brief glimmers of the setting sun peeked into the room through the gently swaying curtains. Someone turned on the music, and the Old Man brought two small cakes with candles—yellow candles for Roman and blue candles for me.

Roman was the first to blow out the candles. He did it in one single breath without the smallest effort. The flames didn't even try to put up a fight but immediately drew inward and disappeared. Despite the joyful atmosphere, I was suddenly overcome with fear. My attempt to blow out the candles resulted in a mournful moan infused with traces of quivering breath. The sound was loud enough for everyone to hear, so the Old Man tried to break the ensuing silence by turning it into a joke. "You're quite weak, my boy."

I smiled a pained and forced smile, as if trying to apologize, and gathered the last remnants of my strength. I tried again. Twelve candles were left burning. Their flames kept warming us for the twelve following years, while the shadow of the eight extinguished candles always followed us wherever we went. It has been eight years now that Roman has no longer been by my side.

X

The preparation for my leave was short, just like the leave itself. When I arrived home, I was overwhelmed by all the work that needed to be done at our old house. The Old Man had forgiven me. Roman sent me four letters, each of which included greetings from the Old Man. He was still angry with me on the day of my departure, but by now his anger had vanished. Five days before my return to the base, Romka called me. Hearing my love's voice, I was suddenly filled with new energy and no longer actively waited for the day when I would leave. I looked at my mother with sadness in my eyes. She would once again be all alone. However, she bravely tried not to show her emotions, so my departure was not too difficult. If only the trains would move faster! It almost seemed that they felt my impatience and kept moving slower and slower. They lingered at each station, and even the sounds of their whistles seemed to say, "Why hurry? We will get there in time." But they always ended up being late.

I arrived in Tallinn on August 31 and discovered that the last train had already left. It meant that I would have to hitchhike and wouldn't get to Roman before morning. I was the last one to leave the carriage. I stood on the platform and tried to get my bearings. The all-encompassing silence slowly turned into music of expectation. The air was warm and still; only a light breeze occasionally caressed my skin. The shadows seemed light and transparent, and the moonlight glimmered like a silvery waterfall. Everything told me that he was somewhere near.

And I was right. At that very instant, Roman appeared at the end of the platform and started running toward me with his arms wide open. His careless joy drew the attention of the few remaining passengers. I felt rather than saw him in the dim reflections of the streetlights and, whispering his name, ran to meet him. In less than a minute we were bathed by the glow of a streetlight that previously had barely shone any light at all. We held each other tight and kissed with such passion that it seemed we were trying to make up for the days of separation right where we stood. In his eyes I saw the unending will to love and also the remnants of his longing for my nearness. We didn't have to say a word. Our eyes, hands, and lips—everything that I had longed for during my nights away from him—said it for us and then repeated. The platform was now empty, and it became our own little planet in the middle of the endless earth, and it held us there with the unsurpassable force of gravity.

"Let's go," his lips whispered.

It seemed that he wanted to add something, but I managed to guess it. "Pilot?"

"Yes, he is waiting for us. It's a surprise."

I didn't ask anything else. I never asked him many questions or tried to make him reveal something he was unwilling to tell. If he was calling me, I knew that he needed me. And I needed him every single minute. As soon as Pilot saw us, he wanted to run and greet me, but Roman gave him a sign to stay, and the dog obeyed. Only his rapidly wagging tail betrayed his excitement. When I saw the car, I realised that there was nothing Roman couldn't do. It was a really old army car that he had started to fix in order to occupy himself during my absence. There was no front passenger seat, and it made the car look bigger and cozier. The back seat was covered with dark-red plush and looked like just the place to sit down and relax. What used to be a grey blanket was now turned into a carpet. The whole car was immaculately clean. I barely dared to touch this symbol of Romka's love and care.

Meanwhile, he was trying to get the engine started. Even though it was obvious that he was having some difficulties, he never swore or lost his temper like the other army drivers. His impatience was only betrayed by the quiet puffs through which he expressed just how unfortunate it was that the car wouldn't start. The only thing that likened him to other drivers was the oil on his hands and face—the face that I loved more than anything in this world.

Finally, the engine growled almost like Pilot (the dog looked around in surprise) and apologetically started to gain power, ready for our departure. Romka couldn't find his wiping rag and stood with his dirty hands slightly raised in hope that he would manage to locate it. He smiled at me. I rushed into his arms and started kissing him with abandon. At first he was afraid to touch me, but then his feelings could no longer be contained. I put my face against his dirty cheek and inhaled the scent of his skin. Our lips were frantically tasting and enjoying each other.

When I finally stopped to take a breath, I noticed a small rag in the open glove department of the car. It was enough to clean the last remnants of the machine oil from his face. Romka wanted to clean my face as well, but Pilot let us know that someone was approaching.

The parking lot was empty. A policeman came up to us and asked if everything was all right. Yes, we were all right, but our bodies were buzzing with the need to be close to each other. We got into the car. Pilot and I sat in the back seat. Then we drove off. Romka told me all the news from the base, informed me about the flights, and with great satisfaction let me know that the soldier I had been training in my line of work finally seemed to really understand his responsibilities.

Lost in the conversation, we didn't notice that the city was now behind us and that we were driving on an almost empty highway. Faster! In front of us was a small woody patch covered in firs and pines. Roman was telling me about an argument he had had with a drunken technician who also happened to be the chief technician of Roman's squadron, but I barely heard him. My lips were kissing the nape of his neck, and I could barely control my hands. My breath was hot and uneven, and my whole body was tense from expectation.

A moment later he seemed to have absorbed my desire through his skin. The car made a rapid turn and drove into the shelter of the nearby trees. I opened the door. Pilot quickly jumped out and disappeared into the darkness like a moving shadow. Roman turned around, and our lips met in a soft union of love. I felt I would never be able to let them go, so desperately I kept reaching toward him.

Roman moved his seat back and pulled me onto his chest. In the silvery moonlight, I saw the expression of wonder in his eyes. A smile of anticipation slowly appeared on his face, and his lips quietly whispered, "Mine! You are mine…" He kept kissing my eyes, my cheeks, my forehead, my eyebrows and eyelashes, then my neck, and again my eyes.

Slowly and beautifully our clothes were leaving our bodies. We were listening to the symphony of our bodies and getting ready for its final notes. I knew what would give him the greatest pleasure. I dug my face into his coal-black hair and felt his body tremble as I licked the beautiful cleft on his chin. He moaned, quietly screamed out, and kept gulping air in unadulterated pleasure. Afterward, he kissed me in gratitude and whispered, "So good…So good…"

The big car suddenly started to feel too small—everything was in our way—but finally, our bodies were filled with such desire that space and time disappeared, and we no longer knew where we were and what we were doing.

"God, it feels so good…"

How much I had missed this beautiful and warm body, so eager to love and to be loved in return! His hands, lips, and tongue kept caressing my skin, and we felt comfort in the way our bodies became one single entity. Our breaths flowed in unison, and we kept getting lost in the fog of enjoyment.

Once the fog slowly started to clear, we regained our senses and unwillingly returned to the world that surrounded us. Oh, just how good it was! Roman opened the back door of the car, and we were greeted by the cool rain of late summer (now almost autumn) that invitingly called us outside. Completely naked, we stepped out of the car and let our bodies be caressed by the gentle droplets of rain. The moon, surprised at such a sight, looked at us with its round eyes. I looked at the sky, held on closer to Roman's body, and whispered to him, to myself, or maybe to the moon, "We are crazy!"

He started laughing, kissed me, then looked at the sky and yelled, "No, Seryozhenka, no! We are happy! Moon, listen to us! Forest, trees, animals, and birds—we are happy and in love! We are happy because we are together! We are the luckiest people in the world!"

"Romka, not so loud."

"No, Seryozhenka, I want everyone to hear that I love you. I want everyone to know. Nothing will ever keep us apart. Am I right, Pilot?"

The dog replied with a loud and happy bark as if to confirm Roman's statement or to scare away the approaching grief.

Later that night the Old Man met us at the gate of the base. Once he saw our tired but happy faces, he immediately understood everything. He briefly greeted me and sat silent in the car until we arrived at the doorstep of his house. He then reminded us, "Don't be late tomorrow."

As he was about to enter the house, he suddenly turned around and did something that we had never seen him do—he crossed himself and said, "God, protect them!" With those words, he left. When the door closed behind him, the first yellow autumn leaf fell next to our feet, once again reminding us that autumn had come.

XI

I was surrounded by the mysterious and eerie dark-blue silence of the slowly approaching morning. The air was fresh, clear, and pure. Dull and hesitant light showed its pale face in the window. Soon enough it would increase in strength and burst into bright sunlight. On those rare mornings when I was the first to wake up, I asked Pilot not to disturb us or let him outside for a morning walk and then watched the beautiful face of my sleeping Roman. His breathing was always calm and even, and his heart was beating in a strong and steady rhythm. If his arms were not wrapped around my body, they were thrown back above his head. His left arm was always folded under his head, which he never failed to turn in my direction. His expression changed with the dreams he was seeing, but mostly there was a gentle smile on his face. If he saw a bad dream, he frowned and tried to dispel it or turned on his side facing me, pulled me close, and became still.

After the night of separation, our lips joined in greeting before we were even fully awake. We smiled and continued sleeping, knowing that we would wake up happy just because we were together. Sometimes I accidentally woke him in my attempt to get a better look at his face, but he was never upset. When I noticed that he was awake, I quickly lay down, covered my face with my palms, and continued peeking at him with curiosity. He smiled, raised himself on his arms, removed my hands from my face, and kissed me. Sometimes, right after this playful exchange, he fell asleep. When I was near him, I felt calm and protected. The heady smell of his body reminded me of the way he made love to me—with so much tenderness and care.

However, even in this blissful peace, I could not fall asleep. With my eyes closed, I thought about how benevolent nature was on the day of his creation. He was the proof that one person can be beautiful, smart, charming, and gentle, and display all these qualities in perfect harmony. There are not many people like him in this world. His whole body—his dark curls and surprisingly blue eyes, and even his large but gentle hands—was complete perfection.

I had never met anyone who was that beautiful inside and out, and sometimes it scared me. More and more often I caught myself half expecting some misfortune. I could almost feel it approaching like a wild and dangerous animal. I tried not to give in to this strange premonition.

But there was another thought that would not give me peace—Roman must have known how handsome he was. But then why was he so detached from his looks? He never seemed to notice or care. Maybe it was just temporary? And I also kept asking myself—what was it that held us together? I still don't know why, but I never had the courage to ask him.

Exhausted by the nagging questions, I fell asleep in his tender embrace, where all the worrying thoughts slowly melted and disappeared.

The morning when the dangerous animal of misfortune caught up with us started in blissful peace. Trying to save ourselves from its claws, we almost fell into a deadly abyss. The unity of our souls helped us survive, but the fairy tale of our love ended that day. The wounded and bleeding animal didn't retreat but kept its vigil for all the years to come. We constantly felt its heavy steps and burning breath.

It started on September 10, 1972. It was a day of beautiful Indian summer when the spiderwebs gently sway in the breeze, the air is crisp and transparent, and nature sinks into peace and quiet restfulness. The programme of the test flights was very simple and well structured. Even though I was a private, I was given a task usually reserved for the officers. It happened because of my sharp memory—I alone was able to carry out all the tasks usually allocated to three different soldiers. I was given a table in the corner of the room, where I patiently awaited the time when I would be called into action. Meanwhile, I looked through the papers of the pilots I was responsible for and observed the officers who were sitting in front of me. It was a varied group of people: some of them were young; some were older; some of them were calm; some seemed desperate; some of them were handsome; but some—not so much. I knew all these pilots and noticed a similar trait in each and every one: when they were on the ground, they always longed for the sky, but once they were up there, their faces looked at the ground with hope and faith. Some of them were not destined to return.

Those who truly love their profession are almost unstoppable. Even if they are falling off their feet from exhaustion and barely have time to rest, the presence of colleagues gives them energy to return to their responsibilities. There is nothing that can change it. I could witness it on the bus that took us back to the base after a long day of test flights. There was about five minutes of silence, but then the conversation restarted and naturally shifted to bombardment strategies, loops, spins, targets, and the experiences of the day. I felt proud that everyone looked at the black folder in my hands with a secret hope. Not all officers liked my presence, but they were all quietly telling me, "Don't let us down!" And I never did. I was happy, and happy people are always good, even though, as Oscar Wilde remarked, "when we are good, we are not always happy." The most important thing was that everyone would return alive and unscathed, so whenever I disagreed with one of them, I knew that it was for their own good. When the Old Man offered me this post, he repeatedly told me that to save a pilot's life in the sky, I would have to protect him on the ground.

And again I am avoiding the actual story. I saw that day in my worst nightmares for a long time. Even years later I would wake up screaming as if it all happened just yesterday. The first row on the bus was occupied by the older pilots. Many of them were still flying, including our commander for political affairs, Zaharich, whom everyone called Saharich (a wordplay with the word "sahar," meaning "sugar"). He was so kind and obliging that there was a joke going around the base: if someone happened to run out of sugar, all they had to do was ask Saharich, and he would surely be able to help out. I'm not sure if he would really give you sugar, but any private or officer could always turn to him with any questions or concerns. People rarely choose to share their happiness, but if Saharich was involved, we would always make an exception. No one missed the possibility to talk to him. He undoubtedly was the heart and soul of the base. And he also was an outstanding pilot.

The Old Man—Saharich's best friend—often said, "If a pilot is kind, his performance in the air is better." When their mutual friend Lanchik—the regional general who showed up for inspections or in cases of extreme problems—was visiting, I often had the chance to see how strong their brotherhood was, how sharp their minds were, how strong their will and desire to do good in the world, even though each of them had seen his fair share of evil and misery.

At the beginning of the evening, Lanchik was not at the base. He arrived in the middle of the night when the whole base was still abuzz with the tragic turn of events.

I then looked at our medical officer, whom everyone called Hotabich. He also was a good friend of the Old Man and the other two, and he was older than each of them. His patronymic was Adamich, but he knew that everyone called him Hotabich and seemed to prefer it. He was to us like a kindhearted genie who always appeared by our side when we were sick and suffering. He put his hand on our burning foreheads and mumbled some words we could never make out, taking away the pain and easing the fever. Upon his departure he would always leave a chocolate, an apple, or a biscuit that reminded us of home, childhood, our father, or grandfather. Whenever there was a meeting, he always told us the same story about the way he,

Saharich, and Lanchik managed to escape a siege. No one would ever interrupt his story or let him know that we had heard it before. This story was a tribute to the unsurpassed honour of his generation, which allowed them to withstand even the hardest challenges.

And soon enough Hotabich would have to demonstrate his skills as a doctor yet again. During the bus ride, he was dozing off. Saharich kept trying to wake him up, but Hotabich just opened his eyes, mumbled something unintelligible, and dozed off again. The last one sitting in that row was the manager of army headquarters, not a pilot but always wanting to give advice and orders to everyone. He was a bitter and quarrelsome man serving out his last year (the Old Man couldn't wait for the year to be over). Because of a funny incident that took place during the first days of my arrival at the base, everyone called him Peewit.

This is what happened. I was on night duty at one of the hangars. That night Saharich was the responsible officer, but Peewit always thought that Saharich was too kindhearted, so he decided to come and check on us himself. Since we were part of the headquarters security team, he considered it his responsibility. He tried to enter the hangar but couldn't remember the password. All he could recall was that it was the name of a bird. He stood outside for an hour, braving the November cold, and called out the names of birds from all over the world but didn't guess it right. Exasperated and overcome by anger, he showed up at the Old Man's door at three o'clock in the morning. The Old Man could barely keep his eyes open and accidentally told him the wrong bird. Once again I had to deny him entry, and he left swearing and threatening to show me my place. The password was simple—"peewit."

The second row. Hmm…how strange the seating was that night! It seems that some invisible force placed everyone in their exact spot. A young lieutenant sat right in front of me and kept looking into my eyes. Later this young man would touch both Roman's and my life by becoming the one who…no, it's even worse than the moment I am trying to describe. But in that instant, he was just Volodya.

During his first flight in the dual cockpit with the extremely daring and hotheaded Captain Arzakyan, Volodya almost lost his life. As I turned out to be the one who saved him, for a while he didn't stop looking at me. Romka was the first to notice. He immediately understood the reason for Volodya's interest and smiled at my embarrassment. This is what happened: during the last segment of the flight, a seagull crashed into the plane, broke the strap of the engine, and remained wedged in the metal carcass. I noticed that something was wrong and used my authority to stop the flight, but Arzakyan's vanity was even stronger than his recklessness. He decided to complete the assignment and once again took off. I immediately informed the Old Man, but he was doubtful about the facts that I provided him with. Nevertheless, I insisted on my conclusions, and all the flights were canceled. Arzakyan and Volodya were called in to see me. Arzakyan's body radiated anger and discontent, but Volodya seemed lost in a premonition that something bad could have happened. All the evidence in my possession was laid out in front of me, and we awaited the arrival of the technician. My fingertips grew cold, and my throat was completely dry.

Under the table I was holding Roman's hand, and its coolness calmed me. I had specifically asked him never to get involved in my conflicts with other pilots, so he quietly mumbled something that no one could hear or understand. His self-restraint left nothing to be desired. At that point we didn't know that soon enough he would have to face an even greater ordeal.

The door opened, and the Old Man brought in the mechanic. The mechanic was a young man whose hair had greyed prematurely. Not long ago he had lost his brother in a similar incident. He confirmed my suspicions—soon enough, the engine would have stopped working.

Arzakyan started cracking his knuckles with such force that it seemed his fingers would snap. He got down on his knees in front of Volodya and whispered, "Son, please forgive me!"

The shadow of fear appeared on the face of the young lieutenant. He looked at the captain, then directed his bewildered gaze at the Old Man, the technician, and Roman, and finally settled on me. A sudden creak of the half-open door made the Old Man react. He put his arm around Volodya's shoulders and led him outside, saying, "Everyone should rest now. We will deal with this tomorrow."

As soon as the door closed behind them and Roman and I were finally alone, I broke out into hysterical laughter. Romka held me close and tried to support my trembling body, all the while repeating, "Well done! It was very well done."

Oh, Roman! If only you knew…

In the meeting room, he was sitting next to Volodya. His eyes were full of love, and I smiled at him. When I later recalled this scene, I was struck by the realization that each of us has our destiny, and there is nothing we can do to avoid it.

"Officers!"

Everyone got up and started leaving the room. My black folder of instructions was empty.

XII

I will let my heart tell the memories of that day. By now the pain has subsided and mixed with the silence of my loneliness. All the memories of what happened are locked away in my heart, and the memories of the heart are much stronger than those of the mind. I hope you won't judge me too harshly if you discover that my words seem to go against reason. I will let love be the judge of my recollections.

Misfortune is like an abyss—you fall right in without any warning. The test flights were almost over. During his break Roman came to see me. Despite the presence of another soldier, he put his hands on my shoulders and smiled. He then sat down and waited for me to finish my assignment. The soldier who had unwillingly become the witness of our closeness smiled to himself. Roman saw it and fixed his eyes on the technician. I knew exactly how this duel would end. A minute later the technician was no longer smiling but seemed to be staked to the wall by Roman's probing eyes and looking for a way to escape. His red fingers were desperately probing the wall behind his back.

After a moment of struggle, he loudly swallowed, cleared his throat, came up to my desk, and gave me the details of Volodya's flight. His technician had moved squadrons to serve with his brother. Not only did he bring the information with a considerable delay, but the documents were also covered in machine oil, which prevented me from establishing the time and the speed of the flight. His clearly untrue story about the reasons for his delay made me angry, but I didn't say a word. One look at my face, and he understood everything. He pressed his thin lips together and left. After every encounter I felt like airing the room and washing my hands. I found his presence extremely unpleasant.

Roman saw that I was trembling in rage, so he held me close, kissed me, and tried to calm me down. "It's all right. He left. Everything will be all right."

His eyes, hands, lips, and whole body made me relax and forget about my sorrows. I was standing with my back pressed against his chest. I looked up and met his eyes. Oh, God! My heart clenched even harder. There was something in his face that signaled approaching danger.

"Roman!"

"What? What's wrong?" He sat down, held me, and started rocking me like a baby.

"What's with you today?"

"I'm afraid of something."

"What are you afraid of? Of him?" He let out a quiet laugh and pointed his hand toward the door.

"I don't know. I'm just afraid."

"There's no need to worry. There is only one death. Besides, you evaluated my flight and gave me the top mark. That means I'm good at my job, right?"

"Yes!"

"You see? What will be your evaluation if I'm late for the flight?" He started to spin me around the room in hopes that it would calm me down.

"I have to go. Don't be so sad. I'll see you in an hour, and we'll have two days to ourselves." But something told me to stop him.

"Roma, wait!"

"Seryozhka, my love, I am already late. Smile! Please, smile. You see?"

I smiled at him through my tears, as if we were saying goodbye forever. He quickly touched his lips to mine and left the room.

The first half hour was very busy, and I managed to keep calm. But after the commander of the quadroon had run into the room several times and each time left without saying anything, my old worries returned. In the white pages on my table and the blue ribbons containing the data of the flights, I saw Roman's eyes. It seemed that they were trying to smile at me, say goodbye, and at the same time fight destiny.

When Rzhanovskiy entered again, I could no longer take it. I turned to face him in hopes of getting at least some information, and what I saw confirmed my fears—his body was shaking. He was always calm and collected. He was strict with everyone and never allowed any unnecessary show of emotion. Besides, he always treated Roman and me with distaste that he didn't even bother to hide. At that moment, however, his body radiated tension, and his eyes seemed fixed on a spot on the floor. He tried to force a smile, came up to me, and asked, "How is everything going?"

I tried to get up and run to the door, but fear gripped me, and I sat back down.

"Sergey, don't worry. It's not that bad. He can't engage the landing wheels, but we are doing everything in our power to help him. Besides, Romka is an outstanding pilot, and…"

"No!" My scream was so loud that the air seemed to quiver with the power of my voice, and for a second I couldn't hear anything.

"Seryozha, don't worry. It's not that bad. It happens. He will manage. Together we will land the plane."

But I couldn't hear him. I felt the wild animal of misfortune crawling closer and closer to my heart. I could feel its breath on my skin. I gathered all the energy I had left in me and screamed, "You can't have him!"

The air seemed to become unbearably dense. I suddenly saw the tiny red eyes of the technician with a gleeful fire burning in them.

In my mind they turned into two bottomless pits that were ready to swallow my Roman. Rzhanovskiy saw my condition and waited for me to regain my senses. To hasten the process, he grabbed my shoulders, briefly shook me, and said in a gentle but determined voice, "We can save him. We will do it together. Do you understand?"

I understood and sat down by the communication panel. The light immediately went on, as if it had been waiting for my touch. It was no surprise. During extreme flight situations, the only communication that went through was between the pilot, the control tower, and the communication center, like the one I was working at.

At first the Old Man's voice was so quiet that I could barely make out what he was saying. But just a minute later, the sound became louder, and I, barely holding back the tears, heard him speak very slowly, enunciating every word: "Roma, son, there is only one option—you have to increase the altitude and eject from the plane. Do you understand? It is not an order. I am asking you like a father..." His voice broke.

"Commander, what about you?"

"Roma, I don't need anything. I have lived my life. You are still young and have to continue living."

These words were followed by silence and the sound of the plane moving farther away from the unwelcoming ground, but the sky was not ready to welcome it either. I guess that really is the state of being stuck between heaven and earth.

Then, through the noises of the aeroplane, I heard Roman's calm voice. "Colonel, I am asking for your permission to attempt a landing."

"No! Roma, no!" There was a brief pause. "You are a very good pilot. An outstanding pilot. Son, you are the best of our pilots, but in these circumstances, you won't be able to land."

"I will try. I will use the emergency landing field. There are nets we can use and arresting barriers."

"Roma, no! Forget about the plane! I need you to return. Alive!"

"We can still save the plane. It is possible. I was practicing this same move in the simulator."

"No!" The Old Man's voice turned into an agonized scream. "No! Lieutenant, I order you to eject from the plane in the area of…"

I couldn't hear which area he meant; I only heard the coordinates of Romka's location.

"Commander, there is a farm and a school. What about the children?"

"We warned them."

"You won't get there on time."

"Why?" The Old Man's voice suddenly became quiet. As soon as he asked the question, he knew the answer.

"How much gas do you have left?"

"Not much."

Then I heard that the plane that had been circling the communications tower once again increased its altitude. The Old Man's voice froze. The insistent blinking of the communication light told me that he had become aware of the fact that I was listening. Before he could think of what to do, Roman's clear voice announced, "Commander, I will take the risk. You can't die twice."

The Old Man had given up. He knew there was nothing else he could do, but suddenly, despite the fact that the whole base was listening to the conversation, he said, "Sergey! Please, ask him."

"No, don't tell him. Spare him the pain."

"Too late, Roman. He heard everything."

The communication stopped for a while. The plane flew to the side but then returned. The Old Man asked, "What did you decide?"

"I will land the plane." His voice sounded like he was going on a parade instead of plunging to his death. Then he called out my name.

I was holding on to the communication microphone as if it were my last hope. It was the last thing that linked us together. Trying to hold back the tears, I whispered with parched lips, "Roma, I am listening."

"Seryozhenka, please forgive me. You are closest to the quadrant of my landing. You can help me."

"Roman!"

"Baby, hold on! I will see you soon. I promise. Remember when we had the same mission in a simulator?"

"Yes."

"What did we do?"

"We decided to use the nets."

"Exactly!"

"But we were in a simulator!"

"It doesn't matter. Make sure that as many are raised as possible. Hurry!"

His voice disappeared again. It was swallowed up by the sky. If the instructors who spent half a year trying to teach me at least something about technology had seen me that day, they would have been very surprised. Rzhanovskiy and I ran out of the building. Pilot ran after us, but I told him to stay. We jumped into the car that always stood near the flight house and drove to the place that Roman had indicated. A couple of minutes later, I had raised all the old but still substantial nets and watched the approaching aeroplane with a trembling heart.

During the demonstration flights, Lanchik always told the new pilots that these aeroplanes were far from becoming obsolete. He insisted that good pilots could do miracles.

Right in front of my eyes, Romka's MIG-17 reached the ground. To decrease the velocity, the plane was manoeuvred on one side. The tarmac scraped the wing like it was made of soft butter. A moment later Roman turned the plane and repeated the same on the other side. He then straightened the plane, and it sped ahead toward the arresting barrier, tearing up nets that stood in its way.

Once the plane stopped, I immediately started running in its direction. The nose and the tail were on fire.

"Nail, try to extinguish the flames," I shouted at the driver, who was standing still from surprise. I desperately tried to reach the cockpit. With bleeding hands I tore away the remnants of the barrier, which was made of fabric, leather, plastic, and pieces of metal. When I reached my destination, I saw that Roman's head was lying on the dashboard, and I felt that it was I who was bleeding out and dying. I still don't know wherefrom came my strength and agility. I quickly pressed all the right buttons and opened the front entrance to the plane. I hadn't been able to do it even during my final exams. At that point I had no idea if Roman was alive, but I knew that I had to hurry and get away before the possible explosion.

I looked at Nail and saw that he was praying. He was obviously not going to extinguish the flames. I pushed, pulled, and tore at all the cables and belts that connected Roman to the seat and to the dashboard. When I finally managed to release him from these restraints, I pulled him out of the cockpit, threw him over my shoulder, and climbed down to the ground with such agility that it seemed I had been doing it my entire life. As soon as I got down, I started running as fast as I could toward the closest trees. Suddenly, I felt him gently hit my back.

"Thank God, he is alive," I thought, but then…oh, God! He was about to suffocate. I had disconnected his breathing tube but forgot to remove the helmet. I put Roman down on the grass and quickly got rid of his helmet.

His eyes opened, and his lips were already seeking mine. "Hello! I'm back," he whispered.

"Roman!" I moved him closer to my body, and I held him up like a child. His face was so near. I started kissing it while tears streamed down my face.

"Seryozhenka, it's all right. We are together."

And then he moaned. I carefully started checking his body, looking for a break or an open wound, but Roman was lying still and showed no signs of pain. I decided to check his head. As soon as I removed the soft hat that protected him from the hardness of the helmet, I screamed out in surprise—on both sides, thick strands of his hair had turned grey.

He noticed some grey hairs on the inside of the hat and understood my reaction. "Don't worry; I'll dye it," he joked and then fell silent. Only his restless hands betrayed his fear and nervousness. Then I heard the screeching of the brakes. It was the Old Man, Hotabich in his ambulance car, and several firefighters. When Roman heard the noise, he held me so tight, as if he were trying to hide inside my body.

"Roma, don't worry. They are here to help." It was now my turn to calm and reassure him. But something was happening to him. His eyes seemed the same, but in their depths, there was something frightening that made me fear that the worst had happened.

Nail ran up to us and announced, "Praise be to Allah. The fire is out."

The Old Man sank down on his knees, took Roman's head in his hands, and whispered, "You're alive. Thank God, you're alive!"

But Roman quickly freed his head and frantically held on to me. He barely looked at the Old Man, who was trying to hold back the tears. I looked at him in confusion and hoped that Hotabich would be able to do something. He was approaching us, followed by a young medical lieutenant. He was holding a syringe and fearfully looked at Roman. Hotabich looked at Romka and stopped his young colleague. "Oleg, wait! Let me examine him."

But Roman wouldn't let him. He shook his head and strained against my body.

"Go away! Please, go away!"

"Roma, son, we at least need to give you an injection for the heart. You went through a severe trauma."

The Old Man kept talking, but Roman's eyes looked crazed, and he kept begging to be left alone.

Soon also Saharich arrived at the scene. He came up to us, bent down over Roman, and started crying. "What are you doing?"

Hotabich led Saharich and the Old Man aside and desperately tried to convince them about something.

Meanwhile, Roman calmed down. His body relaxed, and the tension seemed to disappear. He was smiling and trying to move as close to me as possible. The young doctor approached to give him the injection, but Romka immediately tensed up. I took his face in my hands, covered it with kisses, and whispered through my tears, "Roma, it's for the best. Hold on, my love."

My words seemed to calm him slightly, and the doctor managed to inject something that looked like camphor. We waited for a couple of minutes, and the young doctor measured Romka's pulse. Satisfied with the result, he returned to the car and started preparing stretchers. When Roman saw what he was doing, his body was immediately covered with sweat, and he pleaded, "Don't let them take me away! Please, don't let them. I don't want to leave. I want to stay with you. Seryozhenka, please…"

He tried to get up but collapsed in my arms. His body was shaking with violent tremors. His lips were moving, whispering my name, desperately trying to smile.

"Hotabich!" I yelled at the top of my lungs. I could no longer look at him. "Do something!"

Oleg approached us with the stretchers, but Hotabich immediately told him to stop. Oleg slowly moved back, clearly unsure what the old doctor intended to do. I wasn't sure either. Roman had calmed down again and seemed to regain his senses, but his dear blue eyes still looked unfamiliar. Invisible forces coursed through his body and brought to the surface waves of fear, despair, and something else that I couldn't recognize. And again, all we could do was wait. The Old Man and Saharich tried to convince Hotabich of something, but he shook his head and announced, "It is my decision." Then he returned to my side.

Roman had raised his body and was now half sitting and leaning against my chest. He didn't protest at Hotabich's approach but squeezed my hand so hard that I almost yelped. The only thing that stopped me was the look of fear that had yet again appeared in Roman's eyes. Later Hotabich called this state "post-traumatic stress syndrome." I managed to free my hand and instead wrapped my arms around Roman, who was sniffling like an unhappy child. Hotabich stepped aside and called me to join him, but as soon as I moved…

"Don't leave," Roman whispered.

"Roma, I'll be right back. Trust me; I won't leave you."

"Don't go," his lips whispered as if he hadn't heard me.

Hotabich saw Roman's pleading eyes, outstretched hands, and desperate attempts to stop me from getting up. He quietly came up to us, and while Roman seemed to disappear inside his thoughts, quickly told me, "Son, don't be surprised at anything and hold on."

"But I…"

"Quiet! Don't say anything and listen. We will help you, but right now he needs you to stay sane. Do you understand that?"

"Yes, but…"

"You have to trust me. If you will take my advice and do everything that Roman asks, soon enough he will once again be the person you know and love. But now you have to be patient, we beg you."

I looked at the Old Man and Saharich and realised that it had been decided. Roman's desperate movements made me nod my head in agreement. Quickly and quietly all the people and cars left the area. Only Nail was still quietly praying on one side.

Roman opened his eyes, raised his body, stretched slightly, and sat down without my help. He almost looked like his old self, except for the eyes. He felt that I was trying to move my legs, stiff under the weight of his body, and rolled on his side. He used his arms to get back to a sitting position, and I realised that his legs were not moving. I immediately started pulling off his overalls to check them.

"I'm all right. My legs just feel a bit funny from knee down."

"Roma!"

"Don't worry; it will be all right."

"Roman, Hotabich said…"

"Hush…" He covered my mouth with the palm of his hand and pulled me closer. His arms were still strong.

"Let's not talk, all right?"

"All right, but…"

He felt that my patience was running out and silenced me with a passionate kiss that reminded me of the very first one we had shared. I was ready to do anything to return calm and confidence to his eyes, to make him look like my Roman. But how could I do that? Before his departure Hotabich told me not to rush Roman. All I could do was wait. But the chilly September air, the sparse clouds, the wailing cry of a nocturnal bird, and the damp mist rising from the nearby bog made me wish for the warmth and comfort of my room. I looked at Romka and suddenly was overcome with thoughts about loneliness and the realization that I had almost lost him that night.

My soul filled with tenderness and sadness, and I reached for Romka, who was breathing deeply and seemingly enjoying another moment of calm. And suddenly the most obvious thought came to my mind—love is never easy, but it does exist. And it can touch not only a man and a woman but also two men or two women. No one has any right to judge people just because they feel good together. Rzhanovskiy once told us in anger that we were like the white crows— we stood out among everyone else. And Roman replied, "Yes, we are white but also clean. The crows only take pleasure in flying and not in the misfortunes of others and jealousy. Those traits remind me of vultures and hyenas."

Roman was watching the clouds and quietly smiling. I didn't dare touch him. I bent down, looked into his eyes, and almost felt like crying—they were still the same. His heavy breathing and the eerie edge of his smile told me that he was far from being all right. The wild animal was still close, just waiting for the right moment to attack.

I helped Roman to his feet. It was obvious that standing up was hard for him. He asked me to help him get to the closest birch tree, which he then held on to and told me to step back. He tried to straighten up and fell. I immediately ran to help him, but he stopped me. "I'll do it myself. I have to."

He clenched his teeth, grabbed the trunk of the tree, and got up. "Call me! Call me!"

But I was choking with tears, and strange, tortured sounds escaped my mouth. I spread out my arms, inviting him like a child who is about to take his first steps. I was ready to catch him.

"Roman, my love, my life, come here," I finally managed to say.

"No, Seryozha, no! It's not what I need. I need to feel your anger. It will help me walk. Please, shout at me!"

"Roman, how can I shout if you are begging me?"

We both realised that we couldn't change our feelings, so we started smiling and then laughing. And then Roman made the first step. It was a small and shy step, and he was still holding on to the curious tree. The next step was longer and more confident. I wanted to run up to him, but his eyes told me to stay where I was. He finally let go of the tree. The branches seemed to follow him and offer desperately needed support. The ground under his feet suddenly was covered with golden leaves. He rested a moment and got ready to take the next step. He started approaching me but still didn't let me touch him. His smile lit up like a lighthouse and illuminated the path that would take us out of this dark misery. Finally, he reached me and fell into my arms. His body was covered in sweat, and he was breathing heavily. After a moment's rest, he straightened his back and made another step, but his foot sank in the bog that was hiding under the grass and moss. He started laughing.

"See? I told you I can do it myself."

"Roman! Roman!" I held him close and felt that his shirt was soaked through with sweat. "Roman, we have to go. It's already dark."

"Yes, Seryozhenka, we are going. I also want to return to our house."

"No, Roma. First we have to go to Hotabich."

Suddenly his features contorted.

"Damn it!" I realised that I shouldn't have said that. Hotabich had told me to do everything that Roman wanted.

"All right, Roma. All right. We are going home. It's time."

He wrapped his arms around me and said, "I knew you would help me. You are mine. Mine…"

"Yes, Roman. I am yours. Only yours."

I felt that his strength and confidence were slowly returning. He was unbelievably gentle and kept kissing and caressing me. It calmed me down, but the cold wind and the dark shadows made us hurry to the car. I signaled Nail to start the engine. As we were leaving, the wild animal suddenly discovered our absence and tried to break the birch tree in its futile anger. But the tree fought back—it hit the animal with its bare branches, whispering, "There! Don't even try. You won't succeed."

The animal realised that it couldn't fight the tree and started running after our car. When we reached the flight house, I discovered that Pilot was not there, and his food was still untouched. We were met by the woman who came to clean the flight house once a week. I was surprised to see her at such a late hour. She had lit the stove, made some tea, cleaned the whole house, and was now waiting for us. I could see that she had been crying. When she saw that I was helping Roman to come inside, she immediately wanted to assist me, but Roman moaned and refused her help. I still couldn't understand why she was there and politely asked her to leave.

"Yes, of course. I'm already going."

She tried to say something else, but her tears made it impossible. I concluded that it was a natural reaction of women in face of difficulties. It was only when she left that I suddenly remembered that she was the mother-in-law of the technician.

I put Roman in bed, calmed him down, covered him with blankets, and sat down to watch his every breath. Finally, he fell asleep, his left arm under his head and his right hand holding mine.

Nail entered the house. He sat down in the corner and nervously looked at us. The phone rang. I picked it up and looked at Roman. He was having a nightmare. His head was thrashing on the pillow and there was a deep frown on his face, but he didn't have the strength to turn on his side. He couldn't wake up.

"Yes?"

Hotabich's voice was worried, but he didn't say much. "Is he asleep?"

"Yes."

"When he wakes up, give him something to eat. Maybe also something to drink. Lanchik's cognac is in the cupboard. I'll tell you the rest later. Hold on; it won't be long now."

"Hotabich, but what…"

"Hold on, son. Be patient." The conversation was over.

I was ready to hold on and be patient. I was not afraid. I would have done anything for him. I would have given my blood, my skin, and my life, but none of it was necessary. I had no idea what the Old Man was planning. I had no idea what was happening.

In my helplessness I started preparing dinner. Nail had already understood what needed to be done and was busy cleaning potatoes. We had been planning a visit to Tallinn, so there was no meat at home, which made me upset. Nail once again understood me without any words and left the room to return with a large parcel containing a hake. I found some carrots, onions, herbs, and butter and started frying the fish. It was one of Romka's favourites. I made some sauce with garlic, and the smell woke Roman from his restless sleep. He opened his eyes, inhaled the aroma of the food, slightly raised himself, and smiled.

My hands were covered in flour. I went up to him and saw that his shoulders were more relaxed, his eyes seemed to have gotten warmer, and the grey strands of hair no longer stood out so much. I smiled at him. He drew me close, sighed, suspiciously looked at Nail, and whispered, "I am so hungry. Just like back then…"

"Roman! Oh, Roman!" His words made me laugh and cry at the same time.

And what a feast we had! Roman had a glass of cognac and then attacked the food with such voracity that I almost couldn't fill his plate up in time. Nail was sipping tea and looked at us in surprise. When Romka was finally full, he lay down on the couch and said, "Thank you so much! It was so tasty."

"Roma, that' s it. Now we have to go."

"No, let's wait a little bit longer."

"You sound just like Hotabich. What are you waiting for?"

"Seryozhka, I don't know. I just feel that it's not over." For a moment he was completely silent. Then he made me sit down next to him and slowly started speaking. "You know, when I was up there…"

"Roma, please don't."

"No, I have to. Don't worry. Everything is all right now. So, when I was up there and it seemed like I wouldn't make it…"

"Roma!"

"Please, wait and listen. I suddenly remembered and almost saw my mother and father."

I didn't interrupt him in his sudden confession. We had known each other almost for a year, but he never talked about his past. Normally, he wouldn't say anything. Normally, I would consider it an honest and simple conversation. But I could still feel the cold shadow of the frightening events and remembered what Hotabich had told me. Roman was looking at me intently. Then he continued. "When I was three years old, they were killed by an avalanche. A teacher at the orphanage showed me their picture and told me that they had gone on a long trip but would definitely come back. And I waited. We all waited and didn't want to admit that we are orphans. So many years passed, but today I saw my parents again. And then a cloud carried them away. Then I saw my teacher—Christina Pavlovna. Every evening she used to read us stories, kiss us good night, and say something kind and tender. Only then we could fall asleep. When she passed away, we—the boys—carried her coffin and sat the whole night beside her grave. It seemed that we could hear her quiet whispers coming from beneath the ground: 'Children, everything will be all right. You just have to believe it.'"

He stopped talking and pressed his body closer to mine. I kissed away his tears and waited for him to continue. A minute later Roman continued. "I had a friend—Mishka. Everyone called him Foundling. He didn't mind. Only if someone was getting really tiresome in their teasing he would say, 'Better a foundling than someone who was left on the doorstep.' But then he would immediately run to me, tuck his head in my chest, and cry. His dark eyes looked so sad that I would start crying as well."

Romka drew in another breath and pressed his face against my shoulder.

"We would cry our eyes out and then fall asleep together. We did everything together—ate, played, studied, and dreamed. And then he was adopted. He didn't want to leave without me. He kept making up excuses in hopes that the family would adopt me as well. But no! A flu epidemic broke out. I was placed in a hospital, and Mishka was taken to his new parents by force, in the middle of the night. A year later he ran away from home and disappeared."

Once again Roman's eyes were filling up with tears. His lips trembled, and his breathing sped up. His hands were nervously running up and down my body.

"Roma, my love, don't. It pains you to remember."

"No, Seryozhenka, it's not the past that pains me. The pain is inside me, somewhere here." He pointed to his chest. "It burns and suffocates me. I can't even see clearly."

"Then talk, Roma. Say everything you need to say."

"I remember Mishka very well, even though I never saw him again. Seryozhenka, why did they all come today? My parents, Auntie Christina, Mishka? I got so scared…so scared…if I hadn't heard your voice…"

"Roma!"

He stopped talking. The room was quiet. Nail was praying to his God. Romka's head rested on my shoulder. When he raised it and I looked into his eyes, I knew that the crisis was about to reach its culmination. He was strong enough to continue.

"The last person that I saw was you." He smiled.

"Me?"

"Yes. Your blue eyes are the colour of the spring sky. Your cheeks are the colour of the sunrise. Your warm lips. You were reaching for me, and I understood that I have no right to leave you, to go against my word. You are mine, and I am yours. Forever. Right?"

"Yes, Roma. Yes!" I almost screamed those words. I couldn't stand the fact that he was in pain but I was not able to help.

During our emotional exchange, we almost didn't hear that Pilot had returned. He started howling outside the door, and his howls almost resembled an eerie dirge. I opened the door and let him in. He slowly crawled into the room, lay down on the doorstep, and continued howling.

"Pilot, be quiet," I admonished him with tears in my eyes.

The dog crawled closer and stopped in front of Roman. Oh, God! Why didn't you teach animals our language? But Pilot's eyes, filled with tears, spoke louder than any words. He licked Roman's hand and whimpered, feeling the approaching misfortune.

The door suddenly burst open, and the wild animal was laughing at us. The dog felts its presence and growled at the doorstep on which death was not standing. Roman stood up, his eyes changed again, and he seemed to be looking at something.

"Don't let it take me," he screamed. Then he moaned, found my chest, hid his face, and started crying. I held his head, sank down on my knees, and whispered soft and soothing words to calm him down. Nail was praying again. In my thoughts I turned to God and begged for his mercy, but this time He didn't listen. Roman's body was heaving with pain. Tears rose up from his chest and spilled out of his eyes, choking him and draining him of strength. It seemed that after all the years of holding them back, he finally felt that he could let go of his burden.

I understood now what Hotabich meant when he said Roman needed only me. I held Roman's head to my chest and gently rocked him until he was all cried out. Within fifteen minutes my shirt had turned into a wet rag. That night I died and came back to life with him. I understood that there is never just happiness or pain in life— everything is linked; everything has a beginning and an end.

Several minutes passed. Roman opened his eyes, and I understood that we had won. The wild animal was defeated. Roman's eyes were once again blue, warm, and alive. He looked around, and for a moment it seemed that he barely recognized the overjoyed Pilot and Nail's smiling face. Then he started laughing and finally truly returned to this miracle that we call life.

XIII

And that was how we lived—sharing our joys and sorrows. One month followed the next, and soon a year was drawing to a close. My time in the army was about to end. Many things happened, but I only want to remember those that are close to my heart. Memories are falling like autumn leaves, gathering at my feet in layers. Desperate to be seen and heard, they whisper, "Do you remember?" I do. Of course I do. I remember the Old Man's face and his brief warning to the technician when his wrench was pulled out of the area of the broken landing wheels.

"Get lost, or I'll kill you!"

The technician's face was ashen grey, his thin lips were no longer visible, and his legs shook so hard that he was not able to move.

I remember how the day after the accident, Hotabich drove us to the nearest hospital in Lanchik's personal car. He left us in the care of another old and kind doctor who, after close examination, announced that all Romka needed was proper rest.

I remember how the Old Man and Saharich regularly came to visit us with baskets of fruit and boxes of chocolate. Romka, unlike me, was not used to taking medicine, so the chocolate helped him swallow the bitter sedative mixture that a medical professor from Riga (brought to the base by Lanchik) prescribed him.

I remember our walks in the hospital garden and the unwillingness to let go of the green summer leaves that were still trying to fight against coming autumn. On one of his visits, the Old Man brought

Pilot. Oh, God! His reaction was so amusing. Everyone who saw us stopped and watched the large and extremely happy dog with light brown fur and a black "bow tie" jumping up and down, licking our hands, and trying to stand on his hind paws. With every passing day, Roman's eyes became clearer, and sometimes I could even see a smile on his face.

But the most important thing was the fact that we were together. We had a double hospital room and immediately moved our beds together. None of the staff showed any surprise or disapproval. Every day before going to bed, we were given a sedative mixture, which helped us sleep. And Roman's tenderness only seemed to increase with the return of his strength. As soon as our lips touched, his hands were already wandering up and down my body, caressing and exploring. We enjoyed our closeness and intimacy to the fullest. Sometimes I started missing him as soon as he got out of bed.

"Roman!"

And immediately his hands reached for me, and he returned to kiss me and whisper, "Seryozhenka! I love you! You are mine."

I remember the day when two nurses brought unexpected visitors—two women and an infant. It was the wife and the mother-in-law of the technician. At first Roman started to shiver but the calmed himself and offered them a seat. The women had not expected such a positive welcome. They immediately started crying and asked forgiveness for their husband and son-in-law.

Romka turned his face to the window and could no longer contain his shivers. Up until that moment, I had been watching passively, but I eventually asked the women to step out of the room. I saw a smile in the wife's eyes, and it reminded me of the way her husband had smiled on that fateful day, except her smile was not malignant but, rather, servile. She quickly slipped past me, ran up to Roman, and held out something in front of him. The sound of paper and Roman's expression told me that it was money. He started shaking so hard that it scared not only me but also the child, who let out a heart-wrenching wail. However, the mother was undeterred. She pushed the child closer to Roman and said, "For her! Do it for her!"

Roman took my hand and pulled me out of the room. In the hallway we ran into the Old Man. He pushed us back toward the room and said, "So they made it here before me. I'll take care of it."

"Commander…" Roman said in a strained voice.

"No, Roma. There are many things one can forgive. Not villainy."

He entered and saw the wife hurriedly gathering her money.

"Out!" he yelled.

He didn't say anything to the nurses who immediately appeared in the room, but immediately addressed the doctor. "I told you not to let anyone in."

The doctor looked at the nurses, apologized, and left without saying another word. Then one of the nurses turned toward the mother-in-law and asked, "So you are not his mother?"

The woman quickly apologized to Roman, started crying, and ran out of the room. The wife of the mechanic followed her. Roman grunted and lay down on his bed.

I remember the night before the trial. I woke up, and Roman wasn't there. I waited for a while but then understood that he hadn't gone to sleep that night. He was thinking about the fate of the man who had so profoundly affected our lives but was now at Roman's mercy. He was standing in the half-open door and smoking.

"Roman?"

He immediately put out the cigarette, turned to me, and held me close. "Romka!"

"I'm sorry. I won't. I thought it would help, but it didn't." And then he fell silent.

Pilot came up to us, sniffed the air, licked our hands, and started wagging his tail. Roman hugged both of us and repeated, "I'm sorry. I won't."

I didn't interfere with his thoughts. I had to concentrate on holding back the tears, but eventually I couldn't. When Roman felt them on his cheek, he looked at me, wiped my tears away with his index finger, kissed me, and said, "Don't cry. Go to sleep. I will come soon."

But he only came early in the morning. He saw that my eyes were still open and sighed. He pulled me into his chest, kissed me, and whispered, "Sleep. Sleep, baby. You're so tired because of me."

"No, Romashka. No!"

Our eyes met. Roman smiled. He knew what I wanted to ask him and needed my support in fully making his decision.

"I can't let little Galina grow up an orphan. That way I can do something good."

"You just need to have faith," I whispered with tears in my eyes, and we both fell into a restless sleep. I was the only one who knew how hard the trial was for Romka. The technician publicly admitted his blame and asked for forgiveness. Romka looked at Galina, who was playing at her mother's feet, smiled at her, and said, "I forgive you." It was a victory like no other.

The technician received a dishonourable discharge and an order to pay for all the damages to the plane. That evening we had dinner at the Old Man's house, which Lanchik also attended. Roman was very quiet and only spoke during Lanchik's toast, asking him to say "we" instead of "he."

I remember his first flight after a long preparation and the triumph in his eyes after landing. That night was quiet and light, just like that April night so long ago. When I returned from the shower and slid under the blanket with my skin still damp, he put his arms around me, and I understood—his desire to love had returned.

And once again the moon was the only witness of his gentle touches, which made me quiver with pleasure. Even now the memory of that night makes my heart sing with happiness.

I remember our first trip to Tallinn after the accident. We had two nice and relaxing days, and once we returned…

"Did you manage to have a rest?"

"Yes."

"Well done. Did you sign the documents?"

"Yes, sir."

"Good. You did service to the whole regiment. And how about my request?"

Roman looked at the Old Man in genuine surprise. I was desperately trying to remember what he had asked for. Then I realised that it really made no difference, since we hadn't bought anything. I didn't want to upset the Old Man, so I said as believably as possible, "Unfortunately, there were none."

The Old Man looked at Roman, who was trying very hard to keep a straight face, and then settled his eyes on me. My face didn't betray anything, and he almost believed me, but Roman could no longer contain his laughter, "Nothing was available." He bit his lips and sat down on the couch.

"No pencils in the whole city?"

Suddenly, I remembered the Old Man asking for them and made a gesture that gave me away.

The Old Man gravely shook his head. "You are hopeless! What were you doing there?"

But we no longer heard him. We were both laughing unstoppably. Saharich entered the room, smiled at the scene before him, and asked, "What's going on? By the way, do you have a spare pencil?"

The Old Man sat down on the edge of the couch and started laughing as well. Finally, he replied, "No, we don't have any pencils. None are available." With these words he fell to the floor, his body shaking with laughter.

Saharich looked at him, went up to the Old Man, and said, "Give me a pencil. I'm sure you have enough."

The laughter grew even louder.

I remember that we brought the Old Man his pencils sometime later, after the visit to the Russian Theatre. I had carefully selected all those who would come with us and included Timosha. He was a man of large build, originally from Siberia. He had spent his whole life in a tiny village sharing a house with his father. He had never seen a big city, not to mention a theatre, so every sight and turn was a surprise for him. He knew nothing about compromising. He had always lived in tune with nature, calmly and sensibly, and he made us think about our lives and the way we approached them. If someone was laughing about it, he never got offended. He just put his large hand on the person's shoulders, smiled, and asked, "Is something the matter?" And then add, "Is it? And what are we going to do now?"

Oh, Timosha—Timofey! Your innocence was so captivating.

I remember our excitement when the Old Man told us about the decision at headquarters to make Roman a captain in gratitude for his heroic actions.

I remember the letter from my mother that arrived in December telling me about the death of my grandmother. The Old Man gave me a leave of absence that he was actually supposed to take himself. He next appeared when Roman and I were pooling our resources. To be honest, I didn't have any. I only received 3.80 rubles a month, which always made Roman laugh. When I showed signs of embarrassment, he pulled me close and said, "You are priceless." And then he added the money from his lieutenant's pay.

At that moment the Old Man appeared. He squeezed my shoulder in support and gave me the document and also some money. "It's from all of us," he said.

I looked at him with tears in my eyes, thanked him, and was whisked away to the airport. The Old Man had already called and told them to prepare my ticket. As we were passing the area of the test flights, an army car overtook us. It was Rzhanovskiy (time really does make people change). He gave me a little parcel and said, "This is from the pilots." When he saw that I was about to cry, he pressed my hand and added, "Be strong!" I will always be grateful to everyone who helped me back then.

I remember the eve of 1973. The officers' club was being reno-vated, so the Old Man invited us to his house. His daughters were joyfully dancing with me and Tolik but in the presence of Roman couldn't move their feet. Not even during a slow dance. It made the Old Man grumble, "Now it has happened to them as well. Move, girls! Move!" Then he picked up his youngest daughter and spun her all around the decorated Christmas tree. When he had completed the circle and saw that Masha or Tanya still couldn't move, he clapped his hands, announced a change of partners, and took Roman's place. But then the same sequence of events had to be repeated with the other daughter. Only the Old Man's wife, Susanna, showed no shyness or hesitation. While she danced a passionate tango with Roman, the Old Man said to his stupefied daughters, "It comes with experience. Learn from your mother."

I remember the frightening day in the middle of January when Arzakyan returned from his leave earlier than planned and found his wife in bed with another man. He couldn't cope with his feelings, so he flew his plane into the frozen waters of the bay. All he said on the radio was, "I'm sorry." Three days after this event, I still couldn't eat anything. Roman was visibly upset but, as always, didn't say a word. It seemed that the life at the base had suddenly stopped. Those were hard and dark days. We all felt how fragile human life is and how inconstant our attachments are. The test flights were stopped for a long time. The Old Man was called to headquarters, but Lanchik settled the situation, and with the first days of spring, we slowly started coming back to life.

My demobilization was approaching. I should have been happy, but all the smells and sounds and the songs of the spring birds reminded me that Roman and I would soon have to part. At the beginning of April, Roman received the order to move to another squadron and test the new supersonic aircraft.

The ten days that we were given to say goodbye started in an interesting way. The Old Man, who had aged considerably since the death of Arzakyan, told us about the order separately. Roman was sure that I didn't know anything, and for about a week tried to think of a way to tell me. By then I was getting used to the idea of parting and curiously awaited the day when he would finally tell me. I didn't show that I knew what was coming and in his presence acted as always. However, during those days I was often the first one to wake up, and then I gazed at his face in sorrow and tried to commit it to my memory. It took all my patience and willpower not to say anything.

The Old Man was convinced that the pain of the parting would reduce us to ashes. On the evening of the seventh day, he was surprised to see our smiling faces but initially didn't say anything. When the dinner was over, he finally asked Romka, "Did you tell him?"

"No."

"And he?"

"What?"

"Well, he knows. What is his reaction?"

"He knows?"

Roman accidentally sat down on Pilot's back. The dog growled but didn't move, trying to hold up his saviour. I opened the curtain to see what was going on and couldn't contain my laughter. The Old Man's face looked like a big question mark. Roman's face looked like an exclamation mark. Pilot somehow managed to reflect both. Thus it went on for an entire minute.

Pilot was the first to break the spell—he pulled himself free from Roman's body and ran outside. Roman barely had time to catch his balance. He started laughing and reached out his hand. "My love, why didn't you say anything?"

"Why didn't you?"

The Old Man sighed, tried to smile, and said, "You deserve each other." Then he said goodbye and left.

The next two days flew by in endless test flights. All we had was a long April night and the brief hours before the departure. Even though our hearts were heavy, the night was filled with boundless love.

XIV

O h, what a night it was! After the noisy farewell dinner with everyone who had become close to us, we stayed alone and enjoyed our closeness. We inhaled the fresh aroma of spring, which was mixed with the bitter taste of our parting. It was so quiet that we could almost hear the grass breathing in its sleep and the tiny leaves whispering to one another.

The shadows of the night didn't look as dark as they used to. With every passing hour, they kept filling up with light until they disappeared completely. It almost seemed they didn't want to disturb us or the approaching morning.

But the dawn was still not that close. The smell of some mysterious flowers that only bloom at night but are not visible during the day increased in power and mixed with the more familiar smells of nearby trees and cold water. Everything seemed so confusing, mysterious, beautiful, and simple. But at the same time, something solemn quivered in the air. We were surrounded not only by life and beauty, but by the smells and colours of life itself, and we felt that our future was still ahead of us.

The cheerful voices of the awakening birds told us that a miracle was waiting for us. In moments like these, I feel sorry for those who were never in love in the early years of their lives or who were loved with restraint, never learning the sweetness of pure desire.

We didn't even think of sleeping. Oh, no! We went out into the darkness that was briefly interrupted by the sounds of the night and walked to all the places that held meaning to our love. The wine diluted our sadness, and at times it even made us laugh loud enough to keep back the tears of despair. Old memories kept resurfacing, and when one of us asked, "Do you remember?" the other one immediately replied, "Yes!" And we just kept remembering and recalling, trying to bring back the sweetest memories.

The peaceful glimmer of the moonless sky, the enchanting pull of the old places, the quivering spring air, and the joyful barks of Pilot, who refused to leave our sides—it all filled our souls with endless happiness. We went back to the house and surrendered ourselves to the last night of love. Oh, and what a night it was! These memories are still very clear and make me shiver. Roman was always so loving and tender. He never prepared or planned our moments of closeness (as it sometimes happens in a different kind of relationship). They seemed to naturally flow out of his magnificent soul. Slowly and gently, like the light of the waking sun, he unfolded his desire. When he saw how brightly the fire burned in my eyes and how my body reached for his, he let the gentle spring of our love turn into a stormy ocean of desire. No matter how strongly the storm was raging, we were never afraid to drown and drag all our weaknesses and sins to the bottom of the ocean simply because love knows no weakness, and our love was true and courageous. I had loved him and desired him from the very start. I used to dream about the possibility of belonging to him fully. When my dreams finally came true, I found in him not only strength and beauty but also a storm of human emotions so particular and present only in him—my Roman. This mysterious and heart-wrenching night was different from the rest, probably because it was the night when we said goodbye. It was the night when he fulfilled all my dreams…

Accompanied by the buzzing sounds of a beetle and the impatient whistle of an invisible bird (I think it was a blackbird) who seemed to be telling someone a bedtime story, we took a shower together one last time. We were loud and happy and tried to turn it into a game. Then we returned to the cradle of our love—the old couch. I saw my reflection in the clear-blue lakes of his eyes, and his face reflected in mine. There was another pair of eyes watching us. The pain of our parting was always present in the room, and there was nothing we could do to hide from it.

"Don't be sad," begged Roman's eyes.

"I won't," my eyes replied.

We brought our bodies closer together, entwined our hands, and pushed the sadness away. And then it all started anew. It was just like our first spring, our first night together. Suddenly, everything seemed so new and cheerful. The currents of the ocean of love kept taking us farther and farther away from the shore, and our bodies celebrated the beauty of our love. Oh, what a night it was! We swayed in the blissful waves and thanked fate for all the beautiful moments it had given us.

And while we later enjoyed the bright rainbow of fulfilled desires, the spring air ignited a new spark of passion that we had to chase. Like a falling star, it landed in the darkness and once again joined our burning bodies. That night our love was blooming and singing in the beautiful voices of a thousand birds. It took us a while to remember that someone else was quietly trying to say goodbye. It was Pilot. He jumped on the couch and made himself comfortable right next to our feet. He insistently licked them as if asking our permission to move closer. We didn't want to turn him away on this night that was so hard for all of us, so we got up and moved closer to him. His fur was wet with dew. It smelled of flowers and grass. He looked at us with his understanding eyes and placed his body closer to ours. Many years later I would see our friend once again, and it would be so much harder, but back then I didn't know what was to come and quietly gave in to my tears. Roman put his arms around me and Pilot and brought our heads together. Our quiet moans and whimpers resembled sad farewell music.

But it didn't last long. Pilot licked away our sadness and called outside in the cool air saturated in the morning fog. We were immediately overcome with the feeling of new life and a brand-new day.

The morning unfolded slowly and majestically. The horizon was becoming lighter, and the stars started disappearing from the sky. The wind woke up and greeted the firs by moving their heavy branches. The rising fog pushed the night farther and farther away. The water in the bog shone like a mirror, and flowers woke up and opened their smiling eyes. The blackbird disappeared and let the lark fill the air with its song. The white clouds in the sky looked down on us like white swans. That was the last picture of our life together.

Several hours later, despite Pilot's desperate attempts to stop the car, Roman and I left the base. Then a few more hours passed, and different trains took us in different directions. That was how our separation started. It was April 28, 1973. My military service was over.

PART III

I

And once again it is autumn. The days seem to hurry toward the inevitable end of the year. The cranes are the first to leave. They disappear into the blue autumn sky, leaving behind a trail of mournful sounds. Soon enough, other inhabitants of forests and woodlands will feel compelled to follow. The clouds are becoming heavier; the mornings and the evening are darker. The misty autumn air is often infused with rain. The trees are now dressed in the bright colours of the fall. But nature still fights against the cold, and every once in a while, a brave yellow daisy can be found in one of the flowerbeds. Whenever I see the tiny flower, I have to smile, and it warms my heart no matter how cold and dark the day that surrounds me is.

But right now it's the middle of the night. I am still awake and can't make myself fall asleep. The whole world seems so quiet; only the wind still keeps twirling leaves in a reckless waltz. The dawn is still far away. Even in autumn, the dawn is special with the sound of the first trams, blinking lights in the windows, and slow footsteps of the few people who have stepped outside. But now it all seems so far away. Grey shadows overcome the houses, the streets, and also me. My heart is so cold, and oh, how it aches! I yearn for the warmth of our love. It seems that in the endless darkness, I can feel the presence of Roman. My Roman! My hand touches the window, and I feel his face under my fingers. My warm breath fogs the glass. And then I hear his voice in the wind, calling me. Someone is knocking on the window! I remove my hand from the glass and quickly open the window to be greeted by a branch of rowan. I willingly accept this autumn gift. The softness of the berries reminds me of his velvety lips, and as I touch them, my heart overflows with pain and sadness. I am surrounded by a trembling warmth that reminds me of his breath, and I am ready to run through the darkness of the streets like a leaf that's carried forth by the wind just to reach him, get lost in him, or maybe just say a word to my love…

"Roma! Roman! Wait for me!" I desperately scream into the darkness of the night, but he is no longer there. My eyes and ears keep looking for him, but all I hear are the whispers of the dry leaves. The sky seems to be getting darker. Heavy drops of rain are falling on the rooftops and making them shine. Small droplets of water, like teardrops, are running down the window pane. Who is crying? Is it the garden or is it me? The wind picks up the leaves and throws them at me, and I remember, see, and hear the echo of spring—the spring of our love. The trees in the garden have no memories from the past. But I open my window wider and beg for my memories to fly in. My heart is trembling in expectation. There is no love, joy, or happiness in my life. I can no longer tell the difference between the sky and the colour of my love's eyes. Between the sound of the wind and the remnants of my long-lost life. The person who was the center of my universe all these years is no longer here. All I can do is remember him.

II

There was happiness, and then it was gone. Probably that's why I finally want to escape the restricting confines of time and embrace our first meeting. But what to do with the dull and aching bundle of days that stretched in between? The days became long and heavy, making it difficult to recall them. The closer I move to the conclusion of this tale, the harder it becomes to untangle each separate moment. It's not that I have completely forgotten or that the pain of separation has erased all recollection of what happened in between, but our lives were fundamentally so different. Every morning was marked by the gentle touch of our hands and lips. Every midday was like an island that linked the brief and passing encounters of the early hours. Every evening came with sweet longing, and we rushed to the flight house. Every night was passed in a burning desire to be closer and feel our hearts beat as one. When all those moments were no longer a part of my life, I seemed to lose my way. And the more I tried to find it, the farther away I moved. The apple trees were blooming with intoxicating ferocity, and the smell seemed to choke me. Wherever I went, silence followed me. My soul was constantly weighed down by sadness and longing. I heard his voice and steps in the rustle of the curtains, the sound of the falling rain, the howls of the wind, the squeaking swings in the yard, and the twilight of the blooming garden.

Even in my sleep, I was not able to overcome the grief of separation. I often woke up from the sound of my voice calling out his name. I found no comfort in songs, wine, or even friends. The heavy weight of pain was always there. Who knows what I would have done in despair if the constant stream of his letters didn't start arriving on the third day, somewhat numbing my pain and the fear of loneliness. His letters radiated love, care, and similar sadness, and they brought spring back into my life. The air suddenly seemed to be filled with his tender words, expectation, and the joy of the blooming spring. In all the years to come, these letters kept me alive. I read them a thousand times and memorized every single one of them. Even though the wild animal would later take the letters away from me and erase Roman's face from all the photographs, my heart preserves the memory of some of them.

The first letter was written while he was still on the way. The lines reminded me of little soldiers, bumping into each other, pulling apart, and then coming together once again. These lines told me about his love.

Seryozhenka, my love! The wheels of the train are taking me farther away from you. I am sitting by the open window, and now I can feel how bitter the wind of spring is if you are not next to me. But it won't be long. Baby, we will meet! We will definitely meet! I don't know where and when, but we will be together! It doesn't matter how long we'll have to wait, but for now I keep you in my heart, my soul, my memory. You are my secret and my only love. My first love. So honest, gentle, and unspoiled by this noisy and malevolent life. (I have to stop writing so that I can kiss you, and then I will continue.) A year ago you gave yourself to me. Even death will not erase those memories. All the moments of that night and every single one that followed are burned into my heart. I will always be grateful to you. You were so filled with beauty and love. Nothing will ever surpass the way you showed it. My only one! No matter what happens in the future, you have to know—you are not alone. You have me. Even though we are far apart, I can still feel you and hear you. I kiss you endlessly. Your Roman.

In the evening of the next day, I received a telegram with his address and started writing my first letter. While it was still on the way, I received several letters from him and a phone call. And then he replied. But before it happened, I was visited by Volodya. He was a messenger from my army life, and I was extremely happy to see him, though, of course, not as happy as I would have been if Roman had been visiting instead. However, fate chose to entwine our lives. He was headed to the same base where Romka was, and in the many years that followed, he became our courier. When the time came, he did something even more dangerous. But that happened later.

That evening I read Roman's letter and cried, knowing that no one would ever write to me in a similar way.

My love, my joy, my Seryozhenka! There is one bittersweet joy in this new life of mine—to remember you. In my mind I caress you. I touch your hands, shoulders, and face, and when I reach your lips, I kiss them. I miss your lips so much. Oh, how sweet is their taste! I have been thinking about you all the time since that day when I could finally read your letter. I was on the bus, and I already told you on the phone how the others reacted to my behaviour while I was reading. Everything I said was true. My tears mixed with my laughter, and your name was constantly on my lips. This state still had not passed. I have no way of explaining it. I see you everywhere, my baby, my only love. If fate will not come to our aid and let us meet soon, I beg that no one writes to me but you. I am still without you but always yours, Roman.

Meanwhile, life kept throwing me new challenges. My mother was constantly sick. A week later I started to work and prepare for the entrance exams at the institute. I also started to look for an apartment. I could no longer imagine staying in the half basement. All these troubles took away my energy and positive thinking. Often all I felt was complete and utter despair. And again only Roman's letters returned some light and hope. He wrote more and more. When did he have time to write so much? But then I was writing as well. That was our only way of being close to each other. And we managed to achieve the feeling of closeness so well that I almost forgot about the mysterious and malevolent force that had once already tried to break us apart. It hadn't disappeared. It was patiently waiting. Now older and wiser, it was preparing a new plan of attack.

In the letter that I received at the end of June, I could suddenly feel the presence of the same wild, dangerous animal. This is what Roman wrote:

Hello, Seryozhenka! So many things have happened in such a short time. I feel like I have been thinking about you my whole life. And when I do, I feel a strange sadness. (Actually, it is not that strange. I know exactly why I feel that way, but it is not important.) I have to admit that I lied to you. I didn't write the letter on the day that I promised you on the phone. I am writing only now. I hope that you will forgive me. But let's not talk about my silly actions anymore. There are so many different courses to take, and sometimes we take the wrong one. Enough about me now. I see that you are worried about your place in life. It is understandable. It is a very difficult problem that not everyone comes across. I think it is good to be faced with it; however, there is a danger that it can lead to a different set of worries that can end tragically. I hope (I am sure) for you it won't be the case. I am talking too much. Actually, I still like to be quiet. I like to sit quietly by a warm fire, but not alone…I will soon have to travel to a place that is close to you. I will do everything in my power to see you, at least for a day. I feel that otherwise something bad can happen. I am not really sure how you are doing. Be patient with your mother. Maybe her age and the illness make her so demanding. If that's true, try to understand her. Be supportive. You are such a good person, my baby. You know everything better than I do. I hope that every single day, for at least a minute you will be rewarded with your mother's smile. Don't stop dreaming. I'm sure there will always be in you something from

Seryozha that I know, love, and dream of meeting. That will be all for now. Goodbye! I send you my kisses. Your Roman.

PS. Something happened to me. I will write about it soon.

But the animal read our letters and made sure that the long-awaited meeting didn't happen. I went to take my exams but failed. I then rushed to Roman but didn't find him. On that very day, he had received an order to leave. He couldn't leave a note with his address because he didn't know it himself. I was not able to write to him either. I was upset with the constant ups and downs of life, which lately seemed only to bring me down. I didn't go home that night but returned to the town where I had studied before the army. I made a spur-of-a-moment decision to start working and went to a company that offered me a post in a faraway town in Siberia. I felt like running away and hiding from everything and everyone. Then I went home for my official notice, but I didn't have the courage to tell my mother I would be leaving again. I immediately checked all the new letters. Only two were from Roman.

Hello, my Seryozhenka! I can imagine that your eyes were full of tears when you received the note about my sudden departure. Baby, please forgive me. That's what the army is like. But you know that already. I wanted to write you immediately but got distracted, so I'm only writing you now. And even now I can't express my thought freely since I am in a meeting. Writing in a quiet environment would be better, but somehow I feel that, if I don't write now, I will postpone this letter for several days. I know how impatient you are, so I better write now. I'm really sad I didn't see you. I am desperate to be close to you. I had to try really hard not to do something I would later regret. I'm sorry; I keep losing focus. I will be waiting to hear from you. And I promise that I will soon send you a letter that will explain everything about my life (I know that your insightful heart already feels that something has changed). You will get that letter soon, I promise. I love you! Your Roman.

I had a strange premonition that our love was in danger and we were losing each other. I opened the other envelope. This letter was even shorter: "My love! I hope you can forgive me. I really hope so. I know I promised. You probably won't believe me, but I'll send the letter soon. Thank you for being mine. A kiss. Your Roman."

The promised letter didn't arrive for a long time. Roman's silence made the atmosphere at home even more unbearable. I couldn't take it any longer and called him. I didn't actually think that he would pick up the phone. He did, however. He was in a good mood—he laughed and joked—but didn't tell me anything I wanted to hear. An invisible wall stood between my Roman and me, and I did nothing to break it down. In my mind I said goodbye to him.

I was leaving on October 9, and on that day I received the long-awaited letter. It wasn't sent by post—Volodya brought it. He was only passing through town and had very little time. He was shy and confused. He tried to convince me that everything was all right and Roman was very busy, but…he got tangled in his own words and suddenly fell silent. The sad howling of the wind seemed to finish his sentence.

When Volodya was leaving, he finally gave me Roman's letter. I saw that he wanted to say something, but he pulled me close and tried to kiss me. His attempt was boyish and clumsy, and his lips landed on my cheek. I was so dumbfounded that I didn't even try to push him away, I just whispered, "No, Volodya, don't."

His arms were still around me and his lips sought mine, but I tried to get away. Finally, he looked at my face. My eyes were full of tears. What a cruel joke of fate—to look into eyes that were not Roman's. "I'm sorry. Please, forgive me for everything," Volodya said and ran away.

The envelope in my hand was like a white flag. I was almost ready to give up. I sat down on the wet bench in the empty garden and started reading.

Hello, my dear and beloved Seryozha! Forgive me if you can for all the time it took me to reply to your letter. I'm afraid this letter won't reach you on time. But after all, fate will decide. Sooner or later you will get this letter. Isn't it ironic? I don't write, but I often think about you. Actually, you are all I think about. It is now one o'clock in the morning, and I am alone. I will try to explain some of the things that I previously held back. Sometimes I don't tell all the truth, but it doesn't mean that I am lying. It's been like that since early childhood, but now that I am older, this trait is becoming more pronounced. Your phone call really upset me. Something in your voice once again told me that it's over. I'm sorry about that. But not everything is what it seems. Yes, the events of these past months have somewhat changed me, but I have made no decisions. That is why I don't want to reveal anything quite yet. Maybe everything will pass. No matter what happens, it is very hard to take away hopes and dreams. The longer our dreams don't come true, the more we hold on to them. The day you called was a very good day. Thank you for thinking about me. I'm sorry if I made you feel bad. Volodya will take this letter to you. Seryozha, he is a good person. I was happy to do something for both of you. You have a lot in common. On the thirteenth I will have to leave the base, but I would be happy to hear your voice or read your letter upon my return. I hope that I will have that chance. That's all for now. Now that I looked over this letter, it seems strange and unsatisfying. Please, try to understand. It is not my intention. Try to read between the lines. For some reason I feel very sad. You know that I am rarely upset. A while ago it was raining outside. The weather seems to reflect my mood. The most important thing is—nothing can stand in the way of dreams. I like your determination and faith in what you are doing. Never change! But maybe try not to show your true self to everyone who is looking on or trying to get to know you. My experience tells me that it can turn out to be harmful. Goodbye for now! I will be waiting for a long reply. I already know that I will be happy to read it. Please, don't be too angry. Tell me everything that you are thinking and feeling. Roman. And…

PS. Forgive me, if you can.

When I finished reading the letter and carefully put it back into the envelope, I didn't cry. Instead, I smiled with the realization that I would always love him, no matter what. I knew it with every fibre of my being. At first I had felt confused and worried about his words, but then I understood that he would come back to me, and our separation wouldn't be forever. All of a sudden I had grown up. I felt stronger and more confident, but I grieved for lost youth and happiness.

I turned toward a church. The domes were glistening from the recent rain. Barely moving my lips, I started praying. I prayed for him.

"Dear God," I whispered. "Please, help him! Don't let any bad people near him. Don't let him lose his beauty. Don't let his soul be tarnished. Let anyone who wants to, truly love him. Let him be healthy and successful. Don't let him hurt anyone or make them cry. Not a single person! And then we will meet. We will definitely meet. You won't let him forget me. I beg you, don't let him forget me!"

I sank down on the yellow grass, and at that moment the air was pierced by the bright sound of the church bells. The sound enveloped me as if trying to warm me in the wake of extinguished love.

"Thank you, God! Thank you for believing that I still love him desperately. I will never love anyone like that. Please, bring him back to me; otherwise, my days on this earth are wasted."

The bells kept ringing above my head. My prayer became part of the story of human destinies.

III

Time was passing. People say that time heals all wounds, but my pain kept getting stronger. My days were filled with enjoyable communication with new people. I was happy at work, and I loved the nature of Siberia, but with the coming of twilight, the memories of my love always returned. Even the rare letters from Roman couldn't stop the pain. He sometimes still talked about meeting, and I patiently waited for this miracle. It wasn't that I was trying to fool myself into thinking it would really take place. I was just being patient, hoping my patience would be rewarded sooner or later. Oh, no! I never wanted him to be unhappy in his new life, but I also never asked about it. I was waiting until he was finally ready to tell me himself. I knew that it was becoming increasingly hard for him to make new friends. Volodya was still a faithful friend to us both, even though he was now at a different military base at the other end of the country.

At the beginning of 1975, some circumstances that were unknown to me crushed Roman's spirit. He must have thought that he could change the course of his destiny, but life proved him wrong. He once again started to confide in me, and I immediately felt the weight he carried in his heart. Here is what he wrote:

You asked what worries and torments me. Oh, what a person you have grown into! I should have let you go while I still had the chance, but I didn't do it. Now I am happy to know (yes, I admit it!) that you always were and always will be in my heart. There is nothing I can do about it. My only happiness is with you. To talk to you, to smile at you, to argue and disagree. Only with you! It is obvious that I still love you, even though I am not sure it is right.

I did more than just reply to his letters. When he grew silent, I sent him postcards and tried not to talk about anything that could hurt him. Sometimes I gently tried to push him into answering. Every once in a while, his reply resembled this one:

Hello, my dear Seryozha! Thank you for your letter. It arrived at a time when I was starting to consider myself a real bastard. And it's true—I hurt you, but you still have not given up on me. Please, forgive me! Trust me, I often remember you, and these memories make me very happy. I'm glad to hear that you are well, even though I don't believe you. I have the feeling that you are sick

Oh, God! How did he know? I wrote him a letter from the hospital where I was recuperating after surgery, but I didn't mention anything.

Maybe I am just too suspicious. Probably I should believe you. You mentioned that your mother and aunt were visiting and left happy and content. However, I know how sly you are. You could have pretended that everything is all right to save them pain. You know, a little while ago, I thought I was going crazy. I wanted to drop everything, leave, and go somewhere else. Actually, not "somewhere," but straight to you. I wanted to cry and be comforted. I wanted to fall asleep in your arms. Everything is all right, yet this life is not what I want it to be. I constantly feel underwhelmed, and I don't even know how to explain it. Or maybe I do, but I am afraid to admit it. I don't want to hurt you. I feel like I'm falling from a high mountain, but I don't want to fall into an abyss. I'll be waiting for your letter. If you'll allow me, I'm sending you a kiss. Roman.

His letters became more frequent. It seemed that the artificial dam that had appeared between us out of nowhere was finally breaking down, and his feelings, like a strong current, were bringing him closer to me and to our meeting.

My dear, loving, and always forgiving Seryozha, I once again have to ask for your forgiveness. For everything! It is all my fault. I am such an evil person! But I think that I am able to change. Please, don't forget me. Your postcards always make me happy but also sad. I always wait for them impatiently. Sometimes I am so afraid to lose you. I want to write you all the time. I need to see you, to talk to you before I have lost everything that's left in my life. My love, I am growing old. I feel like so many years have passed. My memory is not what it used to be. I remember you, but I don't want to let anyone else in. Maybe I am a hopeless dreamer. If you can, please write me another letter. I wish I would receive a letter like you once used to write me, in those days that now seem like a thousand years ago. I often see you in my dreams. I call you and look for you, and then I wake up with tears in my eyes. You know that it never used to happen. I don't know what else I can say about my life. There is no use saying that life is complicated; you know that already. I guess at some point I learned not to worry so much. I learned to compromise and live with greater ease. During the day even my conscience keeps quiet. But not everything is lost. I often dream about something far and intangible, knowing all too well that it will never come true. Probably, something is happening to me. Maybe I am losing connection with my life. What else? Oh, yes! I was at our old base. I was visiting the place where our love was born. The Old Man is still there. He asked me to return, and maybe I will. He asked me to send you greetings and tell you to write him a letter. That's all for now, baby! Till tomorrow, then. If I can even wait that long. Maybe I will start to write another letter this evening.

I received this letter in the middle of June. In my reply I told him that I would spend the whole of July in Magnitogorsk. The very next day I received a telegram:

My love, there is God after all. I will be in Magnitogorsk from July 1 to 7. I will find you no matter where you will be. See you soon! A kiss. Your Roman.

The bright sun of our love was about to rise once again.

IV

In this complicated yet so simple world, time twirls us like snow-flakes in the wind. The only way to stay on your course is to love and believe with passion like ours. You have to learn to forgive—not only others but also yourself. And you have to be sure you never truly believe that your love is dead and gone. No, our love was alive! It was alive! Like an eager bird after years of captivity, it followed our trains and aeroplanes to finally find itself in the blooming spring of our love. It was an early morning in July. I was in an overcrowded square where the locals were celebrating, singing, and rejoicing. I desperately tried to find the face I was looking for, and then finally I heard his voice. "Seryozha! Seryozhenka!"

"Roman!" I replied before I even saw him, and I kept frantically looking around. And then the compass of love finally made our eyes meet. He was trying to get to me through the dense crowd of happy locals. It almost seemed like a dream to me. I was moving slowly, pushing against the hands and the bodies of dancing couples that seemed to restrain me. I kept whispering his name and moving in the direction of his voice, but suddenly I could no longer see him. It seemed like the moment lasted forever. All the while he kept calling my name. I could see all the years of separation quickly move in front of our eyes. Some quivering inner fear told me that once again we wouldn't meet. I had to fight against it, so I moved in the direction of his voice, screaming, "Roman! I love you! I love you!"

The crowd suddenly stopped in its movement and opened up, finally letting us see each other. A second later Roman enveloped me in his arms. He kissed my trembling hands and whispered, "My baby! My miracle! Hello! Hello, Seryozhenka!"

His eyes were filled with tears. His lips were warm and moist but still probing and determined. He didn't let me say a word but kissed me passionately right in front of everyone who cared to see. And all the while he kept whispering, "My soul! My happiness! My life! Finally, we met."

Our hearts were beating so loud that the sound seemed to echo through the whole square, but then, suddenly, we were surrounded by complete silence. For a single moment, the touch of our hands took away our surroundings, and all I could see was him. We had managed to overcome our separation, and finally, I could simply enjoy his presence. With a happy and glorious smile on his face, Roman slowly opened his eyes, and I was consumed by their blue depths. I noticed that he was still blushing like he used to. And then the wind started playing in his black curls, which now showed strands of silvery grey, and moved to my light wisps of hair. We were caught somewhere between the morning and the night, between the dawn and the twilight when life brings into this world only pure and happy thoughts.

"Two brothers have met," exclaimed an old lady standing right next to us. Something in her face reminded me of Alekseyevna.

"The two brothers" just smiled at her and stood still, trying to prolong the sweet minutes of their long-awaited meeting. During those moments my soul was once again full of memories. I couldn't tear my eyes away from his lips, his hands, and his eyes. He was the only one who mattered in this world. I felt like turning to all those who were judging or pitying us and saying, "Don't judge us! Don't pity us! Don't think that we don't know how to live our lives. I have no regrets. The fire that kept our love alive stopped burning for a while but was not extinguished by the long nights of loneliness. It was still warming me with tenderness and care toward the only person I ever loved. I hope that God will someday let you taste the sweetness of mysterious and exhilarating love. Maybe then you will understand why we were so happy on the morning of July 1 in the big and noisy square."

V

During our days together, I was torn by conflicting feelings of happiness and suffocating sadness, blissful peace and wild desire, and I don't even know what else. We didn't leave the square alone. Two majors came up to us, and Roman introduced us but then immediately pulled me away. I was holding his hand, and at first all I felt was warmth. But suddenly my skin touched the cold surface of metal.

Roman realised what had happened. While Andrey and Valyera were still trying to catch up with us, his eyes asked me not to say anything and promised to reveal everything later. My eyes wordlessly agreed.

When Roman's colleagues finally found us, we had already made our deal and went to the hotel with smiles on our faces. Roman, Andrey, and Valyera's hotel was across the street from mine. The events of the previous hour had taken away all our energy. All four of us dreamed about sitting down and having a minute of rest. We made it to their hotel suite just before the rain started. I knew Roman well enough to understand that he had planned this meeting a while ago. The large table could barely fit everything that Roman took out of three briefcases. He had brought fruit, different kinds of snacks, champagne, and even roses in a beautiful crystal vase. Even if he had asked what I thought about this feast, I would have said nothing. I kept remembering everything that we had been through and watched the mysterious smile on his face. I felt that everything that used to bind us together was gone and lost forever but that we still had that simple and casual link that we tried so hard to preserve. He noticed and understood what I was feeling and tried to hurry the feast along so that he would have the chance to prove that I was wrong. His friends were not sure how to interpret Roman's mood, but they supported and respected their commander. The lines from Afanasy Fet's poem came to my mind:

Love is a state of boundless bliss!
God, let us love forever.

I prayed to God that I was wrong about Roman and everything that stood in the way of our love.

We had just started eating when the phone rang. Roman answered, listened carefully, and then said that he was on his way. He took a folder, returned to the room, and announced that he wouldn't be long. He refused the help of his friends and asked us to save some food for his return. He took my hand, looked into my eyes, and said, "There's nothing I can do. You know what the army is like. Don't worry; I'll be back soon."

And then he left. We sat at the table in complete silence. We didn't know what to say or how to act. I started carefully observing the two men, who acted like embarrassed guests in their own hotel room. They were identical twins, almost impossible to tell apart, but eventually one of them—Andrey—started smiling at me. His smile grew bigger, revealing the strong and slightly yellow teeth of a smoker. I felt a natural need to smile in return. Valeriy's smile appeared slowly and seemed to increase only by degrees. He kept rubbing his nose, cheeks, and eyes with the back of his hand. When he noticed our quiet but smiling faces, he finally broke out into a glorious smile that only Roman could surpass.

We repeated this silent exchange of smiles three times but then started laughing and eventually also talking. The topic of our conversation was Roman. These young men knew only the outlines of our relationship and, without even knowing, revealed information about the years Roman and I had spent apart. Valeriy was the first to speak. "Sergey, I imagined you exactly like you are."

"What did you imagine?"

"I imagined you were just like you are now—tall, kind, always with a smile on your face…"

"Did you know about me before?"

"Yes," Andrey joined in. "However, Roman never says much. Sometimes he starts talking, especially when he remembers Estonia. We put all the tiny pieces of information together and understood that he has a brother or a friend—a person that he always longs for, even after the…" Valyera's warning look made Andrey stop, but he added, "Why are you looking at me like that?"

"I am sure you already know the circumstances of his marriage."

I didn't really nod, but I managed to play my cards well enough to convince him that I knew. Andrey stopped talking and smiled at me. Valyerka was watching me carefully but couldn't fully understand what was going on in my heart. He changed the direction of our conversation, but it still revolved around Roman.

"Can I give you some advice?"

"Of course."

"Don't write to him often."

"Why?"

"When he receives your letters, he becomes impossibly kind. The men on the base use his kindness and ask for anything they need, knowing all too well that he won't refuse."

"But that's a good thing!"

We started laughing.

"Yes, it is, but then he always gets in trouble. And when there is trouble at work and also at home…"

Now it was Valyera's turn to suddenly stop talking. Andrey looked at his brother disapprovingly. I was tired of this game, but again I revealed nothing. Keeping as calm and collected as I could, I said, "Why do you keep interrupting each other? You don't have to tell me anything. I didn't ask."

"No, we just…" Valyera started the sentence, but Andrey interrupted him. "Never mind! Roman suggested that we…"

If they were not wearing their army uniforms, I could easily imagine them lying on their backs in a meadow and carelessly chatting away. And then I understood what they were worried about. I fixed my eyes on both of them, paused for a moment (during which they kept looking at each other), and asked, "Are you married?"

It almost seemed that they had no idea what I was talking about.

"No. So what?" they answered me in unison.

"Nothing," I answered with mock seriousness, barely able to contain my laughter.

The half-opened bottle of champagne could no longer stand our fits of laughter. The cork exploded out of its neck with a loud hissing noise, and the bubbling drink spilled down the sides of the bottle. Our attempts to salvage the situation were interrupted by Romka's baritone. "Well, well…three against one."

"Romka, help us!" I was holding two glasses filled with champagne, ready for a toast. Still standing on the doorstep, Roman said, "Up and down! Move away and pull in! Cheers!"

The intoxicating nectar revived the quiet echoes of our passion. Our eyes met, and the joy of the long-awaited meeting lit up our loving hearts.

"Hello, Roman!"

"Hello, Seryozhenka! We are finally together."

VI

I loved silence. I was thankful for the silence that allowed me to watch his face and listen to his breathing, all the while thinking how lucky we were to be together. He woke me up with the sunlight in his eyes, watching me till I saw my own reflection. But why was his face so full of worry? Why were tiny question marks swimming in the blue waves of his eyes? I felt that his soul was still reaching toward everything that was good, gentle, and kind, but his doubts and sadness kept taking him away to dark, cold, and open spaces. I pulled his body impossibly close, trying to warm him with the heat of my heart and guide him out of this fog of madness. I tried to continue the conversation we had never started. "Roma, Romochka, Romasha! Don't stay silent, my love. Say something. Anything. Just don't stay silent."

He shivered and pressed his body closer to mine and covered my face in kisses but then fell back in despair and exhaustion. I could see the shadow of everything he was holding hanging over his face, the silvery strands in his formerly coal-black hair, and his still-youthful but no-longer-as-lithe body.

"How can I help you? What can I do for you? Roma, please answer!"

Despite my insistent pleading, he was still quiet. Every once in a while, I could see in his eyes a brief glimmer of the unbearable need to unburden himself, but then it disappeared in the faraway depth of the fog. I felt there was nothing I could do to bring him out of this state. His new wounds were invisible to the eye. I could not heal them with my presence.

Magnitogorsk had greeted us with joyful sunlight, but on the second day, there was only endless rain and silence. Neither my entreaties nor my tears moved Roman. He was torturing both of us with his dark silence, and I kept begging fate to bring any kind of resolution.

Unexpectedly, there was hope. Time had played an evil trick on us but now offered a new possibility. We only had five days left, and suddenly Roman came back to life. He held me close and whispered in my ear, his breath burning hot with love, "Seryozhenka, let's leave. Let's go anywhere you want to just get away from here."

My eyes immediately filled with tears of joy, but these same tears prevented me from replying.

"Don't cry, my baby! Please don't cry. Don't cry, my love. Smile! Yes, like that. Well done!"

However, he also had difficulties controlling his frantic breathing and had to stay quiet for a while. He exchanged the words for gentle caresses and burning kisses, trying to dry my tears with his soft lips.

"It's all right, my baby. I won't give up anymore. Never! I lost my way. I was tired of feeling lonely even though I'm always surrounded by people. But no one has the warmth and kindness that I am used to seeing in you."

He took my hands and kissed them without saying a word. Very gradually, quietly, and slowly, he started speaking. "Forgive me! Forgive me if you can. I know I betrayed you the minute thoughts of a family first entered my mind. I'm sure you want to know how and when it happened."

His eyes seemed to burn my skin like lasers.

"Roman!"

"No, I will tell you. Please, don't make me stop. I need to tell you everything, just like back then. Now you are much stronger than I am. You are stronger and better. Like a sinner, like a prodigal son I have to confess my sins to you. I have been keeping it all inside for too long. Please baby, be patient. I don't know if you will ever forgive me, but at least give me one last chance."

He stopped and waited for my answer. The look on his face was so distraught that I desperately wanted to protect him. I didn't say a word but held him closer. I knew that all the pain and sorrow he was carrying inside his heart was bound to overspill and wash away the bitterness of all the years that we had lost. I also didn't say anything because I knew that I would forgive him anything. I was ready to give my life to him. I wanted to melt into his body so that we could become one single being and stay together forever.

Roman looked to the side and tried to get his thoughts together. He tried to recall all the events that just a minute later would pierce my heart and leave vicious scars that still have not healed.

"I have been keeping it inside for too long. Ever since the first time I caught myself thinking that our relationship was…that it was wrong. And now this burden of my own making has become unbearable. That is why…no, I don't blame anyone but myself. I don't blame her either. She is the general's daughter. She saw all too well how hard I tried to keep her away but did something so vile that the general himself came to see me. You should have seen him! He was shivering and couldn't speak properly. He went down on his knees in front of me! I tried to make him stand up, but he started to cry and said, 'I am speaking to you as a father, not a general. Please, show mercy! Don't make me live this shame. Marry her or go somewhere far away. I will help you.'"

Roman noticed my surprised look. He paused, and a sad smile appeared on his face.

"Don't even try to understand. Only a woman can do something like that."

He let out a pained laugh and added, "It was unbelievably stupid. She put a mattress in from of my window and wouldn't leave for three days."

I raised my eyebrows in disbelief.

"Yes, my dear. She even slept there, using a raincoat as a blanket."

"I guess she really loved you."

"It wasn't me that she loved, Seryozhenka. It wasn't me. Only I understood it much too late."

"And what happened?"

"What happened? Nothing. There is a saying: Passion can make promises burn like dry stalks of hay. That's exactly what happened to me."

He moaned, put his head in my hands, and started shaking it.

"I took pity on her old father. I wanted to feel like a real man." His bitter laughter returned, followed by just as bitter a smile.

"I betrayed what was sacred. That's how my married life started. During those early days…" He turned his face away from me. "I banished you from my thoughts, and for a while it seemed…" He moaned again. "Forgive me! I thought that I had found happiness." His voice was no more than a whisper. "I thought it was time to forget you."

He gently laid his head on my shoulder. He didn't say anything more, so I caressed his hair and tried to smile. But this silence was deceptive. The volcano of his feelings made him get up. Shivering and biting his lips, he forced himself to continue. "Some time passed, but my painful longing for you had not diminished. It became more and more unbearable. It turned into constant torture. I suddenly became aware of my loneliness. It used to be just a nameless and faceless presence, but then it whispered your name. I heard it everywhere. Everything reminded me of you. You were in my heart, my soul, and my life. Without you I couldn't breathe. I couldn't live."

"Romka!"

"Yes, Seryozhenka! Yes! We are two parts of the same being. We were created for each other and have to be together."

And again there were long minutes of silence during which he continued to caress me. He was trying to find the courage to say the words that took all his strength, "I understood that I had betrayed not only you but also myself. And betrayal is always punished. Especially if you have betrayed nature itself."

His eyes suddenly seemed to be looking somewhere in distance, as if he were getting ready to hear the verdict of a judge.

"Then I understood what the expression 'living hell' means. My future father-in-law was paralyzed and had to leave the service. But that was only the beginning. Then the arguments started at home. I couldn't understand what had happened. I tried to find a solution, to get to know her better, to fall in love with her, but it was no use. She became so cold to me, as if there had never been even the briefest period of happiness. Seven months later our first child was stillborn. Only then I found out that she had previously had several abortions. And you disappeared…Seryozhenka, where were you?"

"Roman, I was sick."

"Just sick?"

"No, I was at the hospital."

"At the hospital? What happened?"

"It was not a big deal. Just a minor surgery."

"A surgery?" He quickly put his arms around me and started kissing me. "Dear God, I felt that something was wrong. I felt it! I was so worried. But why? Why didn't you ask me to come?"

"Roma, but you…"

"No, don't say anything. Oh, God! You were alone in a new town. In a hospital room after an operation. A time when everyone needs help. And I was…oh, God! What have I done? I am so guilty. How can I even ask for your forgiveness?"

"Let it go. It's all behind us."

"Is it?" He let out a bitter laugh, wiped away his tears, and continued. "Yes, it is behind us, but what a price we had to pay…I lost my temper. I got drunk and for the first time in my life insulted a person who didn't deserve it. The new commander forbade me to fly and made me work at headquarters."

"Did you write to the Old Man?"

"Yes. And for the first time, I didn't take his advice. He offered me a place. But where could I go with a sick father-in-law and a tarnished reputation? At that time Louisa got pregnant. I really wanted a son, so I let myself hope…"°

"And what happened?"

"Seryozhenka, fate finally showed its benevolence. In May my son was born, and I gave him your name. And I finally started hoping that maybe not everything was lost."

"Nothing is lost. All the hardships in life pass at some point. Roma, why didn't you tell me any of this in your letters?"

"I was afraid. I had betrayed you. I am still afraid."

"It is all in the past."

"It only seems like it is." He shook his head. "Seryozhenka, it only seems like it is."

"What is tormenting you now?"

"I am a stranger to them. And so is my son. She didn't even want to feed him. She was afraid her body wouldn't look attractive anymore. He was crying and asking for milk. I begged her, but to no avail. When she finally came to her senses, it was too late. The milk had run dry. By some miracle we managed to find a wet nurse. I only have you and him in this world, but I don't know how to bring us together, how to hold on to both of you. I just don't know…I am so lost…"

He became quiet and still. It almost seemed that he had died. I felt so scared. I kept caressing him, trying to calm him down, but I was afraid to kiss him. I just kept whispering soothing words. "Everything will be all right. You'll see. You know what they say: 'This too shall pass.'"

Instead of answering, he pressed himself closer to my body, seeking support. I didn't say anything more, not sure what to do. He gently moved away from me and put his hands on my shoulders. His blue eyes were studying my face and looking for an answer. They looked like the eyes of a child who is hurt and scared. I was no longer able to hold back my emotions. I understood how crazy such a step would be, but I was almost ready to scream out my answer: "Let's go! Wherever you want. Just the two of us. Roman, I love you so much!"

His smile was finally sincere. He exhaled and held me tight. "Where do you want to go? Tell me!"

I looked outside the window and saw the dark and wet asphalt. Then I looked into his blue eyes and realised that I needed his love more than ever before. I whispered through his gentle kisses, "Roma, I want to go to the seaside. I want to be closer to the sun and our love."

"All right, Seryozhenka. All right."

He smiled at me, and we immediately understood each other. Our lips met, and we both whispered his favourite saying: "Something good will happen!"

And our kiss echoed, "All you need is faith."

VII

Oh, the sunsets and sunrises of our love! Many of those who are in love right now will not believe it's possible. Time has long since changed the way we understand our feelings. My heart, however, still remembers the heat and sadness of those days. It remembers the voices of the birds and the hushed whispers of the branches swaying in the wind. I will continue my confession hoping that one day the light of the day won't be extinguished.

"Roman, where are we flying to?"

"To the sea, my baby. To the sea."

"But I am supposed to be working."

"So am I."

"Are we being crazy again?"

"No, Seryozhenka. We are happy again."

He smiled and put his arm around me, and all my doubts disappeared in the face of our love. The uncomfortable tears of his morning confession were replaced by blissful sadness (yes, it is possible) and relief. At that moment amid the bright sunlight, the green waters of the sea, and the blue skies, Adler came into our view. The flight attendant came out from her hiding place behind a curtain. She looked like a little angel and reminded me of the girls we had seen at the children's store all those years ago. She told the passengers about the arrival time and the temperature, then wished everyone a pleasant stay and disappeared. I was carefully watching Roman, who was lost in his professional interest—he was listening to the sound of the landing plane. When the landing wheels touched the tarmac and the large aeroplane seemed to glide along the runway, he finally smiled and me and said, "Now you will see someone. It is thanks to him that we are here."

"Who?"

"Be patient."

"Roma!"

"Your patience still has not improved," he added when I impatiently removed my seat belt and was ready to run toward the exit.

"Roma, who?"

"Wait till the plane stops."

"Who?" I stubbornly kept repeating the same question.

"Me," said a familiar voice.

I finally looked away from Roman and saw Klimov—one of the former pilots from Roman's company—standing at the exit. He recognized me but was so surprised to see me that for some reason he said, "You two are unbelievable! However, I am very happy to see you. Especially you." He gave me a friendly pat on the shoulder and added, "Let's go! What are you waiting for? After all, we are colleagues."

Meeting a former colleague in such an unexpected place seemed like the perfect beginning of our escape. With a smile on my face, I happily exchanged the latest news with him, yet I couldn't understand why Roman suddenly looked so embarrassed. When we said goodbye and Klimov was already leaving, he suddenly turned around, looked at us, and repeated, "You two are unbelievable! Roman! Seryoga! Well done!"

He waved at us and tried to catch up with the rest of the crew. Almost immediately the airport bus was approaching. I quickly asked, "Roma, why was he acting like that? What did you tell him?"

"It's not important. Let's go!"

When we entered the crowded bus and Roman was fully pressed against me by the other passengers, he looked at Klimov, who was almost not visible on the other side, smiled at me with pure happiness radiating from his face, and told me, "I told him that I have never been so happy and want to go on a holiday. Apparently, he made his own conclusions. Seryozhenka, we are here! We are going to Sochi, where the sea and wind await us."

"And how are we going to get back?"

"Seryozhenka, we just arrived, and you are already thinking about going back! All right, Klimov will pick us up. All right?"

I wanted to nod, but the bus suddenly swerved, and our lips unexpectedly joined together. That was the only answer he needed. Our agreement was sealed with a kiss. There was a young man standing by the window dressed in a provocatively tight-fitting tracksuit. Something in his face reminded me of Tinu. (Why did I keep seeing everyone we once knew?) From the moment we entered, he kept throwing longing glances at Roman. Once he witnessed our kiss, he sighed, looked at me, and smiled. I could feel his desperate wish to be in my place. Romka was standing with his back to the young man, and only the embarrassment he saw in my face made him realise that our kiss had not gone unnoticed. He pulled me even closer to his body, turned his head slightly in the direction of the smiling man, and whispered, "It is rude to stare."

A quick smile and a confused frown ended this exchange.

The rest of the way, we drove in silence. After a few stops, the bus was no longer crowded, but Roman kept me pressed to the window with his strong body. I was intoxicated with happiness, dizzy from his caresses, and lost in his blue eyes. The look of love that flowed from them reminded me of a poem we had once heard together:

Give blessing as we start this journey
Where our only guide will be
My heartbeat that once was cold and lonely
But now is yours for all eternity.

The fare inspector, who had fallen asleep in her elevated seat, suddenly woke up, smiled to herself for a reason that only she knew, and called out, "Sochi train station—the last stop."

The hands of the station clock were also looking at each other and smiling. It was six o'clock in the evening.

VIII

During the previous twenty-four hours, I had experienced so much that by the time we reached the square in front of the station, I barely understood what was happening around me. I only dreamed about finally reaching the sea. Before departure, we didn't have time to think about booking a hotel, so we tried our luck with the locals who mobbed the passengers from the bus and offered them places to stay. At least five people turned away as soon as Roman told them that we would be staying for three days. After another unsuccessful attempt to bargain, a sudden silence fell over the square.

However, we didn't stop smiling. All we needed to be happy was to be together. We decided to change our approach and moved to a nearby fountain to think it through. Almost immediately we were approached by a kind-looking old lady dressed in an old but festive dress. Over it she wore a white pinafore that made her look like a schoolgirl on her graduation day. She was holding a small basket with flowers.

"Boys, would you like to buy some flowers?"

"Thank you, but we don't even have a place to stay."

The lady was trying to sit down on the ledge of the fountain, but all her attempts were unsuccessful. Roman picked up her basket and then the lady herself and sat her down on the ledge. She sat there swinging her legs, then put her hands in the water and pressed them to her heated face. Then she continued looking at us like an old and kind magician.

"How so?" But then she understood. "Do you want to stay for a week?"

"No, less than a week. Just three days."

Before Roman had even finished the sentence, she grabbed his arm, lowered herself to the ground with the agility of an acrobat, and silently indicated that we should follow her. Seeing our hesitancy, she insistently added, "Why are you being so stubborn? Come with me! You can't sleep here."

Seeing our smiles and readiness to follow, she also started to smile. It almost made her wrinkles disappear, and her face suddenly showed ease and determination.

The name of our host was Elizaveta Ivanovna, and her house was not far from the station. The house was small, clean, and looked a lot like its owner. At the gate we were greeted by a dog who happily wagged its tail.

"That's a good sign," the lady said. "It means that you are good people. Bouquet, meet our guests! Are you hungry?"

The intelligence of the mongrel surprised even his owner. The dog entered his kennel and soon emerged with a bowl in his teeth. He then put it right in front of the door and sat down, waiting for his meal. In my tiredness I forgot that we were not alone. I was so enchanted by the dog's performance that I leaned against Roman's shoulder and looked into his eyes. I saw that he was thinking exactly the same thoughts. We both remembered Pilot, our past, and everything that was lost and could never be regained.

The lady noticed our sad looks but didn't say anything. Instead, she continued talking to the dog. "Yes, Bouquet, I know, but we have guests."

"Can I give him a treat?"

Roman opened his bag. Bouquet's eyes sparkled with expectation. Once his owner had given her permission, the dog pressed his cold and moist nose into my palm to get a biscuit that Roman had handed me. While Bouquet was happily devouring his treat, I thought that the affections of dogs are always so unobtrusive and hopeless.

Then the lady let us into a small outbuilding. In the midst of various household objects stood a very old but still usable couch. I sat down and realised that there would be no escaping our old memories. The couch made exactly the same sounds as the one we used to have in the flight house. The same one that had become the symbol of the happy nights of our faraway youth. I caressed the fabric of the old couch with my hand and barely held back the tears. When I looked at Roman, I realised that I was overcome with the same memories.

"Your brother is so tired," said Auntie Lusya (she insisted we call her by that name), who had just reentered with our bed linens.

All this time Roman had been standing by the door, but he finally came up to me and sat down. He put his arms around me and said, just like in the old days, "Don't! Everything is all right. There's no need."

I leaned against his shoulder. Just as we met the eyes of our host, someone called her from the yard. She put the bed linens on a small table that stood next to the window. Seeing our confusion, she said, "Go and have a swim. I will make the bed. The sea is so calm today. It would be a shame not to use the opportunity. And it's so close… Yes, I'm coming," she replied to the repeated call and went outside.

My eyes were still burning with tears. Roman kissed me and whispered, "Would you like us to look for another place?"

He knew very well how absurd his offer was in the given situation and smiled at me. I started laughing, and suddenly the evening once again became happy and enjoyable. Even though there were still some remnants of sadness in my heart, Roman's eyes and gentle hands lit the flames of desire in my body. The shadows of the past slowly disappeared with the sound of the sea coming through the window. The feeling of the unity of loving hearts once again let us experience the full force of our feelings.

I know that my love for him was lit by a divine power. This love was the basis of my existence. Unfortunately, as we grow older, we never love with the same abandon. Maybe it's good that the fever of our first love cannot be repeated. Otherwise it wouldn't be our first love, and we would have nothing to remember. We would have nothing to compare our feelings to. We would have nothing to worship. On the other hand, at the beginning, our first love is blind, but it grows and changes. Its madness and immaturity suddenly grow into something bigger than the love itself. It becomes something that we have not experienced before. By trying to preserve it in its original condition, we turn our love into something that resembles the reflection in the water—even the lightest breeze can make it disappear. "Why? What for?" The voices of millions of lovers disappear in the cold pathways of centuries trying to find the answers, but they are impossible to find. They are like the sand that flows away and leaves a dark and wet footprint in its wake. But what are we to do—give up on love? Roman!

"Seryozhenka, what's wrong?"

When I heard his voice, I regained my senses and pulled myself closer to his body. Our breathing was becoming slow and even. Maybe it was because of the ticking clock that was attached to one of the walls. Such a natural and calming sound! It was eight o'clock in the evening. We almost fell asleep, but a sudden burst of laughter broke through our tired minds. Roman got up, placed my head on the pillow, and approached the door. It immediately sprang open, and our host came in.

"What? Are you still here? Aren't you going to the beach? Did you come all the way here to sleep?" She kept admonishing us like a mother.

"Get up and go," she said, continuing her assault. "I brought another young man who will join you."

"Auntie Lusya, we'll go later."

"What do you mean—later? It will be too late. Now is the time to go. Get up!" She playfully attacked me with a towel she was holding.

Suddenly, I felt a sweet aroma filling the room. It was the smell of local roses. My tiredness disappeared. To prevent the tears that the old memories always brought to my eyes (even though it was clear that I wouldn't be able to escape them), I forced a smile, and we went outside into the yard. I was surprised to see the young man from the bus playing with Bouquet. He had changed into less provocative clothing. He greeted us with a festive smile; once again tricked the kindhearted dog, who was desperately trying to get a pink ball; and introduced himself. "Good evening! My name is Igor. We are neighbors. If you don't mind, we could all go for a swim."

Neither of us had expected this meeting, especially with someone who was willing to repeat our encounter with Tinu. Before we even had a chance to discuss it, we smiled at him and started to look at him closely. His young face was as smooth as glass. The light dusting of his first mustache added an interesting look to his face. His grey eyes became shy under our insistent glances but soon enough started glowing with curiosity. He seemed to be challenging us, but then he withdrew into shyness and added, "I swear, I ended up here by accident. I have to wait until a place is available at my accommodation. I didn't write to my host before arriving—just showed up. I'm really sorry."

Roman's gaze made him so flustered that he was getting ready to leave.

"Where are you going? Wait! We don't mind."

Roman pressed my hand, asking for permission. I was happy about the decision he made. I didn't want any sadness to hang over our vacation.

"Take him with you as well," Auntie Lusya said and pointed to Bouquet, who was trying to get free.

"Can you see what he's doing? Soon he'll also start scratching himself. I went swimming yesterday."

The dog seemed to understand her words. He immediately attacked his tail with desperate ferocity but all the while looked at us to see if his plans were successful. Roman bent down and opened the dog's collar. He was immediately rewarded with gentle licks on his hands. (Dear Pilot, where were you at that time?) We crossed the garden and followed a path to the sea. It reminded us of what we had experienced years ago, except it was our first time at the seaside. I guess it was apparent (even though I don't know how we gave ourselves away), because Igor finally smiled and quietly said, "When you are doing something for the first time, you have to make a wish."

Oh, the wishes that we made! There were so many of them, and so few came true. Fate had given us such a short time to be together, so we desperately wanted to be alone. Igor seemed to sense it, and forgetting his youthful selfishness, he eventually waved his hand in an impatient gesture of farewell, called Bouquet to his side, and disappeared in the darkness. Please, forgive us! In our hearts we hoped that you would be luckier than us. This was our last hope. Even though the surrounding world was covered in darkness, I felt happiness and elation. It was a strange kind of happiness. It was not the happiness that I was waiting or longing for in all the hours of my loneliness.

But suddenly this calm happiness, devoid of any burning fever or frantic yearning, completely enveloped me in its arms. With the gentle water at my feet, I looked ahead and saw the sorrowful shimmer of faraway waves, which were glowing in bright hues of green. The water was surrounded by darkness that gently lulled everything to sleep, and the reflections of the stars made the sea seem expansive and calm. It reminded me of a large lake—the lake of our love that was now as far from us as the horizon.

Suddenly, my thoughts changed their course, and at the same time, a gentle breeze changed the sea in front of me. It looked like a crumpled map that was trying to straighten itself out but all the while was interrupted by the coming waves. And then it looked inanimate and frightening.

And Roman? What was he feeling? He held my hand and shivered in excitement. What was happening in his heart while he was looking in the distance? Was he trying to understand the boundaries of love, desire, obligation, reason, will, and desperate longing? Was he trying to weigh and understand the meaning of his conflicting emotions? I quietly looked at him and tried to understand what he was thinking and feeling.

A moment later his eyes met mine, and I saw in them worry, sadness, doom, and desperation, which told me that soon we would have to part not knowing when we'd meet again. Maybe never. "No, Roman! No!" I sank down and buried my face in his knees.

He stroked my hair in complete silence. What could he say? I didn't know what to do. Oh, God! How late was it? It seemed that time had stopped and the night was endless. I was suddenly overcome by a piercing headache, and the pain radiated to my eyes. I closed my eyes and pressed my palms to my face.

When the pain finally let go, I opened my eyes. Roman was watching me. Then he undressed, waited for me, and led me into the arms of the dark sea. The air carried a faraway scent of the healing strength of youth. We stepped into the water and tried to let go of our tiredness. The pale faces of the stars reflected in the water promised us a miracle. The velvety caresses of water seemed to heal us, and the air filled our lungs with vibrant energy.

Soon we started playing in the water, and sadness gave way to laughter. We returned to where the water was shallower and tried to rest in the gentle waves. Suddenly, they lost their benevolent appearance. I was torn away from Roman and dragged toward the depth where the stern Neptune was threatening me with his trident. But Roman's arms found me before I could feel any fear. I smiled at him, and Neptune returned to the arms of the person I loved.

When we grew tired of being in the water, we went ashore. It was very late. The sky was filled with stars. Roman and I stood close together, gazing at them, listening to the whispers of the wind, and smiling. And then his palm touched my bare back. For a couple of seconds, he was just looking at me. Then he stretched out his arm and said, "Come to me!"

I crashed into his body, into his lips, which were made cold and hard by the dark air. I sank into his kiss and revelled in the touch of his hands. He kissed me back with passionate abandon and awakened my burning desire. My arms held him so tight, as if I was never planning to let him go. The night covered us with a quiet blanket of darkness, and the wind carried to me his feverish confessions. "You are mine! Mine! Whatever happens, tonight there will be only you. My love! My only one! My Seryozhenka! With you I am so happy. I only need you. You brought me back to life."

"Roman! Romashka! Romochka!" I kept repeating his name, unable to pronounce any other words. My body and my soul suddenly felt so light that I forgot all my worries.

"I am so happy when you are next to me, my baby," I heard him whisper.

Time was no longer measured in seconds. It became a constant flow that took us away from all sense and sanity. I once again had the feeling that I was getting to know him with my lips, my hands, and my whole body. It seemed so familiar and so mysterious at the same time. We were created for each other. I could feel my fate trembling under his palms. He held me impossibly close. My lips drank the cool air of happiness, my head was spinning, my sanity was slipping away. He kept looking at me with tears in his eyes. Light wrinkles of worry appeared on his high forehead. I understood his despair—it was unbearable to think of parting now that we finally belonged to each other. Oh! My heart was clenching with pain. But what could we do?

"I love you! I love you so much! Only you. God, please let us be happy, or let us die together this very moment."

"Roman…" I reached out for him, and our bodies once again came together. I felt indescribable lightness and the enticing call of love, which we answered without hesitation. In the middle of the dark and quiet night, I was drowning in the lakes of his eyes, giving him all of me and letting him love me with unparalleled tenderness. And when our desire reached the point where even the night seemed to cry with tears of fulfillment, we sang an anthem to our love and were consumed by its flames. Later, when we were back at the house and ready to surrender to sleep, we whispered to each other, "Let me dream of you."

"Let me dream of you."

"Seryozhenka…"

"Roma…"

"I love you…"

"I love you…"

IX

It's gone! The brief flicker of sunlight that warmed the cold ground and my loneliness has disappeared. The town is bathed in twilight. The grey air is illuminated by the traffic lights, and their glow mixes with the neon glow of shop signs. Memory is a beautiful but torturous gift. I fully agree with the person who said that the memories of youth are better left untouched. I am ready to wave the white flag of surrender without waiting for the moment when I have nothing left except time. I don't want to wait for the moment when love and pain disappear and take my luck with them on their faraway journey.

Some people will say that I am a coward. But why? I am so full of compassion, kindness, and generosity, but there is no one next to me to share them with. Why should I waste it all on people who think that love should always be easy, that fate gives us those we share our beds with, so it makes no difference what they are like? Why should I waste it on people who can forget the whispers of their loved ones just to respond to the call of money? What is the point? Where can I find strength and happiness if I am living without hope and love—the force that can overcome all our doubts and mistakes? Is it age, weakness, fear, and the cruelty of the world that makes me say these things? Or maybe it is the realization that we cannot fight against loneliness?

"Expel these thoughts," whispers a sweet and comforting voice. "Expel all your dreams, fears, and doubts. Live!" There are moments when we are ready to ask for forgiveness and atone for all our sins. Life mixes everything up—your strength and weakness, your fame and love—and you no longer know whom to blame. Surrounded by the icy waves of despair and loneliness, I am sinking into ever-present silence. The echo of the pain and the noise of my tears rise up in the air and leave me with a tiny glimmer of hope. Under the cover of doubts, I am moving closer to the day that my heart fears to remember. In the name of those who still believe in love and boundless passion, I am ready to step into the fog of memories. But it is getting harder and harder. Every step seems to be bathed in tears and farewells. My heart wants to cling to the days when I woke up in Roman's arms and thought that those who didn't know him never knew true love.

Our days of love flew by like a comet. Wherever we went, we were surrounded by the bliss of our love. Roman seemed to read all my wishes and immediately made them come true. I was surrounded by a feeling of peace and enjoyment. Roman's whole being radiated something deep, serious, mysterious, and touching. His voice excited, caressed, and intoxicated me. His warm lips constantly sought mine and bestowed upon me heated, impatient, and passionate kisses, all the while singing, "You are mine."

I smiled in confirmation and floated in blissful forgetfulness. The rainbow of our love shone brightly above our heads. There was not a corner in the whole city that we didn't visit. Wherever we went, we carried our love with pride. Those who accepted it smiled at us. Those who judged and condemned us couldn't touch us. The pointed arrows of their malevolent glares were conquered by Roman's smile. They returned to their owners and wounded them instead, making their faces even more tired and fearful.

And then the dawn of the last day pierced the darkness. A few minutes before the light appeared, I was woken up by a mysterious glimmer. The silvery moonlight on its way out had decided to stop in our window and look into every corner of the room. One of the tiny diamonds of moonlight had nestled in my palm. I tried to listen to its quiet sound, which reminded me of our inevitable farewell. The night let me hold it a minute longer but then extinguished the unexpected gift and left the room altogether. It briefly stopped on the doorstep, as if looking back, and then disappeared.

I suddenly felt that my palm was wet, and a strange feeling of fear gripped me. I pressed myself against Roman's body. For a minute I felt that we were locked inside a protective circle that kept us away from the rest of the world. Roman woke up, and I looked at him with fear and hope in my eyes. His eyes seemed to say something, but for the first time, I couldn't understand it. I didn't dare ask him, so I surrendered to burning and healing tears. During that one brief moment, I seemed to come to terms with everything that had happened and was still going to happen. The air seemed to become lighter, the room felt warmer, and in the back of my mind, I could hear the final chords of *La Traviata*. But soon the music could no longer be heard. The new day turned our lives into a string of new meetings and expectations.

X

The harder time tried to keep us apart, the stronger was the call of our love. We no longer seemed to feel the passing of time. All we cared about was a chance to meet, to talk, to hold each other, even for just a minute. Whenever we had a chance, we rushed to each other's arms.

Finally, Moscow became our second home. Roman started to study at the academy, and two years later I was accepted at the institute. My studies, together with attempts to find a job, took so much strength and energy that I would never have managed to do it without the support of my love. Sometimes, after another unsuccessful day of trying to find a job (no one was willing to hire a long-distance student), I would aimlessly wander around the strange city. All it took was to think about him, and when I raised my head, his eyes were already looking for me. It gave me the strength to continue my search, which, soon enough, was successful.

It was 1978. Every time I met Roman, I felt my heart clench. The light dusting of silvery grey in his hair was becoming more and more noticeable. He often seemed hopelessly tired, as if all the strength was drained out of his body. His handsome features used to enchant everyone who saw them, but now they made the onlookers uneasy and seemed to warn about some approaching misfortune.

But what else could happen? We both enjoyed our studies. We both had a place to stay. When Roman first arrived, the Old Man found him a room at the academy dormitory. Soon after that, he made Roman move to the two-bedroom apartment of his relatives, who had temporarily left the country.

When my first exam session started, I stayed in the dormitory. Roman came to visit me, and the next day, he took me to his apartment. In the evenings, when we were preparing for the next day of studies, we resembled two first graders. We even kept looking into each other's books. He understood everything that I was reading, but I could barely find a familiar term in his assignments.

Before going to bed, we always went for a walk in the city. No matter how much time we spent outside, the harmony of the sounds and the beauty of our surroundings always gave me strength and energy. Sometimes I couldn't even fall asleep. Roman was my everything, but what did I mean to him?

The Old Man called us every evening, even if we returned after midnight. Then he would jokingly admonish us for walking around so late. More than once he mentioned that Roman's face seemed filled with soft light. And once again I felt like the luckiest person in the entire world. Every day would start and end in Roman's arms. Even on the day of my departure, our love still promised us new meetings.

I never asked Roman about his family. The Old Man told me that his wife, Louisa, insisted on moving to Moscow with their children (by that time they also had a daughter named Rita). Maybe her suddenly resurrected feelings for Roman were true, but Roman kept postponing the move, finding his justification in the workload.

The Old Man often spent considerable amounts of time at his daughter's house in Moscow. He observed everything but kept his thoughts to himself.

Once I happened to return earlier than planned and became a witness to one of their conversations. The Old Man intended that I hear their exchange, and I couldn't understand why Roman was so opposed to his suggestions. Actually, it wasn't even a conversation. They only exchanged a couple of sentences.

"Roman, you are becoming so cruel. Children shouldn't pay for their parents' sins. You should help your daughter while you still can."

At this point Roman had not noticed my presence. He replied, "I am not cruel; she is. She was too busy drinking to have an abortion. I'm not even sure the child is mine. Please, let's not talk about it."

The Old Man gave up, but it was the first time he didn't stay for dinner. Even though he had the keys to the apartment, he started warning us about his visits beforehand.

Time was passing so quickly, yet so slowly. A year later, Volodya also started his studies at the academy. When I arrived for my exams sessions, the Old Man's apartment reminded me of a dorm room, except he dearly loved everyone who lived there. He lived nearby, so every morning he came to wake us and made us do exercises. Meanwhile, he prepared our breakfast. He was equally nice to all of us, but he always treated me with special care. Roman and Volodya, convinced that I didn't notice anything, also went out of their way to spoil me with treats and attention.

All this resulted in the fact that during the first two days of my stay, I was never able to study. During the lectures I often found a chocolate in one pocket of my jacket and an apple in the other. They filled my bag with sandwiches and included also a thermos with tea or coffee.

Volodya also had a room at the dormitory, so in the evenings he tried to quietly slip out of the apartment. However, studies were not easy for him, so Roman made him stay. I never objected to his presence, so the situation was resolved with a handshake.

Roman was almost a part of my being, but it was still difficult to resist his entrancing gaze. For Volodya it was much harder, but he just sighed, smiled at me apologetically, and remained with us.

Our evenings usually had the same pattern: I went to bed, looked at them still studying, and fell asleep, listening to the barrage of army terms that kept flowing from their lips. When the Old Man arrived, he was often shocked to see the three of us sleeping on the double bed, still in our clothes, with books and papers scattered all around us and our arms tangled in a way that made it impossible to tell them apart. However, our innocent waking faces erased his anger. The sounds of the early morning gradually calmed him down.

We all sat down at the breakfast table, discussed our plans for the coming day, and then each of us went on our way. In the evening we were always happy to meet. There is a simple truth that not many people understand: it is less important who you spend the time with than how it is spent.

Oh, the blissful and painful minutes of our destiny! Why is there always more pain than bliss? The approaching end of the year didn't show any signs of trouble. I had passed all my exams with outstanding results, my mother was going to receive a new apartment, and Roman spent a week winking at me in a conspiratorial manner. It meant that he had prepared a surprise.

And then the day came. Roman called me from the academy and warned me that he would return later than planned. The Old Man and I stayed in the apartment together. He was very happy and talkative. He told me jokes and offered various treats and then started placing presents under the undecorated Christmas tree. The Old Man's jolly mood was contagious, even though I could feel that it was forced.

I tried not to pay attention to my observations and held on to the elated mood he had created. While we were setting the dinner table, I shared my thoughts about Roman's situation. I made him understand that I particularly wanted to know why the Old Man, who could finally dedicate some time to himself, was taking such an active part in Roman's life. He replied that problems need to be solved as soon as they arise and added that I should be thinking only about my studies.

But I refused to give up. I felt that the Old Man's words were only partly sincere. I wanted to know what he thought about the complicated triangle in which Roman's family also played a part.

As soon as I mentioned Louisa's name, I immediately regretted it. The Old Man was sitting by the piano, and his fingers suddenly stopped moving. The look on his face reflected profound sadness, characteristic of people of his age. My heart was torn by conflicting feelings. At first I felt embarrassed for acting in such an inconsiderate manner. But then embarrassment was replaced by curiosity, and I repeated my question, avoiding the piercing eyes of the Old Man. I guess it is true that kindness gives you strength but pride brings only despair.

A few minutes later, the Old Man started smiling. He reached for my arms, as if seeking physical support and at the same time trying to find a solution to an unsolvable problem. Then he said, "I don't know what kind of answer you expected, but you helped me without even realizing it. Now I have to choose between doing what's best for you or for my conscience. Of course, in either case someone will have to pay the price. We have some time, but let's talk like we didn't have any. Maybe I'm making a mistake. God knows, I've made so many in my life. But right now we both want to help Roman, so…"

I felt that the waves of sudden honesty were taking him in an unknown direction, but there was nothing I could do to stop it. It seemed that his words were about to reveal something that I previously hadn't noticed or hadn't wanted to notice.

"Sergey, it wouldn't be wise to act in haste, but we don't have much time, so…"

At that moment his handsome and proud face and his slow and deliberate gestures were driving me crazy. I wanted to run away and hide, but I was forced to stay and listen.

"Seryozhenka, if you really love him and wish him happiness, leave him. Leave him right this moment. Please forgive me, forgive him. But mostly forgive me for waiting so long. Trust me, my dear boy…" He saw the disbelief and despair in my face and pulled me closer. "The pain will stop, and you'll find someone else to love. You are young, charming, and intelligent, but he…he is all I have left. I don't think that his plan…"

The Old Man didn't finish his sentence. He felt my body slowly sink down to the floor. He caught me and then sat down next to me. He embraced me and said, "No, no, no! Please forgive me. Don't leave. I have no idea what I'm saying. Whatever will be, will be."

My whole body became numb. I didn't feel any cold, I didn't feel how my body shivered, I didn't feel any heartache. I had lost all feeling. I tried to get up and come to terms with what the Old Man had just said. The thoughts were raging in my head with the force of a violent storm, and I suddenly understood what Roman had planned. The Old Man saw that I was slowly regaining my senses and confirmed my suspicions. "Yes, Roman is at the airport. His family will be here in an hour. You have to make a decision."

I looked in the mirror and saw that my face was as white as a sheet. I don't know what I would have done if someone else had been there instead of the Old Man, but I surely would have stayed. And now the person who once had brought us together was destined to tear us apart. I couldn't scream; I couldn't ask any questions. I barely found the strength to pull myself up from the floor. Then I helped the Old Man and, banishing all thoughts of the person I was doing it for, started packing. My farewell to the Old Man was barely audible. Half an hour later, I was at the train station.

The train was leaving at five past midnight. I had not planned to start the New Year on the way, but soon enough I was on the train. I was almost immediately followed by three young men who happily offered to celebrate New Year together. But I was not able to open my mouth. I fell into a thoughtless and wordless stupor. The three men soon moved to the next compartment, and I heard them opening bottles of champagne. Through the window I could see a bright streetlight that shone with a false cheerfulness and illuminated the snowflakes falling from the sky. A voice in the microphone wished everyone a happy New Year, and I was overcome by a strange and inexplicable feeling.

A minute later the same voice said, "Sergey, Roman is waiting for you at the information stand."

Once I understood the meaning of those words, I immediately tried to remember the number of my platform and the car of the train. I forgot about my baggage. I jumped up and ran to the door, but it seemed that our fate that night was on the Old Man's side. That very moment, the train started moving. I looked outside and saw Roman running after the train, but I could not say a word. I pressed my face against the door and started crying. My hot tears melted the ice that had been covering the glass, and I thought I heard someone knock. I looked up and saw his face—pale, calm, clear, masculine, and full of love.

The train was still moving slowly. I tried to open the door, but even this attempt was unsuccessful. Then I placed my palms against the glass, and Roman did the same on the other side. For a second I could feel their warmth. The train started moving faster, and Roman ran after it for as long as he could. The memory of his hands warmed me for many lonely hours to come.

In the morning I received his telegram: "To say and do, to think and live—it's not the same thing, Seryozhenka. Roman."

XI

Sometimes time becomes more frightening than an execution-er. The silence that surrounded me after the events of the New Year filled my heart with darkness and heavy sadness and made all the days seem exactly the same. Sometimes small rays of hope (my memories of the past) lit up the overwhelming emptiness of my life. I had nothing to hold on to. My nights were no longer filled with love. My days and nights started without his kisses, and my life lost all sense and meaning. And all this time I saw the face of our separation in front of my eyes. It was the face of a wild animal—now older but still strong and dangerous. When I was alone in the dark, silence, and loneliness of my nights, the animal opened its mouth and laughed at me, trembling from rage and hatred. I could hear this laughter even on the days when the bright sun illuminated the sad walls of my apartment, and then it started to resemble the growling of wind that was blowing in the empty corridors of my memories. Four months went by. I was forced to resign from my job and return home to resolve the situation with the apartment. My sorrow gradually turned into hope for a miracle, and the pain stopped on the day when I was holding Roman's letter in my hands.

Hello, Seryozhenka! My love, when this letter reaches you, I will probably no longer be in the Soviet Union. It is my obligation to do that which so many people are afraid of doing. I was given five days to make up my mind, and now they have almost passed. I am happy that is the case. These past months that we have spent apart have been unbearably long and difficult. There is so much to say that I could almost write a novel, but of course I won't. I will, however, at least partly try to explain my behaviour. First of all, I have to thank you for what you did. It made me think and do everything in my power to change. I understood that it was not you I was running away from but myself. It seems I am no longer the person you knew and loved. I had to share myself between you, my family, my studies, work, and the Old Man. I cannot belong to everyone at the same time. And I cannot constantly hurt the people I love the most—especially you. All I can see ahead of myself is the same cursed pattern of being a half husband, half friend, and half son. The person who cannot make a decision and ends up losing everything. So I choose what will always be an important part of me—the sky. And you, my baby…(Please let me call you like that one last time.) I hope you will meet your true love and will be happy. You deserve true happiness. Don't do anything stupid; don't wait for me. You have to forget me. I guess that's all. No, it's not, but I was never good at describing everything I feel. I love you and will continue loving you forever, but you are too good a person to accept only a small part of someone like me. I can't keep torturing you. I have no right. That is why I made this choice. At least I won't hurt anyone. It will bring me some happiness. My love, thank you for all the beautiful years that we spent together. Roman.

PS. You have to do one last thing for me. Forgive the Old Man. The train left without me. Their lights, like a cunning fox carrying away its prey, disappeared as my plane landed in Moscow.

XII

The Old Man immediately picked up the phone. It seemed that he had been expecting my call. When he heard my voice, the only words he could say were "Wait! We will be right there."

But he didn't come. A bit over an hour later, Volodya was on my doorstep. He quickly greeted me and started explaining what Roman was planning to do. I had only one question: Did I make it in time?

"Yes, you did," Volodya replied. "He is leaving in the morning and will go to the apartment to pick up his bags. Here is the Old Man's key. No one will be there. Louisa is in Tallinn." And suddenly, with tears in his eyes, he exclaimed, "Seryozha! Thank God you called. Help us! Make him change his mind. The Old Man and I are in despair."

His voice told me that he expected questions, but what could I ask him? In my head I could clearly see the picture of our meeting, but on the inside everything had turned to ice. While we were driving, Volodya told me to take a nap. "Sleep shelters us from all our troubles," Roman often told me. Sometimes he and Volodya seemed strikingly similar. We were flying to Moscow on the wings of fear and hope.

Having rested on the way, I felt slightly calmer, but when I entered Roman's apartment, I didn't know what to do until he arrived (Volodya went to pick him up at a testing ground). I started looking around the apartment. Even the objects that I knew well seemed foreign. The only thing that reminded me of Roman was the way in which they were distributed through the apartment—every single object had its own place. On the open piano stood a picture of the two of us happily laughing and running toward the sea. It was a pocket-size picture placed in a large frame that made it look very small, and that day seemed to be a part of a very distant past. I took the frame in my hands and noticed that there was another picture in the same frame. It was the picture of his son, Seryozha, who was laughing carelessly and reaching for the camera.

At that moment something pricked my finger. I looked closer and realised that the pictures were pieced with a very thin and sharp hairpin, the ends of which protruded on the other side. I pressed it down on the piano, and the tiny head of a snake appeared. It was Louisa's hairpin. It seemed like she was in the room, watching me, so I put everything back in place. I turned the frame around, and another picture was pinned to it. It was folded, and I knew it was a picture of her. I didn't want to see her face.

Time seemed to be standing still. At one point I thought I heard a car pull up to the house. I opened the window, but all that greeted me was the dark and rainy night full of sounds that reminded me of desperate moans. There was an open book on the windowsill—*Legends and Myths*. I picked it up, and the first thing I saw was a picture of the angel of death with a sword in one hand and flames in the other. The text was underlined with a red pencil: "The ancient Greeks believed that boundless love is a sin that angers the gods. If someone fully gave themselves away to love, the gods would destroy the object of this blind infatuation. Unreasonable and excessive love was equal to blasphemy." I shivered and turned the page. The red blood of the pencil had left its mark there also. The underlined lines were in a language I didn't understand, but at the bottom of the page, there was a translation: "Oh, death! How unwillingly all the evil men remember you. But those who are just think of you in peace and don't fret about their approaching end."

Who underlined these words? Was it Roman? Louisa? The Old Man? It surely wasn't Volodya.

This time the unmistakable sound of an approaching car stopped my reverie. I tried to put the book back in its place, but it seemed to resist my attempts. It seemed to come alive in my hands and expelled something white that fell on the floor. The book had achieved its goal. I bent down to pick up what I had dropped. Oh, God! It was the envelope of the letter I sent Roman the previous October. The letter had been removed and the envelope forgotten between the pages of the book.

My surprise at this find increased when I noticed that there was no return address. The envelope itself had been torn open in obvious haste, but the address was carefully cut out with scissors.

It immediately made me think of Louisa. I put the envelope back into the book, which I now held to my body like a shield. I stepped away from the window and hid behind the curtain. My happiness was ready to overspill, but my muscles and nerves and frantically beating heart would not let it.

Eventually, I gathered all my courage and stepped out of my hiding place. The car pulled away. Roman stepped out of the darkness and moved into a spot lit by a streetlamp. He was standing there with his head slightly bent back—so calm, so strong, so motionless—and looking straight at me. The rain had stopped. Our faces were illuminated by an eerie blue light. The wind tried to tame Roman's curls but then gave up and dove into the puddle at his feet.

We both stood in complete silence. The spring, with its smells and flowers, was talking instead of us. The air was filled with the sounds of flutes, clarinets, and violins. The fresh leaves of the bushes washed by recent rain, the colourful cups of tulips, and the bright daffodils in front of the house exuded their aroma and almost made it tangible. Despite the approaching spring, the air was cool.

Roman stepped over the puddle and opened the front door of the apartment building. Just a few seconds later, he was at the door of the apartment, and I ran to meet him. He entered slowly, almost cautiously, but my hands were immediately on his body, running up and down his chest and shoulders. My touch made him respond with fear, and he pushed me away, but I immediately pulled myself close again. I wrapped my arms around his neck and put my face against his skin.

And then he forgot about everything. His greedy, voracious lips sought mine, and he pressed me closer to his body, trying to erase any distance between us. He seemed so lost and helpless, yet so powerful and determined. It was almost like was drowning in me, trying to disappear. All the feelings that he had been holding back started pouring out of his desperate lips, "I love you. I will always love you, but I…I don't know…I feel so lost. Seryozhenka, I can't do this anymore."

I led him to the couch, removed his coat, and helped him lie down. I sat down next to him, looked at his face, and no longer recognized my Roman. His eyes were no longer black—they were quickly turning grey. Deep frown lines had appeared on his forehead, and his beautiful eyes, once so clear, calm, and sparkling with life and mischievous fire, seemed dark, quiet, resigned, and extremely tired. The lines around his lips were almost frightening in their severity. Roman seemed torn and lost in constant doubt and insecurity. He was calm but unsure. What a dreadful state he was in!

But I was not feeling any better. I had no idea how to help him. Suddenly, I was overcome by almost painful fear. Dear God! The events in our lives were repeating, but this accident was much worse than the one we had gone through. This time it was his soul that was torn apart and destroyed by the cruelty of fellow men. When I held him close to my body, I could still feel it quivering in feeble hope. The indescribable sadness that I felt forced me to get up and smile at Roman. His sleepy eyes were carefully watching me. The brief glimmer of tenderness was overcome by fierce determination. He abruptly sat up.

"I'm sorry; I lost myself for a minute."

"Roma, don't be like that. How are you feeling?"

"Great," he said in an indifferent tone of voice, but a tired gesture of his hand proved otherwise.

"Roma, I'll prepare something to eat."

"Wait! Sit down! Give me your hand. There…listen to me."

"Roma…"

"Please don't interrupt me. I know that you have always been good at convincing me. They know it as well. That's why they called you. Forgive them! Forgive me! I shouldn't have come, but I was not able to resist the temptation to see you one last time."

"Roma…"

"Please! Don't say anything. On the last day, you are not supposed to lie or hide something, so I will tell you everything. Everything!"

But instead of continuing, he stopped talking altogether. The sound of his voice still hung in the air like an executioner's ax.

In my face he saw all my pain and confusion, and suddenly his eyes became softer, lighter, and showed true concern. The same invisible hand that had taken away the black glow of his hair was now trying to soften its blow by letting the gentle tones seep back into his voice. It no longer sounded harsh and commanding.

"Seryozhenka, why are you saying goodbye? Who told you that I am going to die? My baby, everything is all right. Think about it—against all odds we are together again. I am holding your hand. What a miracle…please, continue."

But I couldn't find any words, so I stayed silent.

"All right, then I'll tell you what I was thinking about while we were apart. I was blessed for such a long time without knowing the source of my blessing. But now I know—it was you. I understood that everything that is strong and unstoppable in me is the way I love you. I know that we are not born to experience only happiness. Sometimes we also have to suffer. But I didn't think that my suffering would be so long. You gave me happiness without any fear of humiliating yourself. After your tenderness, I wanted passion. After the flickering flame of your love, I wanted open fire. I can't deny it. She knew how to keep my passion burning with dangerous force. You already know what happened. But once the grindstones start moving, you can no longer remove the grains. That's how I burned myself. And again you were there to comfort me. I should have stopped and protected you, but…"

"Roman, but you must have loved her. You must have been happy with her, at least for a while."

"Happy? Well…what did Shakespeare write? 'Our life is a theatre.' Right?"

"No. 'All the world's a stage, and all the men and women merely players.'"

"That's exactly what I am saying. All our life is spent acting. And it doesn't matter how big the role is. The only thing that matters is how well it was played. Seryozhenka, Louisa and I didn't play our roles very well. It seems that women can either love or be loved. They are not interested in both. Besides, I was used to happiness being long and unchanging, like ours. I didn't want to become the beggar that her love was turning me into. Love has to be given, like you always did, my love. A person shouldn't have to beg for love, but I was forced to at times. I'll tell you more: most of the time, one of us was conquered and forced to cower at the other person's feet. Can you believe it? But I was desperate to hold her in my arms."

"How did you feel?"

"I felt sad. I felt endless longing."

"Who or what were you longing for?"

"I was longing for true love. For our love, Seryozhenka. For a life that has meaning, that is worth living. For a life that has hope, at least for a brief moment." He paused. "I don't see any hope."

"What about little Seryozha? He really needs you right now."

"And you?" He looked into my eyes and asked, "Do you need me? Why aren't you saying anything? Fight for our love! Take me away from them forever. Do it!"

"I can't, Roman. Seryozha is just a little child. He needs you more. At least to make sure that he doesn't grow up to be like me."

"Like you? Why do you think you are any worse than other people? But I see—we are always told that we are not worthy, and now even you are repeating these words. So what do you want from me? You already answered your own question—home is where the heart is. My heart always yearns for you." His voice once again became stern. "However, our wishes have to be in line with our abilities, and that doesn't happen often."

And then his face reflected unadulterated anger. "Life is like a malicious dog. All our hopes and desires are in vain. What is the point of such life? For how long can we stroke the animal's fur in the darkness, not knowing if it is a cat or a tiger? Don't sit there in silence, Answer, if you can!"

My throat started closing from pain and helplessness. The moon was watching us through the window, but seeing our longing and pain, it hid behind a cloud. The cloud swallowed the moon and dragged it away. We were surrounded by silence and darkness that we no longer tried to overcome.

And then the light of dawn slowly started appearing. "The heavy mists are falling away," he whispered, and his hands started caressing my skin.

We had very little time left to drink the last drops of love from the cup of life. Initially, our closeness was sad and uncomfortable, but the old and familiar fire gradually returned, and we were once again blessed with the perfect harmony of strength and surrender. Out of his thick eyelashes and warm lips, out of all the little details that used to seem so important, something new and simple was born. It was the true essence of love that filled us during our last hours together. His hands were so warm, his blue eyes so deep, his lips so sweet, his passion so unstoppable, and his faith in me so complete…that night the whole world was ours. We welcomed this comforting love and listened to its farewell song. The blue morning sky, the glistening tears in our eyes, and the pink rays of sunlight told us a story about happiness.

"Roman!"

"I am here, baby," he said and pressed his lips to my cheek. "Sleep. I am right next to you."

"Roman, I have never felt so good. I am so happy. So happy! I'm not imagining all this, right? I am afraid to fall asleep. Tell me you won't leave me. I will change. I will do everything so that we can be together."

"No, Seryozhenka. I don't want you to change. I love you just the way you are. You are like this garden, full of fresh flowers and shoots. Everything flows and changes. It's the natural circle of life. Our love is just like that. It will always be with us. It is never ending. We will meet. We will always be next to each other. Nothing will ever keep us apart."

"When will it happen?"

"I don't know, baby, but it will. I will find you. No matter where you are. But for now..."

He smiled and kept kissing me for what seemed like an eternity. I tried to put my arms around him, but I could only feel emptiness and cold. I opened my eyes and saw Volodya standing in the doorway, and next to him was the Old Man with his hand on his heart. I turned around and started beating the cold pillow in helpless anger.

"Wait! Come back! Please, come back! You have to come back! I can't live without you. I can't! Roman, come back!"

The only answer was a yellow note that fell from the wall. It landed in my palms, and I read it through the violent torrent of tears. "I have only ever been happy with you. Nothing and no one will ever take your place. I kiss you goodbye. Forever yours, Roman."

They say that death is darkness, blackness, and night, but all this happened on a sunny morning in May.

XIII

O h, the time. After Roman's departure, it stopped. My former life seemed distant and recognizable, my present was lost in a constant fog of fear, and I could no longer see any future. The horror of his departure constantly kept me at the edge of my strength. I was waiting for him to return. My face gradually became cold and immovable, as if it was made out of marble. My lips were pressed together so tight that it seemed like the sculptor had forgotten to include them in my face. I was still like a statue, or at least that was what it looked like from the outside.

Inside me, a profound and significant change was taking place. It wasn't really that I had lost all faith, but something inside had burned out. The day when I first met Roman seemed like a century ago. During the day I was almost sleepwalking, but at night I was not able to sleep. As soon as I wanted to rest, dark and frightening thoughts came into my head. My only companions were the lonely stars—dull and devoid of light, they became my companions till the very morning.

I was twenty-six years old. My youth had given up on me in the face of all the suffering. My life was at a crossroads. My common sense was trying to fight against the torturous pull of my passion, but my memories kept reminding me of all the feelings and desires that used to give me strength and comfort. They kept reminding me about the days and the nights spent with Roman.

But sometimes they could not sustain me. I was filled with worry, doubts, and dark premonitions that kept growing because of Volodya's increasingly frequent visits. My only salvation was the folder containing his letters and our pictures. In the moments of doubt, that was my only comfort. Looking at him, I felt happy, and the blinding pain seemed to take a step back.

I usually sought solitude in the old shed that stood in the yard. It was filled with various objects that I couldn't get rid of because they reminded me of my childhood. I would put the hundreds of his letters and pictures on a table that I had made out of old boxes. Looking at them, I was filled with worry and sadness, but I also felt closer to Roman. Whenever I was overcome with the horror of separation, I would immerse myself in this magical world. I was like a madman who is so blinded by thirst that he greedily drinks poisoned water. The only witnesses to my gradual suicide were the rays of the sun that sometimes sneaked in through the old walls of the shed and illuminated my precious possessions.

I looked at the photographs more often than I read his letters, and in those moments the past revealed the true force of its hold over me. Even the pictures showed Roman's ability to radiate happiness all around him. In his absence, his face seemed even brighter and kinder. I loved him more than ever before, more than I could ever express. The force of our connection surrounded me and at least temporarily dispelled the feeling of loneliness and despair. It returned some of the tenderness and passion, and I suddenly desired to be loved the way I loved him. The whole world seemed to bloom like a rose. Roman left the confines of the pictures and was standing beside me. I could almost touch him and say, "Hello! You're back!"

But when I looked up to see his face, I was greeted by emptiness, and hope once again slipped away from me. The world seemed vast and cold, like a desert at night. The moon hid its face behind the gathering clouds. Another day was drawing to an end. May was followed by June. The area was taken over by a new development, and all the homeowners were given orders to move to new apartments.

For the first time in months, I finally smiled and took the official order to my mother, just for a moment forgetting the sly and vicious animal that was still following me and Roman.

We started to get ready for the move. I spent the day taking our suitcases and boxes out of the spare room and moving them to the shed. By the evening I was so tired that I decided not to open my precious folder. I was almost afraid to tarnish the bright memories with my dirty and dishevelled look. I carefully put it inside my new suit, which I then placed in a white bag. I loaded our possession in the car that we had rented for moving to our new apartment.

I could not have imagined that the calm and warm evening would bring another challenge into my life. Exactly the opposite—all the gloomy thoughts seemed to have taken a step back, and I allowed myself to finally fall asleep in peace.

I had hardly closed my eyes when I found myself at the place where Roman was. I didn't really know what the area looked like, so the majestic desert I saw in my dream initially seemed frightening. Soon the sun appeared, and its rays were scorching hot, not warm and gentle. Red arrows were flying all around me, but none of them hurt me. They all hit the nearby stones and left on them tiny blood-red stars. Then the sand greedily swallowed them, and as they disappeared, they let out a human moan. I was scared, but I knew it wasn't my time, so I kept moving forward. I couldn't see Roman. I wanted to call out his name, but the sand suffocated me and kept me quiet.

At that moment someone's hand grabbed my arm. I tried to shake it off, but the hold increased.

"Son, wake up! There's a fire!" My mother's mournful voice brought me back to reality.

I looked outside the window and saw that the shed was burning. The neighbors' shed had almost collapsed in the flames, but ours had just started to burn. The greedy tongues of the flames happily prepared for their feast. I picked up an old blanket that I had put aside for wrapping a mirror. I dipped it into a bucket of water and ran into the yard to save my precious folder.

"Don't go," yelled my mother. "Let it burn. We'll be all right."

But no one could have stopped me. I didn't have to break the door—the fire had already taken care of it. Inside, there was already a lot of damage. For a while I managed to fight the flames, and I desperately tried to find what I was looking for. In the process I tried to throw outside as much of our baggage as possible. However, I could not find the white bag. Finally, I understood that it was right in the middle of the area consumed by flames and dangerously close to a barrel with the leftover petroleum oil.

I realised that I had to give up. In the dangerous glare of the evil flames, I saw the face of the animal. In the cracking and roaring noise of the fire, I heard its laughter. A falling beam hit my arm, and the smell of burning flesh entered my nostrils.

The shame of my helplessness finally made me react. I removed my burning shirt, picked up a spade, and continued to fight the fire, all the while whispering Roman's name. I asked God not to take away the only thing that still united us.

Somewhere close, another beam fell down. My mother started yelling and ran to me. She grabbed the arm that I had just burned (I'm surprised I didn't feel any pain) and started dragging me out of the shed. I almost gave up and followed her, but then I noticed the white bag I had been looking for. I threw the blanket over it and extinguished the flames. "Let go!" I yelled at my mother and pushed her outside. She fell but was helped back to her feet by the neighbors. She immediately wanted to run back inside the shed, but they wouldn't let her. As the back wall collapsed, I heard her desperate screams. "Save him! I beg you!"

The smoke blinded my eyes and I could no longer breathe, but I was sustained by the hope that the fire wouldn't reach the white bag. But the animal was faster than me. The wind had picked up, and the animal directed the flames exactly to the spot that I was desperately trying to protect. Another burning beam blocked my way, and while I was trying to get out, I heard the diabolical laughter of the animal and saw that the flames were devouring all my precious memories.

Through the mist of my fading consciousness, I heard the sirens of the approaching cars. I grabbed the last remnants of my folder, pressed them to my chest, and started moving toward the exit. I finally collapsed and felt someone picking me up and carrying me outside. Just a minute later, the shed collapsed.

What else do I remember from that frightening night? I remember regaining my consciousness when something silky soft ran over my burned skin. My mother and my neighbor were pouring sunflower oil on my wounds. Someone brought bandages, and someone called an ambulance. I quietly looked at my hand and realised that all the paper had turned to ashes, which the wind immediately blew away. My last hope had disappeared. My lips tried to form words, but I couldn't make a sound. My mother was crying and trying to bandage my arm. And then the darkness consumed me again.

My poor mother! She never found out why I went into the burning shed and what I lost with my suit. I remember the surprise of the doctor when he was trying to clean my burns, but I showed no sign of pain. He told me to scream, but not a sound crossed my lips.

I asked my mother to call Volodya, and he arrived on the same evening. He brought a salve that the Old Man had given him, and it soon helped my skin heal. The earth recovered from its wounds just as quickly.

A week after the fire, small green blades of grass appeared on the black surface. Two months later the leaves reappeared on the branches of the trees. One of these trees—a large and powerful poplar—still stands at the crossroads where our house and the shed once stood. Every time when I happen to be going through that area, I go up to the tree and tell it about my life. Then I lean closer to my old friend, and the whispering noise of its leaves makes me remember the past like it all happened just yesterday.

PART IV

I

Seconds, minutes, hours, days…the days became weeks, then weeks became months, and months became years. And then years followed one another.

When I was with Roman, my days seemed like hours, my weeks like days. When he was gone, everything turned upside down. I had no hopes for the future. I begged time to be merciful, but it never show any mercy. All I could do was wait. I was trying to find a way out or at least advice, but no one was there to help me. Or, rather, I couldn't find anyone whose help I was willing to accept. I was still attracted only to him. Only his incorporeal presence gave me solace. He was still the only one I needed. It almost seemed like the verdict of fate itself: "Either him or no one."

It was the winter of 1984. I had finished the institute a long time ago but still couldn't find a job. I also couldn't leave my mother, who was becoming weaker every day. During the long and dark winter evenings, my eyes wandered around the apartment, which should have felt warm and cozy but didn't. All the colours seemed to be swallowed by the black and always silent telephone on my desk and the just-as-silent dark-blue mailbox two floors lower.

During those evenings I remembered the words that Roman once said to the Old Man. He told him that if he was ever to leave me, it would be forever. He kept his word—his long silence was the proof. Neither Old Man nor I, and not even Volodya, knew what was happening in his life. The unstoppable desire to learn at least something followed me around like a shadow.

It also tormented the Old Man, who had moved to Tallinn to take care of his ailing wife, and Volodya, who had gotten married and moved to Amur Oblast. We exchanged letters and phone calls but remained where we were. Several times during these years, the Old Man tried to get some information about Roman. The reply was always brief: "The lieutenant colonel is alive and well. He is fulfilling his international duties." And that was all! Not a line more. That was how my days passed.

And during the nights in my colourful dreams, we both ran toward the sea. An invisible hand moved the sorrowful clouds out of the way. Then it picked us up and brought us toward our past, which looked like the pages of a heavenly book. The world around and under us was completely empty. All we could see was a blue abyss. Suddenly I was surrounded by its hopeless and frightening depth. I felt all the strength leave my body, and I was afraid (or maybe I was hoping) that I would die there.

And then I woke up screaming. The heartache that had disappeared from the touch of his hands was back. I tried to steady my breath and let my mother know that everything was all right. And then it all repeated from the beginning.

I learned what it meant to fully live just for the person I love. The mornings of all those years were the same. However, the sea of life is always bigger than the river that feeds into it. When the sound of the old clock in the hallway started to falter and finally disappeared, it was replaced by the bright and clear ticking of the table clock. And for a while, my face was once again illuminated by hope. It happened after a telephone conversation with the Old Man. It proved that by extending our lack of knowledge, we can also extend our hopes.

The conversation took place during the first days of March. The Old Man told me that Roman's company abroad would be replaced by another. This information gave me new hope. I went out into the street ready to share my happiness with whoever would cross my path. I was even more surprised to find a letter in my mailbox. I took it out and carefully examined it in the dull light of the March day. I didn't recognize the handwriting. There was no return address. I could barely see the postage stamp of Tallinn. The letter had been sent to my old address, which was crossed out and replaced by the new one. I immediately tried to think of who could have sent it to me, but my mind stopped on her. I examined the bold and slightly curved handwriting and tried to imagine what I would find inside the envelope. Why did this woman suddenly remember me? What did she want to say to me after all these years? It is the destiny of those who are in love to pray for happiness. Then why was my brief glimmer of happiness overshadowed by the old fear? My vision seemed to blur. My eyes and my body suddenly became heavy with exhaustion. The envelope was burning my fingers. At first I wanted to tear it to pieces and convince myself that I had never received the letter. But a voice inside my head told me to read it, so I finally opened it.

Hello! Don't pretend that you don't know who is writing. Read this letter to the end instead of tearing it into pieces and rolling your eyes, as I've heard people of your kind usually do. I didn't address you by first name on purpose, even though I know it very well. Scum like you don't even deserve a name. If you are still reading, I will explain why I am even wasting paper on such a creature. My ex-husband—the beautiful bastard with great ambitions and no intelligence—and your former lover (thank God for that!) finally found what he was looking for. Don't faint! It is not official. For now it is just my conclusion because he hasn't been sending me any money. Maybe he sends the money to you. In that case, you had better return it before I go to the police or take you to court. If I had my way, I would flock all of you together like animals, make you run through the streets so that everyone could spit into your disgusting faces, and then send you to some faraway island where you would gradually die and release this world from your presence. I hope that one day it will happen. I want you to know that I will do everything in my power to make sure that you are punished by law for everything that you have done. Start waiting!

After these lines she had included a return address and an extra line:

Don't bother sending a reply. The address is not meant for your letters. Louisa.

The daylight was slowly fading. The evening was near. The twilight was wandering through the empty streets. The whole world was putting on the mourning clothes of the night. The wheel of my life kept turning. All I could do was wait.

II

The telephone rang almost hesitantly. It seemed like it was afraid to ring so early. My alarm clock showed that it was almost five o'clock in the morning. The energetic voice of the operator betrayed an undertone of compassion and made my heart clench in fear. On the other end of the line, I heard Volodya's voice. "Seryozha! Hello… Seryozhenka, we lost him."

"Volod…no!"

"Yes, Seryozha. Now we are orphans."

Looking for support, I leaned against the frame of the open window and suddenly saw that the blooming spring had turned into winter. A layer of white snow covered everything. My legs gave out. I slowly lowered myself to the floor. Strange and unfamiliar sounds came from my lips—not laughter and not weeping but something in between. The floor beneath my body disappeared and was replaced by a gaping abyss. Every piece of information that Volodya related made me fall deeper and deeper. I could hardly understand what he was saying. I had fallen so deep into the abyss that there was no hope of getting out. Tears flowed down my face in strong and unending currents. I felt like I had aged a hundred years. I tried to get up, but the floor kept slipping from underneath my feet. Black spots kept getting bigger in front of my eyes.

The operator's voice appeared from some unknown distance. "Your time has finished. But you can continue talking. I will extend the conversation."

"Thank you!" Volodya's voice brought me back to reality. "Seryozha! Can you hear me? Say something."

"Who buried him?" My voice was quiet and unrecognizable, but Volodya still answered.

"The Old Man. He sent me a telegram, but I was on a training mission. It took them a while to find me."

"And what about me?" I almost screamed.

"He couldn't."

"Because of Louisa?"

"Yes. Even though he resolved everything, he still asked to wait a bit before going there."

"When can I go?"

"In a month I will have my leave of absence. We could meet in Moscow and go together."

"In a month?" My voice echoed his words.

"Yes. What do you think?"

My silence revealed my decision.

"I'm sorry." Volodya's voice started to disappear.

"Roman…" My eyes were full of quivering tears.

III

The next day, I arrived in Tallinn. Despite the sad circumstances, the day was bright and clear. The transparent air was filled with warm light and the soft smells of spring.

I tried to call the Old Man from the train station, but he didn't pick up. I had to decide what to do, so I went to a nearby square. When the birds saw me sit down, they immediately became quiet and still. The bravest one of them walked in front of me a couple of times, either hoping I would give it some food or gathering information so that it could go back and tell the others of my grief. I put my hand into the pocket of my coat and took out some breadcrumbs, which I offered to the bird to thank it for its bravery and compassion. The bird picked up the treat but kept looking at me out of the corner of its eye, as if asking, "And what about you?"

Indeed, my stomach ached from hunger, but my heart ached even more. And then the bird knocked on my boot with its beak. It seemed to be saying, "Get up and go!"

"Where to?" I hoped that the bird could answer my question. And it did.

"To her," it said.

And then it took off into the sky. I raised my head but couldn't see it. The green leaves of the trees hid it from my sight. All I could hear was a quiet voice repeating, "Go to her! Go to her!"

Then another voice joined in from a neighboring branch: "Don't be afraid! Don't be afraid!"

"Don't be afraid," I repeated. "I am not afraid. I just don't have enough strength to see her now. And she won't take me to his grave anyway."

"She will! She will," the birds sang.

I tried to overcome my wish to go to her immediately and tried to listen some more. My face reflected the mixture of pain and the unexpectedness of my decision. A man who was passing my bench stopped and asked something in Estonian. I was not surprised. The first time I came to this country, everyone thought I was one of the locals. I tried to recall the bits of language that I knew and realised that he was asking about my health. I was not able to give him a coherent answer, especially not in Estonian, so I just shook my head. I don't know how he understood me. He went aside for a minute or so but then came back and sat down on the edge of the bench. He looked into my eyes and asked in Russian with a light accent, "Please tell me what happened. How can I help?"

I tried to collect my thoughts and realised that the face of sorrow is so easily recognizable. And if a person is not completely heartless, the language we speak makes no difference. I was really grateful for his care, but how could I explain that which I couldn't even believe myself?

"Thank you for asking. I am just tired."

"Is that all?" His eyes were carefully studying my face.

"There are some other problems as well, but…"

"But you will resolve them yourself. I can see that. I won't interrupt you any longer. I don't want to annoy you, but remember—for those who are alive, nothing is ever over. Good luck!"

He got up, looked at me with his intelligent and kind eyes, and went on his way.

"Thank you," I quietly said as he disappeared around the corner. I left the square and on my way found a water fountain, which allowed me to quench my thirst and also trick my stomach into thinking I was no longer hungry. I got on a trolleybus and soon found myself at the one place where no one wanted to see me. During my conversation with the stranger and after his words of advice, I gradually let go of my fear and regained my strength.

However, when I entered the apartment building, I suddenly stopped. The two flights of stairs that separated me from the apartment seemed like too big a distance for me to cover. They say that people who are on the way to their own execution site never look around. On my way up, I hardly noticed anything, but it did cross my mind that this five-story building was different from all the rest—the yard was clean, the bushes were even, the flower beds were well looked after, and the paths were covered in gravel. The building had several entrances with two apartments at each. The thought that he had once gone up the same stairs helped me continue my ascent. Finally, I reached the door of the apartment. The sound of the doorbell reminded me of a fire alarm.

I was hoping that it would be a long wait, but almost immediately I heard careless laughter and an enticing voice. "I'm coming, Carl. Just a second."

My mouth immediately became dry. My eyes were burning, and it was difficult to breathe. I heard the movement of light steps down the hallway, and then…her eyes immediately met with mine, but she didn't understand who I was. A couple of seconds passed in complete silence, then she started to examine me with her eyes. There was something unpleasant and probing in her eyes, which seemed to be undressing me. Her manner was cold and haughty, reflecting her despotic mind. Her face lacked elegance and harmony, but most importantly, it lacked the warmth of true beauty. Of course, having read her letter, I did not expect a warm and welcoming woman, but I could hardly believe that her look could reflect such a degree of highhandedness, haughtiness, and unadulterated anger. I had to ask myself a question: How could my Roman have fallen in love with such a woman?

Once this thought entered my mind, our eyes met again. It almost seemed that Louisa had heard my question, and for a brief moment, she let me see a different side of her. Right in front of my eyes, she removed her hairpins and let a waterfall of jet-black hair flow down her shoulders. Her eyelashes suddenly seemed darker, and her pupils reflected light. Her slightly crooked nose looked perfectly straight, the soft smile on her lips made her face look kinder, and her strong and full arms, partly covered by her hair, seemed light and graceful. Her dress made her body look particularly…

"Yes, a woman like that could ignite passion with her touches and kisses, and then turn it into sweet but violent love." Her eyes seemed to ask, "So, do I look good? A gemstone doesn't need to be set to sparkle."

She toyed with me a minute longer, like a cat toys with a mouse it has caught. Something in me seemed to provoke her, and her manner changed. She asked, "Who are you looking for?"

"You."

"Are you the driver? I told you to come at ten." Her words seemed strained.

"No, I'm Sergey."

Her eyes immediately hit me with electricity, but I stood my ground. Her whole being radiated pure hatred, but I just kept looking at her. The corners of her mouth seemed to form something that resembled a smile. A wildfire lit up in her eyes. She was ready to fight to the death. In her face I could see surprise, shame, anger, impatience, and loathing. But then something changed again. Her eyes reflected something cruel, cynical, and stubborn. However, people with rapidly changing moods and personalities can never stay in one role for long. A minute later all I could see in her face was disgust and disappointment, and then everything that made her seem human disappeared altogether.

At this moment I could finally see her true self—she was pale, malicious, and calculating. She was standing in front of me completely changed. His full lips suddenly became two barely visible lines. Her eyes were cold as ice, and her whole body radiated coldness. Suddenly her dress seemed tasteless and made her body less impressive. Just a moment ago, she had seemed tall and elegant, but then the tight dress made her look almost naked and accentuated her age. Her waist was no longer slim, and her hips were rather full. Everything that she had recently experienced had left a mark on her once beautiful face. And it was changing again. (Not even chameleons are capable of what she could do.) She tried to hide her feelings behind a smile but couldn't keep it up. Her eyes suddenly seemed so large in her pale face. She kept looking at me. For a while they showed a strange mixture of pity and distaste but then settled on hatred.

"Louisa, who is there?" A quiet voice came from the inside of the apartment. "Please, close the door. If it's Carl, ask him to come in."

But she didn't even turn her head. She continued to poke me with the daggers of her eyes.

"The fact that you are here proves that you have no sense of reason."

Suddenly her eyes were filled with tears. Her words were cold, but I sensed a degree of sympathy.

"So what do you want?"

Then her attitude changed again. She started speaking in the sweet and playful voice of a young girl, using her words like arrows.

"Do you want to lie down next to him or just bring him flowers?" Her irony kept changing its intensity.

"By the way, where are the flowers? After all, you are going to see the man you love. Oh, right! You were the one who was getting them."

Oh, God! What a performance it was! I knew exactly why I let her treat me like that, but how could my Roman not see that she was a monster who destroyed him and took pleasure in it?

"So? Aren't you going to say anything?" She saw that for a moment I looked slightly conflicted.

"Please, show me where his grave is."

"And that's all? I thought…"

"Louisa, will you close the door already?"

"Father, what do you want?" She replied with a question but then continued. "Why are you always bothering me? What difference does it make if the door is open or closed? When will you finally start to listen to me?"

"Calm down!" I could hear the presence of tears in his trembling voice. "I can't light the fireplace because of the draught. I'm cold." The door of the room was closed, but then another one opened. I could see something familiar in the tiny shadow that appeared through the crack, but a sudden yell, "Get lost!" made it disappear.

There was another moment of silence, and I felt a strong distaste toward this woman who was made up of pleasure, not much intelligence, and no feelings. I heard a key turn in the neighbors' door and a voice telling someone to buy bread. Louisa quickly evaluated the situation and decided to extend a bridge across the chasm that divided us. She suddenly turned into a gentle kitten and said with a slight accent, "Come in! I'm sorry about…"

She even smiled, but her smile was not genuine. The warmth of her voice scared me. I was torn. On the one hand, I felt relief, but on the other hand, I didn't know what she was planning to do. Louisa closed the door, seemed to deliberate for a minute, then looked at me and said in a voice full of hatred, "Apparently, you are not planning to give up. All right, I like strong opponents. Before you go to visit his remains, you will probably be happy to see what he left behind."

At first I didn't understand what she meant, but when she started moving toward the door of the room that had opened just moments ago, I had to grab the doorframe for support.

"Seryozha, come and say hello to this man. You have my permission."

Her face looked triumphant, malicious, and filled with excitement, but it changed again and become somewhat more settled. What happened next probably didn't happen often (it is possible that it happened only in Roman's presence)—the boy immediately listened. Louisa was surprised but immediately moved away from the door and let her father step out of the room.

Then I saw a nine-year-old boy emerge from the room. He went up to his grandfather. His childish and pleasant smile was an exact copy of Roman's smile. At first the boy smiled at his grandfather, but when he saw me, he suddenly became animated and determined and ran to me, screaming, "Did my daddy send you? He is alive!"

I spread my arms and let him come close, but I couldn't say a word. And then a strange shadow seemed to pass over me. I yelled, "Roman!" and slid down the doorframe. The boy did his best to hold me up but ended up moving together with me. His determined voice kept repeating, "No, I am not Roman. My name is Seryozha. Roman is my dad. He is alive, right? Is that why you came? Tell me! Tell me!"

The look on my face scared even Louisa. She was standing completely still. Her father's eyes were filled with tears. I didn't want to scare the boy, who was now kneeling in front of me, so with trembling hands I pressed his head against my chest. I still could not pronounce his name. Instead, I kept saying, "Roma, Roman, Romashka…"

Seryozha broke free from my arms but didn't move away from me. He wiped away my tears with his tiny fingers and whispered, "Yes, he is my dad. My dad. He is far away, but he is alive and will come back. He told me about you. He loves us."

"Stop!" Louisa's voice was sharp as a razor blade. She pushed aside her father, who tried to help us get up, and grabbed Seryozha, who was holding on to me.

Suddenly, he looked stubborn and determined. "Go away," he shouted and bit his mother's hand. Louisa immediately jumped back. That was the first time I saw how lost and confused she actually felt. Then all four of us heard the loud melody of the doorbell and a man's voice with a strong accent. "What's happening? Open the door!"

The clock in the living room struck ten. Apparently, the long-awaited Carl had arrived.

IV

Someone said that to remember means to hopelessly try to answer the question, "Why?" My recollections are approaching their conclusion. When I close my eyes and remember the way I was back then, I ask myself the same question. But no matter how hard I try, the only answer I can find is, "That was my fate." Someone might say, "It's a typical answer. It is safe, generally accepted, and proper." And absolutely correct. The wounds that Louisa inflicted on me have healed. The hatred has disappeared. But back then… back then I didn't know what the Old Man had gone through. His wife died and asked to be buried in a faraway town. As soon as he returned, Volodya informed him about my arrival, so he went to look for me. I didn't know any of this, and my morning seemed long and tedious, almost like the last hour before embarking on a trip—the bags are packed, and you feel like going but still have to wait.

The voice behind the door also continued to wait. The doorbell had stopped working. I was so exhausted that I no longer saw, heard, or felt anything. Seryozha and I got up (the boy refused to let me go) and moved away from the door. Louisa's smile was eerie and distracted, and it made her look even older. She tried to regain her composure and then opened the door. The man who stood on the other side was heavily built. His grey hair was cropped short. His neck was bright red and so deeply set into his shoulders that it was barely visible. He was dressed casually, yet it was clear that he had picked out his clothes with care. He was wearing a colourful shirt, a grey jacket, and trousers of the same colour that looked like shorts. His black boots were impressively big and heavy. In his hands he held a cap with a picture of a ship and a hungry seagull. The cap, the seagull, and he himself looked confused, funny, and sad. I noticed it because he entered with a mask of complete carelessness on his face but a minute later seemed to be asking, "Should I be here right now?"

He was blessed with attention usually found in salesmen, politicians, and con artists. He immediately took in everything he saw and seemed to understand the situation. His little eyes, hidden behind glasses, carefully evaluated each and every one of us and helped him detect the recent fight. Louisa, who had spent all this time fighting with two invisible tigers—jealousy and despair—was the first one to break the silence. "Carl, we were waiting for you. Seryozha had a little tantrum. We are ready to go, but let's have something to eat first. Oh, right…" She looked at me. "You don't know our guest. He is Roman's friend from the army. Do you mind if we stop at the cemetery on the way? He would like to visit Roman's grave."

Her slyness, harshness, and cruelty were nothing in comparison with the lewdness that suddenly appeared in her eyes and took over her entire body. She invited the man to go for a walk, but her eyes were calling him to her bedroom. I wanted to get away from the apartment as quickly as possible, but little Seryozha held on to me even tighter. His little heart was beating against my chest like a hammer.

"Don't go! Please…"

"What to do? How can I help him?"

I looked at Louisa's father, hoping for at least some support, but his silence left me even more confused about what I should be doing.

"Dear friends, come to the living room! Christina has the day off, so I will prepare everything myself. Carl, will you help me?"

I didn't hear Carl's reply. He and Louisa went to the kitchen. I looked at the little boy, who had inherited all the best of his father's features—the dark and curly hair, the dark eyebrows, the unbelievably long eyelashes, the short and straight nose, the sensuous lips, and the tall body. But he had his mother's dark eyes. I guess Mother Nature had run out of blue.

"Seryozhenka…" But I couldn't say anything more.

The grandfather was watching us carefully but then got up and went to his room. The hallway reminded me of a long and empty tunnel. Only Seryozha and I stood at the end of it. We were almost like two conspirators, and suddenly I had a wish to leave with him. But then his hand, so tiny in my palm, just like my palm used to be in Roman's hand, started pulling me somewhere.

"Let's go to my room!" Even his voice, still childish but already enchanting, reminded me of Roman. Seryozha took me to his small but comfortable room, carefully closed the door, and then led me to the bookshelf. His eyes were so full of love that I immediately realised—he didn't want to talk about books. His small body shivered, but then he smiled and asked, "Would you like to see daddy?"

I don't even know how to call my reaction. It was a mixture of a moan, a scream, and crying, yet I didn't say a word. My breathing almost stopped. All I could master was a barely perceptible nod. He carefully removed the first row of books and put them in my numb hands. Then he pulled out the cover of a notebook that the Old Man had given Roman on his birthday. This cover contained what was a treasure for both of us—a small picture from Roman's old army licence. It still had the dark-blue stamp on its edges. My eyes filled with tears. The books started falling out of my hands. Seryozha caught them and kept repeating, "Quiet! I don't want mom to see it."

"Seryozhenka, where did you get it?"

"Grandfather gave it to me. Mom burned everything, but this one was in his room. She doesn't know about it."

He gave me the picture and picked up the fallen books. I couldn't ask him for the picture. I just kept looking at it and memorizing the familiar features. Seryozha must have guessed what I was feeling because he suddenly asked, "Don't you have a picture of daddy?"

I swallowed the lump in my throat and shook my head. I returned the picture to the boy and turned my face to the window. Seryozha seemed to deliberate for a little while, but then he reached out his hand and said, "Here. You can take it."

"No, Seryozhenka. No. I can't…" Once again the words failed me.

"Take it. You also love my daddy." He kept trying to give me the picture.

"I'll find one. Don't worry."

"Where?"

"I'll visit someone who might have it."

"The Old Man?"

"Yes. How do you know about him?"

"Daddy told me. When I was little, he came to visit us and let me sit on his lap. He always called me grandson. The last time I saw him was when we buried daddy. Mom didn't want me to go, but my grandfather and the Old Man insisted, so I…"

He could not hold back his tears, so he pressed his face to my body and became quiet. A minute later he looked at me with his moist eyes and continued. "I still don't believe that daddy is gone. The coffin was closed. I didn't see him, so it seems like someone else was inside. I feel like daddy will come back."

What could I tell him? I also kept hoping that he was alive, even though I was not as full of certainty as this little boy who already had been through so much.

We were both quiet. In his silence I saw my Roman. Seryozha was remembering the time when his father's strong arms threw him so high in the air that he could almost reach the sun. And when he was afraid, the same arms held him close, caressed him, and calmed him. And then Roman's moist lips kissed him and whispered, "My son! My Seryozhenka!"

I also remembered Roman's hands and lips, just as vividly as little Seryozha. And at that moment, Roman returned and united all of us saying, "I love you! Don't be sad."

We smiled at him, and our joined hands felt the touch of his skin. We didn't move, trying not to scare away Roman's spirit. A moment later Seryozha asked, "Where is Old Man now?"

"He's in Tallinn. He was not at home, so I came here. Tell me, is the cemetery far from here?"

"No, not really. Sometimes I go there with my grandfather. Mom doesn't know…"

Seryozha was interrupted by the quiet opening of the door, but he didn't look afraid, so I realised that was his grandfather. His gloomy look still didn't look welcoming, but Seryozha saw it as a sign.

"Yes, Grandfather, we are coming."

He smiled at his father's picture and then put it back into the hiding place behind the books.

"Let's go! I will soon have to go to school."

He smiled at me with the same smile. It revealed his strong, quiet, and beautiful heart. "Will I ever see you again? Will I ever find you?" I looked at him and asked myself these questions. He interpreted my look in his own way. "Don't worry; I will never forget daddy. And I will never forget you. I swear!"

The grandfather once again appeared in the doorway, but this time his smile was warm and welcoming. The boy whispered to me, "Grandfather is very kind. I love him very much."

Then we went to the living room. The fire in the marble fireplace was much warmer than Louisa's and Carl's smiles. I waited for her to treat me with disdain and cruelty. But the old saying is true—success really makes us generous, and wine makes us kind. Her look was peaceful and satisfied. She started laughing, and Carl laughed with her. Carl's laughter was quiet, but Louisa laughed with her whole body, desperately trying to draw Carl's attention to her and the glass of wine in her hand. When her fit of laughter passed, she put her glass down and said in a seductive voice, "I still don't believe you. Say whatever you like. You can't even try to convince me that the water is wet."

Louisa's voice was becoming unpleasant and capricious, but Carl paid no attention to it. Despite her changing mood, Carl still kept smiling. He found her answer suspicious.

Louisa filled her glass with wine, drank it, and continued. "The month of my love that later did so much damage clearly proved to me that I am not interested in real and passionate love."

As she said the last words, her eyes stopped at the level of my knees and refused to look somewhere else. The grandfather was watching her closely but didn't say anything. He made sure that Seryozha had eaten everything on his plate and then took him closer to the fireplace. I could see from his stance that he was not comfortable with the scene that was unfolding in front of his eyes.

"I need a man that I can love," Louisa continued. "Remember, you told me that in the cinema, the screenwriters are very important, but we don't need to know their names. It's the same for me—if I like the man, I don't care who he is."

Little Seryozha offered me tea and a slice of bread, but I still had not touched either. He reminded me of a ray of summer sun. I knew that his thoughts were in his room, next to the bookshelf, with his father.

"Louisa," Carl interrupted her, "love starts with common interests. Sex is like a garlic sauce—it tastes good, but you can eat the meal without it."

Louisa, who was pouring more wine into her glass, pressed her lips together.

"Don't you agree?" Carl repeated his question in a careful voice.

Louisa didn't answer. She was still drinking.

"Roman, so that's what your life was like," I thought. I was sitting at the very end of the couch, and I used this opportunity to look around the room. Every once in a while I looked at Louisa, but I didn't hear her. It was as if she were talking on a muted TV. I could easily imagine how hard it was for Roman to pretend he was happy during such evening gatherings, when some people talked about metaphysics or poetic nonsense while the others could only converse about hunting. I could imagine how this life could have suffocated his hopes and dreams and driven him toward his tragic death.

My reverie was interrupted by Louisa's voice. "Carl, there is no need to argue. As you know, sometimes an old story can seem brand new if looked at from a different perspective." She turned to me with a smile on her face. "This young man could tell us about his first passion." She challenged me with her eyes and started laughing. "Apparently, when it comes to love, he was unsurpassable."

"Louisa, you've had too much to drink."

"No, Carl. I know when to stop. Besides, wine is like a magic wand. It helps you get rid of everything that stands in your way. The darkness disappears, and the future suddenly seems so bright. But now I would like to return to the past and clarify something else." Her voice was quivering with anger. "How could he choose him instead of me?"

"Louisa!"

"Father, stay out of it!"

"Think what you are doing! Your son is in the room."

"Good! He should know what his father was like."

"Louisa, don't—"

"Carl, wait! I'm not blaming anyone. I just want to understand why he slept with me but called his name in his sleep. I want to know why he put his arms around me but felt him. And even when he kissed me, my husband's lips were looking for him. Why?" Her voice broke. She started coughing and sat down.

"Mom," Seryozha screamed and ran out of the room. His grandfather followed, throwing an angry glance at his daughter.

The room fell silent, but I could feel that the real explosion was still to come.

"You see, there is something else that I can't understand. Why doesn't anyone believe what I am saying? Where are my answers, Carl?"

"Louisa, this is not the right time or the right place."

"You think so? I want this lucky man to tell me why my ex-husband, going on the last flight of his life, took his picture with him and not mine. Why?"

"How do you know?"

"Now you are surprised? None of you know the whole story. Here, look at this!"

She opened the bottom drawer of a small desk and took out a half-burned picture, which she angrily threw on the table. It was the picture of us running toward the sea. I tried to hold back a scream by biting my lips, but I couldn't prevent myself from saying his name. Her face immediately was in front of mine.

"Yes, that's you and Roman. Or rather—that's what's left of him. Do you recognize the picture?"

In her face I saw confirmation that she could actually kill a person. Carl stopped moving altogether. At that moment a car honked outside. Our eyes met again. Louisa's eyes were full of anger, but Carl seemed frightened. He said in a quiet voice, "Louisa, that's our car. We have to go."

These words seemed to cool her temper. She replied in a calm and collected voice, "All right, just a second. Let me get ready." And then she left the room.

Carl got up, but his movements seemed strange and forced. When he reached the door, he turned around and asked, "Are you coming?"

I nodded and in my mind said goodbye to Seryozha, who had already left for school. Then I went downstairs. On the polished surface of the table stood the blackened proof of our love.

V

On the way to the cemetery, we kept looking at one another but didn't say a word. Louisa's maliciousness had disappeared, and inside the new Volga, she was polite and welcoming. How naive I was! I didn't realise that her eyes were full of desire to take revenge. I never said I understood women. I was not worried about Carl's sarcastic interest.

We arrived at the cemetery, which looked like a big park. Only the church that stood at the far end revealed that this was the final resting place and a place to be faced with memories. In all directions I could see monuments that guarded the loneliness and silence of the cemetery. I was surprised to see how empty the cemetery was, but I was also happy. All I wanted was to be alone with him.

The car stopped. Louisa didn't move. Carl got out and ran to open the door. Only then did she gracefully get out and start walking toward the gate. Carl and I followed her. I hardly had enough strength to move; he had no desire to do so. Next to the entrance, a young girl was selling flowers. Louisa passed her and then stopped. When she saw the red tulips in my hand, she forced the sad smile of a widow. Then she took six yellow daffodils out of Carl's hands and asked me with a warm smile, "You like poetry, right?"

Suddenly a question rose in my mind. "What now?"

"Roman also loved poetry. Sometimes he read it out loud to me. I think it was Fet."

The devil in her was once again ready to play.
One of the poems I remember particularly well:
We don't need the river, the fires, the nights
My breath will find you and ease my flight.

"No, you won't do it."

"Why not? Who will stop me? Your loving heart will show you the way. You have the flowers. And these sad daffodils I will put on your grave." The flowers trembled in her hand.

The devil himself couldn't have laughed with more satisfaction. She turned around on her heels and started walking back to the car. I looked at her with eyes devoid of tears, devoid of hope, and devoid of life. When Louisa reached the car, she lit a cigarette and kept watching me. Every once in a while she said something to Carl, who wasn't listening to her. I turned my back to them in horror and despair and tried to understand what to do. The answer frightened me—I had to start looking. But a voice inside me kept repeating, "You will meet. You will definitely meet." So I took the first step.

The bright and sunny day here seemed like twilight. The light was playing with the shadow, but it was not a malicious game. The path reminded me of a long, white ribbon. I could almost hear the sound of the sea. I could also hear the gravel under my boots. I had the feeling that I was walking barefoot on broken glass. I didn't cry, didn't think, didn't feel anything. The pain in my chest was asleep. There was no one who could help me. I just went ahead and kept looking.

The grass and the leaves were all bright and cheerful. My eyes kept scanning the sea of graves, revelling in their silence. Once again I found myself under the gaze of Louisa, who had not stopped watching me.

Then I stopped. "Oh, God! Roman, where are you?" The question came out like a moan. My whole being was expectant. I kept listening and looking. I shivered. A cool breeze ran through the alley. The branches of the giant firs swayed and then moved upward, covering the sun. At the same time, the sun hid its face behind a cloud. For a moment the midday light was overcome by evening mist. But then the sun got free, and its rays hit against the bright domes of the church and illuminated my path to his last resting place.

But even then I didn't see him at once. In the beginning I just heard the opening notes of *La Traviata*. The music was pure and touching. I moved in its direction and heard a distant voice calling me: "Seryozha…Seryozhenka…" And nothing more. But it was his voice! It was so familiar and beautiful. It was the voice of my Roman calling me so mournfully, passionately, and insistently.

"I'm coming," I replied. It came out as something between a scream and a whisper. "I'm coming."

I was just a few steps away when a black and scary spider, lying in its net, stopped me. But the voice of my love kept calling me more insistently. "What are you doing? Come here! I'm waiting."

My head was hurting. My legs were heavy. I could barely breathe. My heart was frantically beating in my chest. Silvery silence entered my ears and made his gentle voice seem quiet and distant. The names on the other tombstones were quivering in front of my eyes, which were now filled with tears. They mixed together until all I could see was just outlines of flowers. And then I started to pray. "I will no longer meet him on this earth. At least show him to me. Take me to him, and I will not lose my faith."

Everything seemed frozen in despair and expectation. And then my love, still calling me with his familiar voice, told me what to do. So I opened my arms like I had opened them to Roman on that square, and shouted, "I love you! I love you!"

In the burning sunlight that shone through the branches, I heard Louisa scream, "That's impossible!"

The spider, the darkness, and the gloom disappeared, and my Roman smiled at me from the picture on the gravestone.

"Hello, Roman! Did you call me? I came."

"Seryozhenka!"

"Roman!"

I kissed the cold marble and put my head on his heart, which was no longer beating. I felt so happy and miserable, so sad and overjoyed. I could no longer understand what was happening to me. The tulips slid out of my hands and fell like a wreath on the light-yellow surface of the marble. There they mixed with light-blue forget-me-nots, and this mixture of colour seemed to tell the story of Roman's short life. I knelt down and caressed the blue flowers, which reminded me of his eyes, his face, and his lips. They became a part of him. The flowers moved their pretty faces and invited me to sit down on the small, low bench right next to them.

"Don't cry," he said. "Don't cry. You see? We are together again."

With the hands of a light breeze, he tamed my hair and dried my tears.

"Roman, these are tears of happiness. I am crying because I found you."

"Seryozhenka, I am also happy." He continued to talk to me, and his sigh moved the flowers.

"Sit a while, let's talk! We have a lot to say to each other, right?"

"Yes, Roman."

"My baby, you are tired. I know how much you have suffered. I'm sorry I tormented you. I didn't mean to." A branch of a tree caressed my face with fresh leaves and pressed them to my lips, leaving behind a taste of a kiss.

"Seryozhenka, do you remember these lines? They are so well suited."

"Which lines?"

No one now can judge us harshly,
Our time on earth is done.
All is gone and all is pardoned,
And we don't care, 'cause we are gone.

"No, Roman, we do care. I am so sad for both of us. Why did you leave that morning?"

"I didn't leave you, Seryozhenka. The anger of people tore us apart."

He grew quiet and resigned, and his curls—the soft leaves—touched my shoulders. I pressed my cheek against them, and our silence became sad and uncomfortable.

"Baby, why are you so quiet? What are you thinking about?" the leaves asked in his voice.

"I'm thinking about the fact that it will all happen again, just not for us. Neither the summer nor the autumn or winter moon will ever look at our games. But now we can meet whenever we want. Yes, Roman. That is all that life has left us."

"Seryozhenka, don't cry. If you love someone, that is a lot. Think about it—we spent years together, and we had everything. We had smiles and sadness, meetings and parting, but we always loved each other. And even now—God knows how—we are still together."

Little violets raised their sad faces and smiled.

"That's what Fet wrote."

"Yes."

"Seryozhenka, read me one of his poems."

"Roman, I can't remember."

"Try!"

We were forbidden to go closer,
We were forbidden to be near.
We were told by someone wiser,
That our love will end in tears.

"More!"

The vicious crowd can tease and hurt us,
But we won't feel it, we won't see.
We are together, love will warm us,
And there is nowhere else to be.

"More!"
"I can't remember any more. Really!"
"All right, don't worry. They didn't kill our love. I left this world
with your name on my lips, and you came here with mine. It means
that we are together. Nothing will ever tear us apart. You are the only
one I pray to. We will love each other forever."
"Roman, I remembered another one."
"I'm listening."

You are so far from me, so far forever,
But are given something true.
We'll never be apart. Oh, never!
I only live when I'm with you.

"Thank you, my love. I always knew that you are mine."
"Mine," said the flowers.
"Mine," whispered the leaves.
"Mine," sang the wind.
"Yours, Roman. Only yours. And neither the waves of life that
took you into your grave, not the breath of death that extinguished
your heart will make me stop loving you. I don't care what the rest of
the world thinks. My heart will continue loving you. Nature doesn't
care about laws and customs. It only gives true love to people who
carry it with them for the rest of their lives, like you and me. That
is why we belong to each other. And if God can hear us, let him tell
the malevolent world that only love can save it."
As soon as I said these words, all the branches and leaves reached
toward the sky. The storm was coming. The air was filled with almost

transparent raindrops. Gradually, they became stronger and larger, until they turned into a wall of water that was seeping into the earth.

"Love," said the rain.

"Love," said the drums of thunder.

"Love. Love," answered the lighting.

"Love," said the whole sky.

Forever! Scared! Pure! That is what true love is like. The whole of nature talked of love. "Love," repeated Roman, the invisible Fet, and I.

All that you will try to forbid,
And banish from my heat,
Will once return from the place where it hid,
And tear all your doubts apart.

LOVE!

VI

I will not describe the last meeting in this tale and on that day. The time passed quickly, even though usually at a cemetery it almost stands still. The orange-and-red light of the evening sun told me that once again it was time for us to part. The last apologies froze on our lips, the recent happiness was replaced by sadness, and we were not able to let each other go.

A car pulled up to the cemetery. Many cars had come and gone while I was there, but this one stopped very carefully. The elderly man who got out of it came in my direction with quick and sure steps. I didn't pay any attention. Only when a familiar but faraway voice greeted me, I finally looked up. It was the Old Man. His face was full of despair and profound sorrow. It reminded me of an old lamp that no longer carries any light. He bent down to the picture and kissed it.

"Hello, son!" A heavy teardrop fell from his eye and ran down Roman's face. "Finally, we are all together again. Volodya sends his greetings." He bent down his head and stood in silence. "I'm sorry; we have to go now. The gate will be locked at any minute. Come, Seryozhenka! Let's go!"

His inner strength was still in perfect balance with his kindness, except now he seemed weak and sickly. He took my hand and pulled me in the direction of the gate.

"Goodbye, Roman," I whispered to the picture.

The violets bowed their heads.

When we got into the car, the Old Man became silent. For a long time, we didn't say a word, but I could see that he desperately wanted to break the chains and start talking. I didn't try to push him but patiently waited for him to say something. When we reached the house, he asked, "When are you leaving?"

My only answer was a shrug.

The Old Man turned to the driver. "Yura, come pick us up tomorrow around lunchtime. And please buy a ticket to Moscow."

"Yes, Colonel." We drove up to the front door.

"Will you come in?"

"No, Colonel. At ten I have to be at the base."

"All right, go then. Thank you, dear." The Old Man's eyes started glistening with tears.

Yura gave him a small bag, and we entered the house. When we entered the dark apartment, I felt someone's presence, but I didn't pay attention to it. I helped the Old Man take off his coat. Then I noticed that he opened a door and let in a dog. The dog was so old that it could barely bend its paws, and its eyes were full of tears. He pushed his nose in the Old Man's palm. The Old Man turned the dog's head in my direction and said, "Look who came to visit us!"

The dog's ears started moving, and I understood that I was looking at Pilot.

"Pilot!" I called him. "Pilotushka!"

The dog started to whimper and tried to move his hind paws but couldn't, so he started crawling in my direction, using the front paws.

"Pilot!" When he was finally in my arms, my eyes filled with tears. He recognized me. He continued to whimper, and the sounds reflected excitement, tears, pain, and loss at the same time. He licked my face and even tried to get up on his hind paws, putting his front paws on my shoulders. But his front paws were too stiff. Pilot licked my lips and almost fell to the floor. The Old Man went up to him and stroked his back. All three of us were crying. Pilot tried to lick our tears away. He lifted his head, but it was too heavy, and he had to lower it once again.

"That's how we live here," the Old Man quietly said. "Take him to the living room. He likes to sleep by the lamp. And turn it on. I will be right there." He went into the kitchen.

I picked Pilot up (my faithful friend licked me again) and carried him to the room. I placed him on an old army blanket and turned on the light. The dog gently growled in happiness. I moved up a low table and two chairs, sat down, and stroked Pilot's back. He put his front paws across my feet—a sign of gratefulness and trust—and fell asleep. Every once in a while he sighed and whimpered. It seemed that in his dreams he was complaining about his lot. I didn't want to wake him, so I sat still and started to look around the room. I didn't expect any surprises. I looked at the bookshelf. It contained no books. On the highest shelf, he had an enlarged picture of Roman, similar to the one that little Seryozha had. Next to it burned a red candle. I caught Roman's gaze and moved. Pilot woke up, started whimpering, and turned his head in the same direction. Suddenly he got up and went in the direction of the portrait.

"Pilot?"

The dog turned around and expected me to join him. When I went closer, I understood what the dog wanted. On the next shelf, there was a portrait of the Old Man's wife. The candle next to it had burned out, and the black ribbon had slid down. (Poor Old Man! How much he had to go through in those past couple of days.) I put the ribbon back on. Pilot was still standing next to me and whimpering. The Old Man came into the room with a tray in his hands and was the first to start speaking. "Please light the candle. He won't leave before looking at her face."

I lit the candle and put it back in place. Then I looked at Pilot. He gratefully licked my hand, lay down in front of the portrait, and kept looking at the candle.

"She died three days ago," the Old Man continued. He put the contents of the tray on the table. "I was not here. He was the only one who heard her last breath."

The dog turned his head in the Old Man's direction.

"I only went out for a little while. I didn't even lock the door, just closed it. He managed to open it, went into the corridor, and barked till the neighbors came."

Pilot barked in a breathy voice and lay down.

"The neighbors ran to the shop to find me. When we came back, he was lying by the door, overcome with sadness. Right, Pilot?"

The dog sighed and stretched out again.

"Sit down. Let's commemorate the dead. I'm sorry, Sergey. I didn't expect you. But God sent you here."

"That's not true."

"We buried my wife in her native village. The wake was there as well. My daughters are still there. And then Volodya called me. The village is very remote, but they do have a telephone. Volodya knew the number. He told me that you were in Tallinn. You are not afraid to take risks."

"I'm sorry, I didn't know."

"No, I'm not talking about that."

"How did you find me?"

"I was worried about you, my boy. You went straight into the nest of vipers. I guess you forgot, or maybe you didn't know."

"What?" I interrupted him.

"The old saying: 'Beware of a wounded animal and a scorned woman.'"

I stopped talking and raised a full glass. We got to our feet and drank it. That was when I remembered that I had not eaten anything the whole day. I looked in the direction of the table. The Old Man noticed it.

"Eat. You must be hungry."

"No, I…"

"Go on," he said and pushed the plate of sandwiches in my direction.

"I went directly to Louisa's apartment. Her father told me everything."

The Old Man sighed. "I can imagine what she did at the cemetery."

"She didn't do anything," I said with a bitter laugh.

"What do you mean?"

"She refused to show me his grave."

The Old Man's face reflected surprise and disbelief. He even got up to his feet, and I saw that his lips were trembling.

"So how did you find it?" His voice was a mixture of happiness, pride, and anger. All these feelings once again brought tears to his eyes.

"I don't know. I was looking for it, and I found it."

"Oh, God!" He turned to Roman's portrait. "Why would she treat you like that even after death?" His angry fist landed on the table. "What did you ever do to them all?" His breathing was shallow and rapid. "For how long will the world still hate love?"

He sat down again and seemed to be lost in thought. The only sound in the room was Pilot's happy growling. He held the bowl between his paws and carefully licked all the soup from its sides. At that moment I could still see a spark that he had had as a puppy. We wiped away our tears and smiled at Pilot. Then the Old Man's hand touched mine.

"Did you like little Seryozha?"

"Very much."

"He is a good boy. I only have granddaughters, but that's all right. God, give them all good health. You know what they say—you have to drink three glasses, but we still haven't had the second one. Let me add some more. And bring him some water from the kitchen. The boiled water is in the kettle. His stomach is very weak. Our Pilot is growing old."

I took the bowl, went to the kitchen, and returned with water. Meanwhile, the Old Man had cut up some bread and prepared sandwiches with cheese and sausage. Pilot had returned to the portraits and gently whimpered.

"Pilot, stop that! We can't get them back. Better come here and drink your water."

The dog obediently went back, lay down, and started drinking.

"Well done," the Old Man said, trying to encourage the dog. "Seryozha, let's drink!"

We finished our glasses and became silent again.

"How did he end up here?" I nodded toward Pilot.

"The boys from the base brought him over. After you left, he didn't eat and didn't drink. He spent all his time lying next to the flight house. If a car was approaching, he ran to meet it. And then he saw that you were not there…he wouldn't let anyone touch him. We thought he would die. Yes…what a job you left me! It took me a long time to heal him from sadness. After a while he started eating out of my hand. He became more cheerful but refused to live in the apartment. He always slept in the flight house. I wish people were that loyal…"

And again silence.

"And what happened then?"

"Then…Pilot, what happened then?"

The dog raised his head, looked at the Old Man, and turned his head to the picture of Roman. My skin was immediately covered in sweat. I remembered the letter where Roman mentioned a visit to the base. The Old Man seemed to know what I was talking about.

"And some people say that animals don't understand anything. Yes, Pilot! Then Roman came. He immediately asked for Pilot. I told him, 'He is still where you left him.' We drove up to the flight house, and he was sleeping there, as always. I thought it would be a happy reunion, but no! Pilot was barking and didn't let Roman close. Roman tried giving him chocolate and sugar, but it was all in vain. He even brought a bone! Still, Pilot was barking and didn't let him approach.

Roman almost started crying. But as soon as Roman left, he started howling. As if he knew…"

The Old Man sighed and dried Pilot's teary eyes. The dog's head remained on his lap. The Old Man kept on stroking it and continued his story. "And then we both retired, moved to Tallinn, and started living here. He was not used to sleeping indoors and at first always wanted to sleep outside. Gradually he accepted the women of the house as well. And then my daughter moved to Moscow, and you started your studies. I didn't want to leave him, but then I thought that Masha and Ira would manage without me. Dear God! What a performance that was! The girls called me every day, and I could hear his howls in the background. And then he disappeared. My daughters called me crying, but what to do? In my head I said goodbye to him."

The dog removed his head from the Old Man's lap and moved to me.

"He didn't forgive Roman but forgave you. That's from old age. When my wife got sick, I returned to Tallinn. I called the base before my arrival to see if he got back—and indeed! He was still by the flight house. But a car had hit him, and he crawled there to die. We called the vet. He wanted to put him to sleep. While my wife was still walking, she changed his bandages, talked to him, took him for long walks. When she got sick, Pilot stayed right next to her. That's how it happened."

"Pilot, please forgive me," I whispered and kissed the dog. "We didn't want to hurt you. I swear. And forgive him as well. He saved your life."

Suddenly, the light went out. The dog raised his head and went up to the pictures. The Old Man and I stopped moving. There were long shadows on the floor from the candles. Pilot moved to the shadow that came from Roman's picture, put his paws around it, and lay down. The Old Man started shivering. My whole body was covered in goose bumps. The candles were still burning. It was midnight. A new day was starting, but the dog still didn't move. In the last minutes of his life, he forgave Roman. Roman's candle went out, and Pilot was surrounded by darkness. I wanted to scream but couldn't.

The Old Man finally understood what had happened. He said, "He's gone! He is also gone." But then he started screaming, "And who will forgive me?"

"You haven't done anything. There is nothing to forgive," I finally said.

"I haven't done anything? Who else is to blame then?"

"You are tired. You should go to sleep."

"No, Sergey. I must say my confession. I can see that the time has come. I didn't think I'll be confessing to you. But please, listen to me."

"Maybe better tomorrow?"

"No, I'm begging you. I can no longer keep it inside." Looking at his face, I realised that he had never revealed his emotions to such a degree. When he was sure that I would listen to him, he went to the bedroom, and I thought of how I had always admired the combination of strength, benevolence, and suffering that I saw in him.

My thoughts were interrupted by his shadow. He sat down closer to me, and I saw that he had changed. When he left the room just minutes before, he seemed distant and unrecognizable, but he returned ready to do anything to make me believe his words and eventually help him. He had changed his clothes and looked like an old wise man from a painting who had come to confess all his sins. In one hand he held a little box. It was one of the family relics, passed down from generation to generation and often brought in on similar occasions.

Candlelight illuminated the faces of those who were no longer with us. We were all waiting for the Old Man to do something. I almost wanted to pinch myself to prove that this was really happening. The old box didn't contain anything mysterious. There were a couple of photographs and some papers. He put each of them on the table with tears of joy in his eyes, and he started with the one that pained him the most.

"Youth cannot take separation, but I separated them."

"What are you talking about?"

But he didn't hear me.

"They could have both become my sons, but I destroyed them. First one and then the other. Look!" His voice had suddenly become unrecognizable. "Do you know who it is?" He touched a picture that stood in the corner of the table. Suddenly it was in my hands. It was a picture of two teenagers. They had their arms around each other and were laughing carelessly. The other picture showed them in a very different situation. One of them was listening while the other one excitedly told him something about poetry, music, or faith. The other boy was standing up. I looked closely and whispered, "It's Roman!"

"Yes, it is. And the other one is Misha."

"But they…"

"Yes, it is my fault. I killed them." His eyes were bright and feverish. He got up, then sat down and got up again.

"Please, don't. I know you haven't done anything."

Then he took another picture in his hands. "Yes, I have. We are both guilty. Right, Galya?" He addressed the woman in the picture. Then he showed it to me.

"This is my first wife. She couldn't have children, but she really wanted a son, so we went to an orphanage. We immediately liked Roman and Misha. They were not blood brothers, but they were even closer. Nothing could keep them apart. I wanted to adopt both of them, but my wife didn't like Roman. She should have been happy to have two sons, but she refused to change her mind. Some women only bring men trouble, without even wanting it. And I also have to admit that passion can blind us.

"I gave in to her insistent pleading. Misha resisted for a long time. He refused to leave without Roman. We took him almost by force while Roman was at the hospital. We promised to adopt Roman as soon as he recovered, but of course we didn't do it. Misha ran away several times. We always brought him back. Oh, God! I can still see the look in his eyes when he left us for the last time. He didn't shed a single tear. We thought he would return to the orphanage, but he moved to another city and joined a gang, which later gave him away to another one."

Frightening shadows crossed the Old Man's face. I could see that the words were burning his throat, but he kept talking.

"He was killed by his own gang. Stabbed. When I arrived, he was still alive. I bent down, and he opened his eyes. With his last breath, he said, 'I hate you!' And then he died. It was the most horrifying moment of my life. I buried him there. But I promise, if I live that long, I will bring you together again."

He let his head fall on his hands. I put my face to his shoulder and felt that he was crying. The ticking of the clock reminded us of the passing of time. The Old Man raised his head.

"Soon my wife and I went our separate ways. I went to get Roman, but he had moved to another town. Then I swore I would do everything in my power to make him happy. I found him, but I never revealed who I was. I helped him all his life, hoping to make up for what I did to him and Misha."

I could no longer stop myself from asking. "Why didn't you tell him everything? Why didn't you take him to your house? Roman would have understood and forgiven you."

"Seryozhenka, the strongest passion of people is hatred. You felt Louisa's hatred, and I felt Roman's on his graduation night. Thank God, he didn't recognize me. Each of them was asked to tell about their hardest experience at the boarding school. He told everyone about his parting with Misha and cursed the person who separated them. I didn't know what to do. I left the hall, but I felt like I was carrying a scarlet flag of shame. And I didn't know how I would help him from then on. I had spent all my money on his boarding school. I was standing there completely lost when I suddenly heard his voice. He said, 'Colonel, can I talk to you?' I was so worried that I had to lean against a column. He just stood there and waited for me to say something. Finally, he continued. 'I want to become a war pilot. Could you tell me what I should start with?' I felt like fate was giving me one last chance. He was so young and handsome, dressed in the suit that I had sent for his graduation. I wanted to tell him who I was and ask for forgiveness."

"And…?"

"I couldn't. I tried to remain calm. I told him to leave his information so that I could contact him. All the while I prayed he wouldn't change his mind. Then he said, 'No, that's what I want to do after my military service. What could I do until then?' We started talking. I managed to place him in a school. I found him a job and a place to stay. When the time for the military service came, I took him to my base."

He stopped talking. The candlelight was quivering. Our silent witnesses looked at him in expectation, but he didn't say anything and kept looking at Roman's picture. He was still overcome by feelings of love and care. There was no doubt that this confession was very hard for him.

"Tell me about us."

"About you? You know, when we love someone, we also love the time before we met him. Even though I had a new wife and daughters, I missed Roman. And I was still afraid that he would learn the truth. When the test flights started, I offered to move him under my command.

"And then you appeared. Please, don't be offended, but at the beginning, you were so strange. The army was no place for you. If it was my decision, I would have let you go. I read your file and saw that you were brought up by women. You studied drama, and it was of no help in the army. I kept you only because I had to. It was not your fault. Your fragile nature and kindness finally won me over.

"But you truly helped me when Roman arrived and you met. Don't ask how I found out. I felt it rather than saw it. When he started seeking your company, I was afraid to take him away from you like I once took Misha away from him. The only thing that I wasn't sure about was whether you were well informed about what nature had in store for you. I was afraid that he, being older than you, would just enjoy himself and then leave you. I kept watching you and was surprised to discover that not only were you both perfectly capable of profound feelings, but you also knew how to navigate them.

"I have to admit that initially, I was against this kind of relationship. I had come across it during my years in the army, and it was always so dirty and unpleasant. All I felt was disgust. But the warm sunshine of your love made me look at it from another perspective. I came to the realization that it was not a mistake of nature, as most people believe, but that it is nature's choice. A gift to those who are able to love once and forever. Your love was like a constant celebration. It burned so bright that every look and every touch made me experience happiness as well. I felt the pleasure that you took in each other's presence. So I did everything to protect you from those who didn't wish you well. Some people were too shy to express their opinion and followed their malicious leaders. Here are all the reports that were written about you."

He took several sheets of paper out of the box.

"Better don't look. There are many names that you will recognize. Those are people who worked next to you, who smiled and wished you a good day. There were also those who showed their hatred openly. They were consumed by envy. I tried to help you as much as I could, but at a certain point, I was powerless. I have no idea what would have happened if Lanchik hadn't interfered. He was the one with the highest power."

"What did he do?"

"He said that he would investigate and act accordingly, but he was actually looking out for you. Once he received such a vile report that he even wanted to punish those who had written it. And the accident happened…" The Old Man smiled and looked at me.

"You really showed them that time. Lanchik played his role well. He sent you to the hospital and on the next day called everyone together. He put the reports in front of everyone who had written them and acted as if he had made a decision. He said, 'Add everything you want to add.' He looked everyone straight in the eye with an air of expectation. They all suddenly started looking at the floor, but he continued. 'As soon as they are out of the hospital, they will both face a trial.'

"I carefully watched their faces. The room was so quiet that we could hear the phone ring two floors below us. Lanchik kept waiting, still not saying anything. They were breathing heavily and drawing circles on their papers. Finally, some of them started to give up. Pankratov was the first one."

"Pankratov? But he…"

"I told you. Don't be surprised."

"I'm sorry. What happened?"

"You remember what he was like—always so confident and haughty. He wanted to be the best at everything he was doing. But on that day, he was pale as a ghost. He held the paper in his hand and hardly found enough courage to speak up. He said: 'Excuse me…' And Lanchik yelled: 'Silence!' Pankratov started trembling. He wasn't sure what to do. He expected to be promoted and feared for his position. I looked at the rest of them. Oh, God! How scared they all were.

"Lanchik saw that. He stood up and said, 'I see. Everyone is envious. No one has any proof. Well, I am not God Almighty. There are people with more power. Complain to them, if you think you must. And now—go!' He turned around and left the room. I followed him. We felt like saying something but couldn't find the words. We just stood there in silence. Gradually, everyone left. When we went back into the room, all the papers were neatly put on the table. I took them because I wanted to destroy them, but I ended up keeping them. You can have a look if you want to."

"No!"

"You're right. Let sleeping dogs lie." His eyes started closing. "Put the kettle on. I am feeling really tired. I think I want to lie down."

I went to the kitchen. When I returned, he was asleep. His body had slumped in the chair, his hands joined together, his head hanging to one side. I called him, but he didn't wake up. He just slightly changed his position. His confession had finally brought him peace.

I covered him with a blanket and put a small pillow underneath his head. I listened to his even breathing and realised that during these hours I had learned more about him than during my army years. The moon looked into the room and saw that I had put away my tea cup. It chose to rest its head on clouds and go to sleep. The candles had almost burned out. The clock was counting the last minutes of the departing night. The lines of Fet's poem were printed on the calendar:

It all will pass, you cannot love forever,
But sometimes love can make you better.

Tallinn was still asleep. But on the third floor of the old house, I opened the curtain slightly and listened to the weeping rain. I touched my sleepless hands to my head and held it. I tried to let go of everything that I would never return to.

"Roma," I whispered. "I will remember you. You are the true essence of love."

"Good morning, Roman!"

THE END

PHOTO CREDITS

FIRST PHOTO BLOCK: SERGEY'S LIFE
Photos by Sergey Fetisov

SECOND PHOTO BLOCK: FIREBIRD
Photos by Herkki-Erich Merila

ACKNOWLEDGMENTS

We would like to acknowledge all of those who contributed to the publication of this book:

Stephen Fry

Tom Prior
Peeter Rebane
Christopher Racster
Maguire Mount
Marii Joala

Priit Rebane
Oyvind Dino Hjulmand
Kristin Graham
Janne Raavik

The publication of the book was made possible by many contributions to our Kickstarter campaign. Without this support, we would not have been able to fund the editing, publication, and distribution of *Firebird: The Story of Roman.*

Jim Head
Jochen & Christof Beutgen

Kaili Juppets David Johnson Bryan Boeck

Christopher Barrington Orlan Boston & Tomas Mikuzis-Boston
Jingyi Chen

Kirk Dahl
Brett Davies
Kevin Fannin
Bode Ferguson
Michael Hobensack

Hu Jin Jie
David Joiner
Jonathan Latimer
Thomas Lemp
Eugene Louer
Madison D. Pennington
Markus Winter
Randall Withrow
Hadam Zucker

ABOUT THE AUTHOR

Sergey Fetisov was born on August 12, 1952 in Oryol, Soviet Russia.

He served his two-year mandatory conscription (which every Soviet man had to undergo) in the 1970s at the Soviet Air Force Base in occupied Estonia. Here he fell in love with a young maverick fighter pilot, Roman.

Later in life, Sergey graduated as an actor from Moscow's prestigious GITIS institute, but turned down numerous offers from major theaters and took a job as a night mail man instead, after learning about his mother's terminal illness. Sergey nursed his mother to death for 5 years, and for a while did not return to the stage, until a director rediscovered him on a city street.

Besides his extensive theatre career, Sergey acted in over 40 Soviet and later Russian films and TV series, including the Estonian feature film Georg (2007).

He was one of the founding members of the "Russian Style Theatre" in Oryol in 1994.

Sergey published his memoir "The Story of Roman" in the early '90s under the pseudonym Sergey Nizhny. It's his true life story of courage, love and fear during the height of the Cold War, of following his heart in the face of the dangers of the repressive Soviet system, a testament and example of true love, that 'love is love'.

In 2017, Sergey fell ill and had to undergo serious surgery. He passed away on May 3, 2017.

Sergey was a force of love, he lived with courage, joy and wonder at life.

CPSIA information can be obtained
at www.ICGtesting.com
Printed in the USA
LVHW031739050423
743440LV00003BA/356